FINDING HER GONE

Christopher A. Taylor

 **FriesenPress**

Suite 300 - 990 Fort St
Victoria, BC, Canada, V8V 3K2
www.friesenpress.com

Cover photograph "Water and Ice" © David G. Taylor

ISBN
978-1-4602-6202-3 (Hardcover)
978-1-4602-6203-0 (Paperback)
978-1-4602-6204-7 (eBook)

1. Fiction, Literary

Distributed to the trade by The Ingram Book Company

I ask and I am told by a child beneath the pines,
"How should I know where he went?
He's on the mountain somewhere,
gathering herbs among the clouds."

Jia Dao
Visiting a hermit and finding him gone

October

1

Alf didn't understand. He thought gone meant gone. I guess I wasn't very clear. When he clued-in the phone went silent for a very long time.

"I'm sorry," he said.

I must have started to say something because he interrupted me.

"Come here," he said. "We have room. You could stay a week or two – a month – see Edinburgh, the Highlands. Take a side trip to London or Paris. Wherever."

Another pause.

"You need to do something, Kit. You could meet Gem. And Emily. I might even let you win at darts."

"I'll think about it," I said.

Scotland in October. It didn't sound so great. Rain. Wet sheep.

"Do more than think about it," he said.

Sure. Whatever.

"You need a change, Kit."

No thanks. I just had one.

"Come here. Or go to New York. Boston. Barcelona."

Paris. Peru. Iraq. Iran.

"It doesn't matter where. Just create some distance. Give your mind something else to think about."

Like what?

Rain? Wet sheep?

"I'll let you know."

"Not good enough."

The volume was up. He was getting angry.

"Do it," he said. "I'm telling you as a professional – not as a friend. You need a break. Understand? So, do it."

Alf is not a patient man.

"Do it now."

*

I saw a deer a while back. There were trees on either side of the tracks – a small island of forest surrounded by farmland. The deer stood at the edge of the wood watching as the train rumbled past. It was visible for a few seconds – elegant, curious – then gone from view. The train emerged from the trees leaving the deer and who-knows-what-else behind. Since then it has been fields and farmhouses, a cluster of homes every now and then, a road lined with telephone poles heading nowhere. I don't know what this area is called. It could be anywhere. It could be another world.

*

There is a woman with long black hair on the other side of the aisle, one row up. She is sitting in the aisle seat, leaving the window seat empty. Odd. Everyone else goes for the window right away. Maybe she wants to avoid being trapped by some creep who likes her looks. Or maybe she doesn't care for the scenery. Not that it is any better inside. I am at the back of the car so I get to see everything. There is only one row behind me and it is empty on my side. On the other side there is a heavyset woman sitting by herself – window seat, of course. The seats across from me – directly behind my dark haired friend – are empty.

I will call her Alice. I didn't notice her when she came in but I think she is Asian, maybe Japanese. She has a slender build and, from the side, a pretty face. She is reading a book but glances up every now and then and stares for a minute or two into empty space. She is reading very slowly, with long pauses between turning pages. Either she is thinking carefully about what she is reading or she is bored.

What else can I say about her? She is wearing a red top and black slacks. Black boots. She looks to be in her late thirties, maybe forty. Her hands are narrow – long delicate fingers. No rings. Her clothes look expensive. There is an aura of calm surrounding her. If she weren't travelling economy I would say she is wealthy. Instead, I will say she is interesting – which is better.

*

Alf asked how it happened so I told him. He couldn't believe it.

"In September?"

"Yes, in September."

"But ..."

"That's right – it wasn't a very smart thing to do."

"Yeah, but she must have ...."

"I can't talk about it, Alf."

"Sure, I understand. But the water ..."

"It was the Arctic, Alf. The water is always cold up there."

"Right."

Silence.

I could sense the list of questions growing, the self-control disappearing.

"But she must have ..."

"I told you – I don't want to talk about it."

"Okay. I understand."

A pause.

"But, you know, sooner or later ..."

"I know that Alf."

"I know you know that, Kit. I'm just reminding you – that's all."

"Sure."

"I mean – was she upset? Angry? Did something happen?"

"It was an accident, Alf."

"Kit ..."

"A stupid accident. That's what it was, Alf. A stupid fucking accident."

"Okay, okay."

That's right. Back off.

"It was an accident. I understand that. Of course it was an accident. But sooner or later ..."

I don't need this.

"Just drop it, Alf. I hear what you are saying but I can't deal with it right now. Okay? Later. I will deal with it later. But not now. So, drop it."

"Okay. Consider it dropped."

"Good."

"Finished. Done. Dropped."

"Thank you."

"No worries."

Right. No worries.

Not now.

I can't think about it right now. I'll think about it later.

The worries can come later.

But, of course, he didn't drop it.

*

The big woman in the back corner has started to snore. Lightly once, then a bit louder; finally a long rolling rattle that no one could miss. Alice didn't. At the sound she turned around and looked down the aisle, then at me, then again down the aisle. I caught her eye as she faced forward. She smiled vaguely then turned around the other way to try to look through the gap in the seats. The snoring woman wasn't visible so Alice raised herself, kneeling on her seat, and finally got a good view of what was going on. She sat back down, turned to me and smiled again, this time a warm wide sign of sharing and silent, gentle laughter. I held her gaze for as long as I could without appearing rude. She turned, faced forward again, picked up her book and started to read.

Alice has a serene smile. And radiant dark eyes. She is pretty but I wouldn't call her beautiful. She has an oval face and a small mouth. Everything is delicate and well proportioned. Her cheek bones are not as prominent as with some East Asian women but she makes up for it by the way she holds herself, the simplicity of her dress, that aura of calm. She is attractive and, more than that, she is interesting.

I caught a glimpse of her book while she was looking over the seat. It has a white cover with a yellow circle and a trident in the middle. Something like that. I didn't get a very good look. I was checking out her curves and didn't think to look at the book until it was almost too late. I couldn't read the title. Too bad. It might give me a clue.

There is time.

Like Alice, I brought a book with me but I don't have the focus to read right now. Instead, I'm following Alf's advice and letting my mind wander – taking in the scenery, seeing new things, different things – like Alice, for example.

At first I wasn't going to bring anything. I plan to spend my time wandering and watching, jotting and sketching, not reading. I can read at home. Anytime. The whole point is to get away. Break my routine. Open things up. Not bury my nose in a book.

That was Alf's advice. And it sounded right to me. But then a little voice piped up telling me I might need something to put me to sleep at night, something to help shut down the engine, something interesting but not too interesting, enlightening in a soporific sort of way.

I could see the point.

So, I made a tour of the used book stores and came up with a volume on the pre-Socratics, a blue-green ghostly thing with an image of a Greek statue on the front cover. It is a close-up of the statue's face and the nose is broken. Unlike the statue the book is in decent shape. Someone has written notes in the margins but I don't have to read them. And there is underlining in some places – that is harder to ignore – but it lowered the price. I can live with the added emphasis. It's interesting to see what other folks think is important.

*

Alf laughed when I told him my decision. Ha, ha, ha.

I don't like to travel. He knew that. What was so funny?

"You can't walk home?" he asked. Ha, ha, ha.

"It's too far to walk." Asshole.

"Good. That will help. I was thinking of somewhere a little further off, somewhere more adventuresome."

"Montreal is French," I said. "I don't speak French. I think that's a pretty big point."

"Sure, sure. It's a start. It's better than crossing the bridge to … what's that place across the river?"

"Gatineau. It used to be called Hull. Now it's Gatineau."

"Okay, Gatineau. It's better than Gatineau. You sure you can't walk home?"

"No. I can't walk home." Double asshole.

"Good. And, Kit, remember two things."

"What, Alf?"

"First, don't do anything stupid."

"Like what?"

"Well, there's the obvious – which I assume you aren't considering – and then there are all the secondary stupidities. You know them as well as I do."

"I suppose I do."

"So, make a list and read it now and then. If you are getting anywhere close to something on the list, run."

"That's helpful. And number two?"

"Number two. Remember, you won't be alone. It's a big city with a lot of people in it. And at least half of them are just as fucked-up as you are right now."

"That's comforting."

"It wasn't meant to be."

"Okay, so what's the point?"

"Don't give anyone your real name."

2

We are coming into Montreal – the city, not the suburbs. There are low-rise apartment buildings, row houses, old cars and dust. It is a beautiful day – the sun is up and bright – but everything looks tired. Summer is done. And fall is tilting. In the backyard of one of the houses there is a fat woman sitting in a lawn chair smoking a cigarette. A black dog is lying at her feet. One street over an old man is working in a thumbnail garden that borders the railway tracks. He is wearing a white undershirt and looks as scraggly as his tomato plants. He is picking the last of the green tomatoes. So it goes.

*

Alf never met Julia. She was teaching in China while he was studying in Canada. He finished his post-doc – psychology – addiction – a month before she came through Toronto for a visit. It was an awkward time. Alf went back to Edinburgh and repaired his relationship with Gem while I stayed in Toronto and wondered if I had a relationship with Julia. I knew I had something with her – infrequent sex and long walks and boxes of letters – but did those things add up to a relationship? Alf had his doubts.

It wasn't a relationship in the sense of a relationship, he said. It was something else. He never told me what that something else might be but he did say it was curious. That's a favourite word of his. Very curious, he says. And then a smile cracks his lean Scottish face. Sometimes there's more – an observation or a question, occasionally an explanation, or sometimes just a repetition – very curious – and then again for emphasis – it really is very curious, Kit.

My relationship with Julia fascinated him. It had come out in bits and pieces as we played darts and talked about life. He told me about Gem – also known as Gillian Meredith McCaul – and I told him about Julia – also known as Julia. We were, I suppose, a mutual consolation society with each of us facing a GPS challenge – neither of us knew where we really stood.

Gem had made it clear to Alf that if he went abroad to study then their relationship was over. Alf took that as a challenge. He was, he said, a Buddhist and, as a Buddhist, he knew that the source of all suffering was attachment. If he was to be true to his beliefs he could not let his attachment to Gem determine where he would study. He had to decide objectively – on the basis of facts, not emotions – otherwise he would be setting up the conditions for future suffering. Those were his exact words – the conditions for future suffering.

It struck me as an odd bit of reasoning but I didn't see any point in poking at the holes. I just nodded and noted silently that I had now met two Buddhists – both of them on the skew side of life.

Based on Alf's rant it appeared that Gem was less tolerant than me. She thought the whole thing was a crock. Buddhism had nothing to do with it, she said. It was time for Alf to grow up and either make a commitment or move on. And stop trying to dump responsibility on some guy who died 2,500 years ago. Be an adult. Get a life.

Alf did not agree. And he insisted on telling me why. The whole point was that he *was* taking responsibility for his life. He was living consciously, deliberately and taking steps to ensure that potential problems were avoided – problems that would have ensnared both him and Gem in unnecessary suffering – inevitable suffering that would have arrived sooner or later if he had let himself be guided by his attachments. He had to be rational for everyone's sake. There was no immaturity in being rational. It was Gem who wasn't being adult.

All of this spilled out during our second session of darts – once Alf had heard something about my relationship with Julia. In the first session the conversation had circled around more general matters concerning his 'ex' – the woman who had been left behind in Edinburgh – a woman called Gillian but nicknamed Gem – a woman who was a musician – she played and taught clarinet – who had been living with Alf until Alf decided to leave for Canada and she decided to stay in Edinburgh – a woman who was no longer part of his life – she was in his past – gone – absent – nearly forgotten – although, over two hours of darts I learned about her tastes in music – mostly jazz – her favourite food – vegan mush with curry – her preferred painters – Peter Doig and David Hockney – and her personal style in clothing – eclectic with shawls. I also got to hear about her parents and their cats, her brother and his car, a dead uncle, a maiden aunt. By the beginning of the second hour it was pretty clear that Alf's ex was not very ex.

In return, Alf learned about Julia's wandering ways – her ESL life and her allergy to geographic commitment. He knew the type, he said. And he understood why people would follow that route. But he admitted he was intrigued by her technology aversion – she refused to use email. This struck him as a tactic – a way to keep both distance and control. Email and texting were mundane, shallow. Ongoing electronic messages would reveal the thinness of our relationship. But hand-written letters sent weekly – that had an exotic air to it – anachronistic – idiosyncratic – curious. Letters had an aura of intimacy. Not romantic – he didn't like that word – too wet and fuzzy – and beside the point. The physicality of the letters was important but it was more than that. The old tech element was key. It was a cleverly cultivated form of dependence using a centuries-old technology – a postal drip of commitment – carefully administered – subtle and innocuous – very clever, wasn't it?

It all came down to addiction.

Everything does with Alf.

*

The porter has just announced that we will be arriving in five minutes. Alice has slipped on her jacket and now she is gathering her stuff. She has a red cloth backpack with embroidery on it – black and gold thread – curves and cross-hatching and satin stitch. The pattern looks like a bird rising – or maybe a dragon. I think there are flames, although it could be bushes. I can't tell from this angle but it definitely looks expensive.

Everything she has looks expensive. I wonder what she does? She must make enough money to be able to buy stuff like that – but not so much that she travels business class. Maybe she's some kind of consultant – image is everything – that kind of life. Or an academic who consults on the side and needs a decent wardrobe. Or maybe she just likes nice clothes. I don't know. She is a pretty woman – maybe even beautiful – and the clothes don't hurt.

No.

She is more elegant than beautiful. She is a little too hard to be beautiful.

*

Julia wasn't beautiful. I suppose you could call her willowy – long brown hair, slender body, sharp nose – but not beautiful. Or elegant. She was still a student at heart – simple, loose fitting clothes – all natural fibres, natural dyes. Organic if possible. She needed to look respectable for teaching but she didn't need to be elegant.

Casual. Distant. That was her style. Easy on the outside. Wound up tight within the shell. She once described herself as a sniper – watching, waiting. It was an odd thing for her to say and I put it down to her being an army brat. A familiar image. She had a way of standing, a way of holding herself apart that seemed to say – I know about you and I know what I am doing, so let's be adults, please – don't mess with me.

It seemed to work for her. She never had trouble on her travels – at least, no serious troubles, not the way she told it. Little bumps, she said, every now and then. Ripples on the pond. Nothing more. But that didn't stop her going north and getting herself drowned.

I still can't believe it. It doesn't make any sense.

She wasn't beautiful. But she had a way.

*

Alf said I was babbling. Not true. I do not babble. I may have been short on coherence but that's not the same thing as babbling. Babbling has no content. If I had been babbling he wouldn't have understood what I was trying to say – but he did – eventually. It took a while. But eventually he figured it out. Ergo, I wasn't babbling.

He didn't really understand.

That's not his fault. He didn't know Julia. I doubt they would have gotten along. When Alf gets on a roll I let him rant. Julia would have taken him down. She would have stopped him mid-breath and turned the conversation in her direction. He wouldn't have liked that. But it never happened. They never met. If they had, Alf would never have loaded me up with all those stupid questions.

Asshole.

*

Alice is fussing with her backpack, trying to fit her book inside. It came out of the backpack so it should go back in – conservation of space – but take your time, Alice. Do it properly. Turn it upside right with the front facing out. That way I'll be able to see the title – which will give me an opening, a way to start up a conversation as we leave the train. Good idea, right? Don't worry – I promise I won't harass you – just say hello and ask about the book, that's all.

I might ask what you do. And maybe your name. But that's all. I'm not interested in having supper and spending an evening with you. Not even a coffee. Just a hello and a question or two – enough to get a better picture of who you are for my report to my therapist (a.k.a. Alf). I know he will want to know. This whole trip is his idea, after all. He's a man with high expectations. Unlike me. I take things as they come. And go. Understand?

Well, maybe a coffee.

So, turn the book around, Alice. And don't worry. This is just a way for me to keep the world open. I hope that's not insulting. I'm sure you are a wonderful person (or not).

An intelligent woman (for sure). With excellent taste (no doubt). Especially in books (right?). But, frankly, none of that is particularly important. What counts is that you are here right now – if you know what I mean. You don't need to do anything. Just be here. So please turn the book around. I would like to see the title.

That's better. Now move your hand – to the right. Good.

Thank you, Alice.

Hmm.

The Art of War.

3

Alf says addicts are looking for something that doesn't exist – usually happiness – and when they can't find it they get impatient. They want *that something* but it isn't there so they fill the gap with an addiction – drugs, work, sex – whatever. If they knew how to wait – if they were calm and detached – they would recognize that the gaps are part of the scenery – accept them for what they are. But addicts can't wait. They aren't calm or detached. They lack perspective. They lack patience. So when they hit a gap they grab for a quick fix – drugs, work, sex – and end up on the circuit. It is so good. And then it's gone. It is so good. And then it's gone.

Of course Alf doesn't put it that way. He uses words with more syllables and much longer sentences. He tends to go on. And on. Like February. He is a short man but very determined to last longer than anyone else. He does not believe in paragraph breaks. He does not believe in chapters. Everything is a marathon because that is what it takes to free yourself of addiction. According to Alf.

I pass these ideas along because Alf is a friend and a pretty bright guy. He says things worth hearing. I don't always agree with him but I always listen. I pay attention. But, you know, sometimes it is hard.

I am having lunch at a café at Sherbrooke and Parc – smoked salmon on a croissant with a green salad bleeding beets. I ordered a glass of house red and I've been nursing it for almost an hour. I have a coffee to balance the alcohol. When I finished my croissant I took out my sketchbook and did some sketches of my train ride: Alice reading her book; Alice looking down the aisle; Alice kneeling on the train seat looking back at the snoring lady. They turned out pretty well. I also did the deer at the edge of the woods and an old lady I saw in the train station. She had a squashed hat and beat-up suitcase and she was walking in circles around the station talking to herself. Now I'm drawing fish. There's a large aquarium on my right and it's soothing to look at but the fish make a dull subject – all gills and fins – they never blink. I think I'll switch to the flower arrangement by the front door. It is a massive thing with spiky orange and yellow petals. It looks like it might turn carnivorous in its off moods.

I didn't manage to speak to Alice as we were leaving the train. By the time I got my bag and made my way to the platform she was already on the stairs. I tried to catch up but no such luck. She may be elegant but she moves like a thief through a crowd. C'est la vie. I've got notes and sketches – something to report to Alf. See! I'm checking out the scenery. I'm distracting myself. And you never know, maybe I'll bump into Alice again and we can chat about war. Or some other primal instinct. Sleep, food or travel, for instance. Fish or flowers. Coffee.

I'm getting bored.

Okay. This is better. A woman in her twenties has come in and settled at a table by the window. She has a red wool cape that she tossed on the spare chair and now she is taking a stack of papers out of a cloth bag. They look like essays. She must be a grad student with a pile of marking to kill her afternoon. The waitress has brought her a carafe of red wine without her even asking. They are talking but I can't hear what they are saying. The grad student has poured herself a glass of wine. Now she is pointing at the stack of papers and saying something that looks like it should be punctuated with a gob of spit. My teeth are starting to hurt from the intensity. Have a drink of wine, please.

The waitress has moved off and now I have an unobstructed view of the sour one. Her profile is strong – a sharp nose and firm chin, short forehead. She has long earlobes with dangling earrings. Her hair is trimmed up close at the back and spikes out over her forehead. It is deep black except for some streaks of red up front. Her skin is very pale. Her eyes – I can't tell. For some reason she makes me think of Gem, although I have never met Gem. It must be the tension. I can almost hear her yelling at Alf.

*

Second glass of wine and barely a dent in the stack of papers. I have got her face down pretty well but the drawing is flat. She is recognizably the woman at the window, marking papers, sipping wine, staring out the window from time to time. That's fine as far as it goes but in the real world the air around her has jagged edges – I haven't captured that. Her expression is almost placid – must be the wine – and yet the tension comes through when you look at her for more than half a second. What is it? The way she is holding her pen? How she flips through the pages? I don't know. But it is definitely there.

If Alf were here he would focus on the half litre of wine and the fact that the waitress brought it automatically. Addiction on the horizon. No doubt about it. Time for some aversion therapy. Maybe so. But I would rather share the carafe and hear what she has to say. She is intense – that's for sure – and intense can be good – in the interesting sense of good – like Julia, for example. It can also be bad – in the nightmare sense of bad – like Julia, for example. But in either case it is usually worth a closer look.

*

She's started a second carafe. I've ordered another glass of wine. And some cheese. If I don't have something more to eat I will either fall asleep or do something stupid. Alf said I should do something different – but not stupid. This qualifies as different. I don't think it qualifies as stupid. It's not stalking, for example – just watching – and sketching – and mulling the physics of her moods. I've got a few good drawings – her full anatomy – but I still haven't captured those jagged edges. I have come closest with her feet – they are pressed against the center pedestal of the table – scrunched tight like she is trying to push it over. Once the table tumbles she will jump up and scream at the sky – banshee style. That's the look.

Interesting.

*

I think her name is Christiane. She made a call a few minutes ago and I think she said that name – c'est Christiane. That's what it sounded like. She didn't talk for long. And it was all in French so I didn't understand what she was saying but she didn't sound angry. Of course she's had a lot of wine so she may be past angry and into who-gives-a-fuck territory. She finally ordered a sandwich – halfway through the second carafe – and she scarfed it down like a professional. A healthy appetite for such a lean woman. I bet she runs marathons.

She might like Alf.

I've done a couple of quick sketches of the waitress. Not so good. She has curly black hair and a round face and big hips. She seems kind of antsy for such a mellow looking woman. I would have thought she would lounge a lot – or at least hold a pose for more than a minute – but she is always shifting from place to place – picking things up, wiping things down, tidying, straightening. Her employer should be pleased. Although, looking at her, maybe she is her employer. She's old enough to own the place – fifty plus – and she's got that comfortable air of an owner – casual but serious. I wonder. She has seen me sketching and it doesn't seem to bother her. Maybe she thinks I'm an artist.

No such luck. This is therapy, madam.

I could hear Alf raise his eyebrows when I mentioned my sketching. This was via email so I am speaking figuratively. I think his exact words were – You want to draw? What for?

He's a verbal guy. In theory, he recognizes the role of all the arts but in practice he likes words – preferably his own. That was harsh. But true. There is no rule that says the truth can't run close to the line – and nip a few tender feelings as it goes. Total objectivity – that's what I strive for – ha, ha, ha. We can all be assholes at times.

The fact is – I like to draw. It shuts down my language sector and the silence is marvelous. It's very meditative.

Very primal. It makes me wonder if I was meant to live in a cave with a flickering torch and a sharp charcoal stick. See that? That's a bison. And that one over there is a bear. And that one – with the weird ears and wild eyes and spiky hair – is called ... Christiane. Say hello to Christiane.

*

Christiane is studying at UQAM. History. Louise introduced us. She's the owner – Louise. She got curious about my drawing and asked to see. When I showed her the last few sketches she called Christiane over – just like that – without asking – and I was exposed – an anglophone 'artist' alone in Montreal. Neither of them seemed to mind. Even my English was acceptable since I could draw better than a four year old. In fact, Christiane was quite complimentary. I think she liked the sketch of her feet. And Louise's hair. Very democratic, she said. Her English is excellent although her meaning isn't always clear. She's from Quebec City and hopes to go to France when she finishes her PhD. I told her I was from Toronto. I think she would have preferred Vancouver but I've never been there and I didn't want to be caught out. Ottawa is too boring to admit to. I got the impression Christiane feels the same about Quebec City. Parochial. At least, I think that's what she meant. Louise piped in a few times but it didn't help. Her accent is better – non-existent really – but she rushes things, skirts words, flits. Like a hummingbird.

It was pleasant enough. Louise and Christiane chatted in French a bit – I haven't a clue what they said – and then they asked to see my sketches again. They both really liked the old woman in the hat. It's my favorite, too. She was so ethereal. Louise made a comment about Alice – I think she called her skinny or something like that – then they left me to my pencils. Christiane went back to her marking and Louise went back to her tending and tidying. And I went back to my cheese – what was left of it. I didn't feel I could start sketching either of them again – not right away – so I returned to the fish. Boring. I switched to the flower by the door. Not much better. When I finished my wine Louise brought me another glass on the house. I didn't really need more wine but she smiled a hummingbird smile. So, I smiled back.

It seems like a civilized place, Montreal.

*

The last time Julia visited she was in a strange mood. It was only six weeks ago but already those memories are mixing with other times. She had so many moods. I get images of our walking by the river, her talking about going north, her face in the sunlight, the ducks landing on the water. The river was low. It was a beautiful day but she was upset. I didn't know why then and I still don't. She had been angry before – lots of times. Was this different? Maybe. It seemed to be aimed at me – more than usual – but not really. It was like she was angry at me for being me – except she was really angry at herself – for being angry at me? For being herself? I don't know. I think she wanted one of us to change. We had broken off, re-connected, gone silent, resumed – so many times. It was the dominant theme in our relationship – its fragmentation. Neither of us was willing to force a permanent break-up. And neither of us was willing to change enough to make our relationship solid. And so we went on. And on. But we didn't make sense. She was restless. Always. Her one attempt at staying put didn't work – for either of us. It was a mistake. We were a mistake.

Is that what she finally realized after all these years?

Alf and his fucking questions.

*

"You are on vacation?"

Louise is sitting behind me, to the side, so she can watch me sketch. I was trying to draw Julia's ears from memory but I stopped when Louise sat down. There is some kind of sculpture in the far corner – it's made of wood and metal – rebar emerging from a driftwood stump with strips of cloth and feathers hanging on the rebar. It almost looks like a person – in my red wine dreams. So, I've put it in the middle of the page and I'm doing faces around it. No one recognizable – to Louise.

I nod yes to her question.

"How long are you here for?"

That depends.

"About a week."

Louise gives a 'hmm' and shifts on her chair. I expect she will stand up any moment given her restlessness earlier, but she isn't going anywhere yet. Across the room Christiane is powering through her marking. She looks over from time to time just to check out what we are doing. I think she feels self-conscious but her mood seems better. The air about her has lost its jagged edge.

"That's not long," says Louise. "But maybe long enough. Have you been to the Musée yet?"

The what?

"I just got here this morning."

"So you have all your time in front of you." She sits forward and touches my arm. "I can show you some places – not tourist places – interesting places to visit. Good places to eat."

That's an idea. She looks like she knows where to eat.

I smile.

"Good." She stands up.

I knew she couldn't last.

"And you can do my portrait," she says. "A big drawing. Something to frame."

She holds out her hands showing the size of the portrait.

"Maybe just the face. Maybe more."

She gives me a big smile, a wink.

"We can think about that."

4

The stairway from the main path up to the big Chalet should have Led Zeppelin piped in at the landings – the stairs keep going up and up and up. I am resting for the third time and for the third time I have had the pleasure of watching a fifty year old lunatic in spandex going up and down in search of a heart attack. He looks like shit as far as I'm concerned – all tendons and bones with a close cut white beard. I don't know why he thinks this is good for him. He must be a lawyer. Or an accountant.

This is a busy place. A German couple in their twenties just came past wearing matching blue hats with excessively wide brims and earnest exercise sandals. Their hands appeared to be glued together. Lovely. And now here comes a woman who looks to be in her seventies. She has a golden retriever at her side. I've been watching her wend her way up with her dog and she hasn't stopped once. I get the feeling she does this climb every day. I hope she doesn't ask me if I'm okay.

"Oh, thank you. I'm fine. Beautiful dog."

She gives me a pleasant smile and keeps on going without another word.

Thank you, again.

I guess I look tired. I didn't get much sleep last night. I went to supper at a place Louise told me about and it was good but I stayed a little too long and drank a little too much wine. I had a seat by the window and there was lots to watch – high heels and car wars – but I was too tired to sketch so I sat there quietly fading. By the time I got back to the hotel I was done. I went to sleep in a second and everything would have been fine except the folks next door came in laughing around 2 a.m. and decided to finish the evening with some headboard banging. The walls in that place are misleadingly thin.

I turned on the light, tuned the radio to a classical station, took out my book on the pre-Socratics and started to read. By 3:30 everything was quiet and I managed to drift off to sleep half way through Heraclitus – which might explain the weird dream that appeared in the morning: rivers and toes and water flowing over rocks, sunlight on the surface, people floating past. I think Louise went by on a reed raft, relaxing in the nude, but that might have slipped in later. She wants me to start sketching her tonight and I am, shall we say, concerned. I told her I would let her know. She just smiled and wiped another table.

*

This may sound strange but Julia didn't know about my sketching. When we first met there was nothing to know. I had stopped drawing briefly while I was at university – it didn't seem to fit – and when I picked it up again I kept it to myself. I never talked to her about it and I definitely never sketched when she was around. Not sure why. It would have made sense to draw her portrait but I didn't. I don't even have a photograph. Maybe it was the posing thing – self-conscious, artificial. Or maybe it was just too intrusive. I could look and I could touch but I could not represent.

That's not quite right. I would sketch her from memory when she was away. And sometimes I would include a doodle in a letter – a stick figure, face or mythical beast – but that was as far as it went. I suppose it was just one of those things that people do. I have no idea what parts of herself she didn't share with me. She claimed she didn't keep secrets – but what's a secret, after all? Something you intentionally choose not to share. That leaves a lot of room for I-didn't-think-you-would-be-interested, it-wasn't-worth-putting-in-a-letter and plain old I-forgot.

Right.

Alf would love this. I can hear the analysis revving up: client prefers memory over technology – makes vague claims about posing and privacy – no photos – only sketches – all from memory – and nothing shared. The veneer of objectivity suggests an obsession with temporal residues and future avoidance, thereby obscuring the character of the unilateral personal commitment and evading a realistic assessment of the bilateral personal relationship. Open to rational analysis but closed to emotional engagement. Deep structural issues. Formal resistance. Ironic rupture required.

That's curious, Kit, he would say. Very curious.

*

It is a beautiful day – cloudless, bright and mild. I've made it to the top and now I'm sitting on a bench in front of the Chalet. The German couple are by the wall at the edge of the cliff. I can tell it's them by their hats. There are a few other people wandering about. A cyclist or two. More dog walkers. The old woman with the retriever is long gone.

No one has come up to the Chalet so it's my own private resort for the moment. I am sitting in the sun with a light breeze and small white clouds passing overhead. What a view – the city spreading out to the south and in the far distance isolated mountains – miles and miles and miles of open air. If I could sing I would – but I can't so I won't. I have my sketchbook if I get exuberant.

There is a small group of people doing tai chi in the plaza in front of the Chalet. Slow movements, extending, reaching, lowering, rising. The leader of the group is in a pale blue silk outfit that shimmers in the sun. She goes lower than anyone else and rises as if time were measured differently in her life. She must have strong thighs to move like that. I suppose the silk helps. One of her students (green silk) is smooth but she doesn't have the same elegance. Her hands look like they were pasted on at the last minute. They droop. She needs to relax and focus more fully at the same time – no one said this was going to be easy, you know. There is a guy in the back who is pretty good (black silk) but he tends to speed up when finishing his moves. Focus on this moment, not the next. And stop trying to be fluid. It is making you wobble. Yes, we all know you are subtle. Show us you are strong. That's better. But don't overdo it, please. Good, good. Careful. The rest of them? They aren't worth mentioning – beginners with a future but that's where it is – in the future. Someday they may get silk. Or maybe not. In either case it won't be a question of what they are wearing.

So, here I am, all of a sudden, a sunshine-fresh-air-top-of-the-Mountain tai chi critic. Ha. I'll put it down in my report to Alf. It'll give him a laugh.

*

Christiane came past the restaurant last night. She was walking with some friends and stopped at the window when she saw me. I gave her a wave and lifted my wine glass to her. She waved back, made sketching motions and an okay sign, then ran to catch up with her group. A few of them looked back in my direction when she rejoined them. I'm famous now, I guess.

I wonder what she said. Something pleasant, I expect – that guy's from Toronto – an artist – really good. Vanity, vanity. I hope I didn't have spinach stuck between my teeth when I smiled. It's always like that – stuff your mouth and the waitress comes by to ask if everything's alright. I'm sure they do it on purpose. Someday I'll spit out a mouthful and say 'great'. That would be fitting – gobs of half chewed salad on the plate – very educational.

Christiane was smiling a great big smile as she left. She should do that more often. It was like a different person – not quite pretty – but attractive in her way. Of course, she was already looking calmer after seeing my sketches at the café yesterday. Anything is better than marking papers by semi-literates – even second-rate drawings of Louise's hair. Not that Louise's hair isn't nice – very full, very curly – but I expect it's dyed – too dark to be real. But that's okay. Christiane can be too dark to be real, too.

It was a funny coincidence – seeing her walking past. Montreal is a big city but it's a small place at heart. Just like everywhere else. I wonder if she'll report back to Louise. They seemed to be good buddies but, then again, Louise looks like she's good buddies with the entire world. She has that rolling comfort you see every now and then – like the Northumberland Hills. If I could capture that side of her in a sketch – that aura of ease – it might be worth the risk.

Maybe.

Or maybe not. Hours alone with Louise and her long curly hair, her steady smile and her big dark eyes. It is something to think about.

Hmm.

I can see her sitting in a wing chair by a window in the morning sun, cradling a cup of coffee on her lap, smiling, relaxing – fully clothed.

Maybe.

*

Alf said not to do anything stupid. But what is stupid?

Jumping off a cliff? Running out into traffic?

Everything depends on context. He knows that. I know that. And he knows as well as I do that stupidity flows through our veins. It pools in the lower brain stem and spurts up periodically in sudden bursts – like an epileptic shock. Cerebral opacity blots they are called – 'cobs' for short – like inkblots in the brain. It is a sad truth that minor cobs are necessary from time to time if you want to avoid a full blown opacity event – the kind of thing that leaves a stain and often leads to bruises. You don't want to end up there.

He knows that. I know that.

I believe what Alf meant to say was – don't do anything *really* stupid – don't have a major cob. And the best way to avoid that possibility is to let the brain stem vent periodically. Let it spray up minor cobs – the kind you can feel coming and clean up quickly once they are done. Little wincers is what I like to call them. They aren't fun but they aren't disastrous either. People notice, of course. They stare for a moment, but not for long. They are part of life, right?

Everybody has them. Like farts and indigestion. They are no big deal.

Right.

So, Louise, Queen of Ease, I will see you tonight. I will bring my pencils and you can bring your comfort and together we will let the minor cobs flow.

*

Tai chi is over. Smiles all around. The silk is shimmering in the sun. Lots of chatting but no bowing. Hmm. I thought you were supposed to bow. I guess not in Montreal – non-hierarchical and not-into-bowing. That's okay with me. I'm not-into-bowing too. If only I could speak French I might like it here. Unfortunately, that's a very big 'if'. Maybe I'll visit from time to time.

The sun is bright and feels great at the moment but there are a few clouds and the temperature drops every time the sun disappears behind a cloud. Bright/shade. Warm/cold. The lighting effects are great but I am slowly getting chilled. Time to walk.

*

According to Julia a village by the sea is ideal – preferably in a foreign country – but she would take Canada if it was convenient. She liked the surf and the colours of the ocean. The birds. The stones. There was one place in Japan she was especially keen on. I forget the name. She was teaching there a few years back and she tried to get me to come for a visit. I thought about it for a while. She pushed pretty hard so I even checked out the cost of flights. Not cheap. It's a long way from Ottawa and there would have been a transfer or two. I would have lost a couple of days on travel alone. And then there was the language thing. And what to do about my practice. And the cost. I thought about it seriously but there were too many issues. It just wasn't feasible. So, I didn't go.

She was pissed. She called me hopeless – more than once. Maybe a dozen times. I wasn't counting but I got the message. Fine. Sure. I don't like to travel. Understood. You learned that a long time ago. I am not a wanderer. If that makes me hopeless then I am hopeless. Guilty as charged. But so what? What is travel? A fool's paradise. And what is hope? A childish wish for something you don't have today and may never have in the future. It's a distraction. A lure. A trap. An attachment – as Alf would say.

A village by the sea.

Would that have worked? Would she have settled down? She didn't want a city – not Vancouver or Sidney or L.A. – she wanted a village. She couldn't explain why. There wasn't any place she could name. Or she could name dozens but none of them seriously – Japan, France, Wales, Australia, Spain, New Zealand. Yeah, right. How would we have lived? How would we have paid the rent? She could have taught. Sure. But what about me? I would learn Japanese and do what? Sketch?

Hopeless. Sure, that's me. But what did she really want? It didn't make any sense. None of it makes any sense.

*

The runners are out. There was a group a few minutes ago that bounced along very nicely. And a trio up ahead has slowed to a walk which makes for better viewing. I am following at a respectful, non-stalking distance. They are all of them trim but they have very different shapes – long waisted, short waisted, pear and plum – the interaction of muscle and bone and gravity – the undulation. It is too much for pencil and paper. You have to see it for yourself.

Altogether I would say that motion isn't a sketching thing. You can get a hint now and then – blur things a bit, stretch a line, tilt a body – but true motion – the flow of a river slipping past – forget it. That's what walking is for. In motion, admiring motion. Don't draw it. Do it.

So I am.

*

You don't walk, you pace. That's what she said.

It wasn't true. It isn't true. She only said it because I have favourite places to walk – familiar streets, the path along the river. Familiarity breeds contempt – for some. For others it breeds contentment. She couldn't see that. She couldn't see the variety in the familiar. The subtle changes. Day to day. Hour to hour. The details missed. Leaves and litter. Water and stones. Infinite division.

She would deny it, of course – that she was blind to the familiar. But that's what it comes down to – came down to. That's why she had to travel. It was a question of need. She needed the familiar – that was me. And she needed the not-familiar – everything but me. And she wasn't satisfied with either one.

Here and there. Near and far. Now and then. It cycled on and on.

*

Time for a break.

The map calls this place Beaver Lake but it doesn't qualify as a lake in my books. It's just a big pond. There's a building at one end and a path around the outside. Benches here and there, including the one I'm sitting on. It's a pleasant enough spot. There aren't many people but lots of seagulls. A few ducks. Lots of sun. I've got my sketchbook out and I'm doing trees.

A runner came past a few minutes ago. She was moving at a good clip, scaring up the gulls as she went. Nice stride. Steady pace. She was wearing a black running outfit with a red baseball cap. Long black hair tied at the back. Sunglasses. Very sleek. She looked my way as she went past – a long hard stare that made me want to wave hello. I guess I'm a novelty – no one sketches around here – but not novel enough for her to stop and chat. Swish and she was past. Focused. Intense. She didn't look like a lot of fun. But she had a nice back end.

Sketchable?

I don't know. She was lean. Not a lot of wobble. I might do the face – glasses, hat, mouth and chin. And a back view with the pony tail swinging out behind. Shoulders and arms. Full figure receding.

Maybe.

It would be an impression – in multiple parts. Not a representation. There's a difference in weight and definition although Alf doesn't believe in impressions – not the way I use the word. Everything is an impression, Kit. Calling one thing an impression and something else a representation is an error, a mistake, a delusion. All we have are impressions. There's nothing more definite. That's the reality. And the goal is to recognize that fact.

Sure, Alf. No need to get metaphysical. It's just pencil on paper.

I can always erase it.

Julia could be like that – a word tyrant. Friend and acquaintance – that was a big one with her. She had friends across the world – dozens of people she kept in touch with.

She spent a fortune on stamps. I called them acquaintances. Friends are rare, I said. For you, she said. For everyone, I insisted. You're a hermit, she said, so how would you know? It's a question of definition, I explained. And why should I accept yours? Because it's right. If you call everyone you meet a friend then the word becomes meaningless. For you maybe, she sneered and stood up, but that's your problem, not mine. Then she huffed out the door.

Life wasn't easy with her.

*

Start again.

It is a beautiful day. I am sitting on a bench on the Mountain in Montreal. There is a large pond in front of me. Water and gulls and sun. Not many people. I am taking a break – a break from walking, a break from thinking, a break from my practice, a break from my life. I am sketching a break in my life.

The pencil moves across the paper – lines and arcs and swirls and circles. It moves on its own. I watch it as it moves. It leads and I follow. It fills space and I provide time. We work together. We are building a break together. We are sketching a break so I can get from here to there.

Faces. And birds. And clouds. And water. A wind across them all.

I can't draw the wind. Not even the pencil can draw the wind. Motion isn't sketchable – period. The wind will have to draw itself. Waves on the water. Clouds overhead. The wind rises. The sky darkens. A sudden storm. The water turns wild. It is full and dark and cold. The waves are breaking, the water sinking. It rises again. Surfaces and falls. It is cold and dark and empty. No one can draw it. No one can know the whole story.

Fucking Alf.

5

"This is my best side." A pause. A glance. "Don't you think?"
I never take sides.
A worried look.
"Have you got enough light?"
All I need.
"Are you sure this is the best position?"
Seems comfortable to me.
"I can move to the left." She shifts. "Is that better?"
No. But I can live with it. Now shut up and sit still.

*

I have found the zone of discomfort for Louise.
She is sitting in the corner of the restaurant under a single lamp, in a large leather chair, her hair down, her chin up. All the lights are off except for that single lamp. I am sitting with a brand new sketch pad open to the third page. Things would be going well if only she would sit still.
"My nose itches."
"Then scratch it."
She scratches her nose, shifts in her chair, changes the position of her arms, moves them back to their original position (almost), looks at me and sighs.
"This is hard."

For you.

"I don't know how people do it – models, I mean. I guess they're moving most of the time. Flashing their legs, their boobs, their ass. It's not natural – sitting still."

Not for you.

"Think of something boring," I suggest.

"Why?"

"Something dull. Something that makes you feel lazy."

"I never feel lazy. When I get bored I get restless. I need to move."

"Okay, then think of something interesting. No. Something scary. Pretend there's a snake and if you move it will bite you."

Louise gives me a hard look, a look of disbelief.

"A snake is supposed to calm me down? Are you nuts?"

Okay. Maybe that wasn't such a good idea.

"Sorry. How about your favorite meal? A good glass of wine. Something like that."

She looks toward the bar, then at me.

"That's better," she says. She gives me a smile. "I know what I'll think about."

*

I have been sketching for about half an hour. She wanted to go to her condo – more comfortable, she said – but I insisted on staying here. I'm not interested in comfortable right now.

"I want to do some quick sketches," I said. "Then we'll see."

"But what about my clothes?"

She made a sweeping motion at her outfit – stretch black slacks and an orange t-shirt with a black line-drawing of a tree, its branches spread appropriately.

I told her not to worry. All I wanted to do was to see how she would sit. That's all. We would figure out what she should wear later.

She frowned.

"It's late," I said. "This is just a start. Tomorrow we can get serious."

At the sound of 'tomorrow' she gave in.

So now she is sitting and I am sitting and the restaurant is closed with a single lamp on in the corner and it is very quiet and peaceful and ideal for sketching except Louise won't stay still. Whatever she was thinking about to keep herself calm she has eaten and digested.

"You have to stop moving."

"I'm not comfortable."

No kidding.

"You don't have to be comfortable. You have to be quiet."

She looks directly at me.

"You are a hard man to please, Alfred Sloan."

No kidding.

"Louise, if this doesn't suit you we can stop. Let's just forget about the whole thing."

Panic. Waving hands. "No, no. That's not what I meant."

"Then please settle down for another five minutes. That's all I want. Just another five minutes."

"Okay." Calming. Calming. "I will."

She puts her hands together on her lap. Shifts back and forth on her rump.

"I promise."

"Good. I'm glad to hear that."

"Tomorrow we can go to my place, right?"

"Yes." Maybe. We'll see.

"Tomorrow we can get serious."

"Right." Sure. Maybe. We'll see.

A smile. She tugs at her t-shirt and smooths it.

"Okay," she says. "In that case, tonight I will sit still."

She looks toward the door, strikes a pose, her chin up.

"Thank you." I begin to sketch.

She looks at me. "You're welcome."

I nod and smile, continue sketching.

"Tonight," she says, looking at the door, chin up. "I will be as quiet as a nun."

"Good."

I work as quickly as I can.

But, of course, she doesn't sit still.

*

I am up to Empedocles in the blue book. It appears he was big on Strife and Love. Love brings things together and Strife sets them loose again. Sounds plausible enough to me – although I'm not so sure about the Love part. Maybe it was different back then – in Greece – before Socrates. Of course, Empedocles wasn't actually Greek. He was Sicilian – like Louise – almost. He was born in Sicily. Lived there. Died there. Louise, on the other hand, has never been to Sicily. She wants to go someday. Maybe next year. Maybe when she retires. When she has the time – and someone to go with.

Her grandfather was born in Sicily. He came to Canada when he was twenty-one and settled in Quebec City. It was too cold for him so he moved to Montreal where he married and found work building houses. He and his wife had eight children. His middle daughter was Louise's mother. She had five children – with Louise the eldest (of course). The youngest son died in a car accident. All the others are still alive. Two in Montreal. Two in places Louise didn't mention. I didn't ask.

So, Louise is one quarter Italian – Sicilian when she's feeling territorial. The rest is a muddle of old time Quebec French and one stray Dutchman back a couple of generations. Or that's the family legend. How the Dutchman fits into things isn't clear but Louise claims it's a good mix – Dutch and Sicilian and French. The Dutch and the Sicilian are both hard headed, down to earth, but in different ways. And the French know how to live.

She's a survivor, she says. Thanks to her genes. Her husband left her eight years ago for a little shit with skinny legs – I think that's how she put it. It was a rough patch and she considered killing the bitch but that would have left him free and her in the big house so she considered killing him instead. That, she concluded, wasn't worth it. Skinny legs. Skinny ass. He had gone queer – that's what it came down to. Let him go.

That was the easy part. The real challenge was financial. The banks don't give a shit for women. They smile a lot but don't take you seriously. Patronizing, she said. That was the word. She didn't think she was going to make it until she got a new loan officer. Like her, he was part Italian. Him she could handle. So, she managed to hold on to the restaurant and got herself a little condo in the old town – a loft with a view of the water. The restaurant has had its ups and downs but she's Sicilian – and Dutch – so everything has worked out fine. Life is good. It isn't easy. But it is good. Getting better all the time.

I sketched for another ten minutes. She couldn't sit still longer than that. In fact, she couldn't sit still for ten minutes. She stood up twice and stretched, turned around, waved her arms. She sat back down quickly when I glared at her. The third time I closed the sketch pad.

"How do you expect me to do your portrait if you are going to be bouncing around all the time?"

She was standing and it was clear she was not about to sit down again.

"I'm not bouncing around," she said. "You want to see bouncing around, I'll show you bouncing around."

No thanks.

Too late.

She did a little dance, swaying her hips and shaking her breasts. There was a lot of bouncing around.

"Now let's go for a drink," she said.

"I'm tired," I said.

"We'll go somewhere quiet."

I shook my head, no.

She shrugged, waved her hands, then came over and stood beside me, her hip against my shoulder, her hand on the back of my chair.

"Show me what you've done."

I flipped quickly through the pages.

"Not so fast." She leaned over and took the sketchpad from me. "I like to do things slowly."

She turned to the beginning and looked at the sketches one after another, pausing a few times. She handed the pad back to me.

"You've got talent, Alf."

She put her fingertips on my shoulder, let them drift down my arm and into the air.

"Good hands."

6

I bought another sketchbook when I got the big pad for sketching Louise. I'm already two thirds through the sketchbook I brought with me and I have at least a week left in Montreal. After my hike up the Mountain I came down through Westmount and did a lot of thumbnail sketches – houses and gates and stone walls and wooden doors. They are all very fine in their way but not particularly satisfying. There is a lot of around-about-and-up-and-down to Westmount but at the end of the day – or even in the middle of the afternoon – there is nothing you could call exciting or romantic. Lots of impressive stone mansions with neatly trimmed hedges and expensive black cars parked in the driveway. Yawn. It is a slow, staid place suitable for walking a very small dog.

But that was yesterday. This morning I'm in a different city. I had breakfast at a place on Milton and then made my way out to Parc LaFontaine. There was a guy feeding the ducks at the north end of the park. He was about sixty and looked like he did this for a living – beard, long hair, pea coat and beret. The ducks knew the routine. When he started tossing out crumbs they clambered out of the pond onto the pathway – en masse – and crowded around their ageing benefactor, quacking politely. People coming down the path had to walk on the grass to get around the crowd – except for a few determined runners and one dog walker being dragged by a very excited black lab. It was a dangerous place to be when that dog came through. I was sitting a couple of benches away – well out of harm's way – but I swear I could feel a wind from all that fluttering. I thought the dog might drag its owner into the pond. Very nice. I did a few sketches but it was that motion problem again – too many feathers and too little time. I did a decent job on the guy with the beret.

It's sunny today – beautiful blue and bright – but it was clear all night so the temperature dropped and it was too cold to sit in the park for very long. Once the ducks started to disperse I flipped a coin to decide which way to go – north or south? It came up heads so I headed south – down to the old town by the river – Champ-de-Mars, Palais de Justice, Notre Dame de Bonsecours. It was a bit of a hike and I was surprised at how many tourists there were hanging around. It's October. Don't they have some place warm to go? I sat in the big square in front of Notre Dame and tried sketching for a while but my hands couldn't take it, so I am wandering again.

I have to admit there's a special feel to the old town – with the narrow streets and the old buildings built to the edge. You can feel the past leaning over you. Hundreds of years of shouting and laughing and shoving and dying. Shadows in the archways watching the new life go past. It's like there's a trace of everyone who ever lived here or even just passed through. How poetic.

*

I am having lunch at a place on Saint Paul. I arrived early and managed to get a table in the back corner by the window

– plenty of light and a good view of the room inside and the traffic on the street. It's a good spot but, even better, the waitress clued in right away that if she didn't speak English I was going to starve. Her name is Michelle and she's in her late forties and her English is very good. She's thin with a long pointed nose, narrow face, long dark hair. Brown eyes. She's all in black – sweater, slacks, earrings – with black knee high leather boots. It's quite the uniform but she's friendly. And efficient. I took her advice and ordered the daily special – pasta with mushrooms and a rattling list of other things. Sundried tomatoes? Pesto? A salad to start. And a glass of red wine.

I've got the wine. And with the sun through the window I'm okay to wait for the rest. I've taken off my jacket but my scarf is still wrapped around my neck. I think it makes me look local. Or stupid. It doesn't matter. It keeps me warm. Julia used to make fun of the way I dressed. I'm into dull. Dark blue, brown and grey. Black is usually too flashy for me. I sometimes wear dark green. She wore colour. And I wear dull. She liked to travel. And I like to sit. We both liked to talk. We disagreed on most things but we still liked talking to each other. Writing and talking. That was the glue.

*

There's a mix of people here – four Americans at the far end with New York accents and six equally loud Russians much closer; there are some suits – lawyers, I'd say, based on the sheen – and scattered unknowns like me. No one under thirty and no one past seventy. Nobody poor.

I took out my sketchbook while I was waiting for my salad but all I managed to catch was the outline of a hat walking past on the sidewalk – a grey wool cap and the curve of a jaw. The guy was going slowly enough for me to do more but Michelle showed up with my salad. She looked at the sketchbook on the windowsill, then at me, then out the window. The guy in the cap was gone and there was a woman in a wrap and heels strutting past. Michelle put the salad on the table and said 'bon appetit' with a smile. I smiled back and started to eat.

The salad is good – mixed greens with a simple vinaigrette. I don't like creamy salad dressings. I guess I'm a vinegar kind of guy. That was another area where we converged – Julia and I – eating. Simple. High quality. Non-denominational. We had our best sex-free times with cups and cutlery in front of us. Full meals, snacks, coffee. It didn't matter. As long as we were out.

She got restless in the apartment – even after a good meal – but if she was out where there were other people then she could eat and talk and watch and be herself. I mean the self that wasn't wrapped up in wanting to be somewhere else. The here-and-now-engaged-with-reality self. The self that hooked me and reeled me in when we were at university. She was so alert, curious, quick. Where did it go – that earlier self? Did she lose it in the South Pacific? China or Japan? I don't know. It was gradual and it got worse every year – the tension, the restlessness. When she turned thirty there was a quantum leap. Or fall. After that whenever she visited she arrived unannounced, left without warning and in between she was on edge all the time. She wanted to see me – she needed to see me – but then, within a day or two, she turned restless. It was like she wanted to settle down and relax but couldn't. Something was driving her. And something was blocking her at the same time.

*

The pasta was good and now I'm having coffee. Not espresso. I want to linger. I may yet order dessert but for the moment my sketchbook is out and I've got the back of a Russian head in focus – square, solid, short hair and thick neck. He might be a ballet dancer but I don't think so. Not that he's necessarily a thug. He moves his hands as he talks, slowly, fingers spread. He could be a philosopher or a novelist. I saw a Russian violinist once – I think it was the Prokofiev Quartet – he looked like a truck driver – heavy set, sloppy shirt, thick everything – but, wow, could he play the violin. It was beautiful. After that I'm reluctant to judge a Russian by his neck. They are a deceptively subtle people. This one, however, I'm pretty sure he's an industrialist.

The suits have gone – back to billable hours. The Americans were out the door before I even got my coffee. So, it's me and the Russians and the scattered undefined. There's a guy across the room with an artist beard and a book and an espresso. Narrow face. Round wire-rimmed glasses. He must be a poet. A woman is sitting with him but I can't see her very well. She's focussed on her phone. I don't think they've spoken once since they arrived.

Rats. The Russians are leaving. I thought they would hang around longer – more alcohol – but I guess there's business to do, buildings to buy, people to threaten. Too bad. I've got a rear view portrait that says a lot but not quite enough. The density comes through but not the possibility. He could be Dostoevsky with a crew-cut but you wouldn't guess that from my sketch. The hands – I need to work in the hands somehow – but not today. Ah, well. The ears are pretty good.

What now? I guess there's the poet. He doesn't look like he's going anywhere fast. An immobile introvert. The sedentary kind. Julia was the wandering kind. I think that's true. She kept turning inward and sinking the Index. And that's why she needed to travel. She had to shake herself alert. Over and over. It was a compulsion. A holdover from her childhood. Unhappy parents. Unhappy child. Turn inward out of self-defence, then wake up and run outside. On and on.

It is almost as simple as that.

7

It is past five o'clock and my feet hurt. I walked all the way down Notre Dame to the Atwater Market and now I've made it up the big hill to a café on Saint Catherine. This is where I am going to stay until my feet stop throbbing.

I've been flipping through the sketchbook putting in notes for future reference. If I don't do it now it will never happen. And then where will I be? Wordless. The images stand on their own but I still feel the need to annotate. It's a compulsion, I guess. I make notes and spice my letters with the best bits. But there aren't going to be anymore letters. So, do there need to be anymore notes? At the moment, I think the answer is yes.

I already miss writing to her. I suppose I could write letters anyway and just not send them. But that would be sick. I could write up reports for Alf and see what he thinks. He already said he wants me to send him something once I'm back in Ottawa. I was non-committal but, just in case, that's a good reason to annotate the sketches. If I need a reason.

As for Julia, I'll have to find some other way to get the message across.

*

"Do you mind if I sit here?"

Pardon?

There's a woman looking at me. Dark glasses. Dark hair.

"All the tables are full," she says.

I look around. Every table has at least one person at it. I've got a table by the window – a good one to share if you have to share.

"Help yourself." I move my cup and plate closer and motion at the empty chair across from me. "Please."

She smiles a vaguely familiar smile.

"Thank you."

She puts down her café au lait, takes off her jacket and hangs it over the back of her seat. She is wearing a black stretch top and black slacks. A necklace with a red stone hangs like a punctuation mark above her breasts. She sits down and takes off her sunglasses, then looks briefly out the window.

Well, well, well.

With her glasses off it all comes into focus. I thought there was something familiar about her smile. Her hair. Her chin. Is this a coincidence? It can't be. I close my sketch-book then look down at my coffee. It is half empty but I can get another one. Or two.

There are a couple of guys with half beards talking to a woman on the sidewalk outside the café. Alice is watching them and I am watching her. I wait until she brings her attention back indoors and picks up her café au lait.

"This probably sounds corny," I say. "But you look familiar. Have we met?"

She looks at me, holding her coffee bowl with both hands. She is petite and yet her fingers manage to fully circle her café au lait.

"I don't think so," she says. "And this may sound corny but people often mistake me for someone else."

I am sure they do – but not me. I smile.

"I think we were on the train together – from Ottawa?"

She puts down her coffee, looks at a blank space for a second, then at me. She thinks.

"Oh, yes."

She smiles, raising her hand slightly, her long fingers pointing nowhere in particular.

"The snoring lady."

"Yes," I say with a laugh – the snoring lady. "I guess she found it an early start."

"It sounded that way."

She sits back and, with her hands at either side of her head, lifts her long black hair off her shoulders and releases it onto her back. I try not to stare as the necklace and her breasts rise and then settle with the movement of her arms.

"The train is so hypnotic," she says. "I felt like dozing a few times myself."

Not me.

"It's a comfortable way to travel," I say.

I pause for a second.

"Do you live in Ottawa?"

"No. Here." She gestures with her hand, pointing past me. "In Westmount."

Of course. And do you have a little dog?

She glances at my sketchbook. "Are you an artist?"

I laugh lightly and shake my head.

"No. I suppose you could say it's a hobby."

"A hobby is a good thing." A pause. "I play classical guitar. A few friends and I made a CD. Guitar, piano and violin."

Really? Those long fingers. A guitar.

"That's cool."

She hides her smile by taking a quick sip of her coffee.

"That's why I was in Ottawa."

She puts down her coffee bowl.

"We take turns selling the CD in different cities. I've done Ottawa, Cornwall, Brockville and Kingston – and here. My French isn't the best so my friends take the places like Quebec City and Trois Rivières. It's a mental health thing."

Really?

"The CD? Or selling it?"

"Both. I'm a psychiatrist. So are my friends – colleagues, actually. We do the music for balance."

A Westmount psychiatrist who plays classical guitar for balance. You have got to be kidding. God is playing with me.

"And the travelling sales routine?"

There's a slight tightening in her face.

"Well," she says, "since we went to the effort of making an album we thought we might as well try to sell it. Complete the circle."

She wraps her hands around her coffee bowl and raises it slightly above the saucer. I can feel the circle tightening.

"Don't get me wrong," she says, smiling again. "We don't have delusions of grandeur. We're amateurs in the true sense of the word. But to make the album and then let it sit unheard – it's like quitting half way."

She takes a sip of her coffee.

"Plus, it's fun. You meet the strangest people."

"I'm sure you do." And now you have met me.

*

It was awkward at the end of lunch – at the restaurant down on St. Paul.

"Is your name Alf?"

What?

Michelle had come with the bill. She put it on the table and then asked her question. I gave her a puzzled look.

"Pardon?"

She hesitated.

"I've got a friend..."

She looked at the sketchbook and then at me. Her confidence returned.

"She met a guy, an artist, named Alf. And I thought maybe ...."

She motioned toward the sketchbook.

"Are you from Toronto?" she asked.

Alf. Toronto. An artist. Okay. Serves me right.

"Yes, I am."

"Alf?"

"Louise?"

"Yeah, that's her."

Had to be.

And then Michelle gave me a very big smile. I think she was drooling.

Fuck.

*

"Do you mind if I look?"

Alice points at my sketchbook.

"Umm."

I put my fingertips on the sketchbook and rotate it slightly.

"There are notes with the drawings." I pause. "It's nothing odd – just comments to myself – mostly drivel. If you promise just to look at the drawings. And I have to warn you, they aren't very good."

"I don't want to embarrass you," she says. "If you would rather not."

It's now or never.

"No. It's okay. There's nothing embarrassing. Maybe a few stupid ideas – but nothing personal. It's just café sketches and observations."

I slide the sketchbook across the table. She does a double check with her eyes – are you sure? – but she doesn't say anything further and immediately picks up the sketchbook. I glance outside for a second then back at her.

She has opened the sketchbook at the front and is slowly leafing through the pages, sometimes turning back a page or two for another look. Her face is blank. I watch her for a while then look out the window. The woman in the trio by the lamp post is pissed off about something. She is spitting venom at one of the bearded guys. Her hands are shaking and her face is a mass of anger. I look down the street, at the cars, across at the park – anywhere except at that woman. She is seething and the guy is laughing at her. I don't need to see what happens next.

Bang. She just hit him.

Oh, boy. There they go.

*

I can hear the commotion outside but I just remembered the sketches I did of Alice at the beginning of the sketchbook – so all my attention is on her. She seems oblivious to the fight on the sidewalk and if she notices my stare she doesn't show it. She is flipping back and forth through several pages. Her expression is still blank. Not even curious. She is halfway through the book so it can't be the drawings of her. Back and forth, back and forth. A little pause and then back and forth again. What can be so interesting? They are just sketches. They aren't all that good.

Right.

She is reading the comments.

8

There are a few scattered clouds in the south. It is mild but windy and the pages of my sketchbook keep flipping up with the wind. I am tired and I have a slight headache behind my right eye. In the mirror this morning I noticed how my fatigue surfaces more on the right side of my face than on the left. Maybe it's some kind of genetic flaw – left brain decay. Or maybe it hits everyone once they get past a certain age. Everyone with a left brain, that is. I'll have to ask Alf if it happens in Scotland.

I have a date with Alice – Sally – for supper tomorrow night. I didn't tell her that I have been calling her Alice. And I have to make sure not to do it to her face. Sally Hatano. Sally, Sally, Sally. Not Alice. Not Alice. Not Alice. It's kind of funny, though. Alice. Sally. Close enough for horseshoes.

She seemed to relax once she learned I was a psychologist – a kindred but inferior spirit. Psychiatry versus psychology. Music versus sketching. Montreal versus Ottawa. I lose on all counts. But they aren't fatal flaws – just part of a less fortunate life. Oh, well. It happens.

She didn't comment on the sketches except to say that some of them were 'quite good'. Thank you. Perhaps you will play guitar for me sometime. We chatted about running a practice, the need for an outlet (a guitar or a pencil), the diversity of clients and the remarkable repetitions in human behaviour. It might have turned into a real conversation but she had to go, so we decided to have dinner tomorrow. Her idea.

The one odd thing was when she asked if I was married. It came out of the blue – right after she put the sketchbook down. She slid the book across the table, looked me in the eye and asked – blink – no smile – no blushing – head tilted – eyebrows up – blink.

"Are you married?"

I almost stumbled.

"Do I draw like I am married?"

"You draw a lot of women."

"True. There seem to be more of them around."

"I think it's about fifty-fifty."

"I guess I prefer to draw women. Does that mean something?"

"That's why I'm asking."

Oh.

"So, are you?"

"Married? No."

"Living with someone?"

"No. Why? Does it show?"

"Yes. I think so."

*

I would say we hit it off but we didn't. She is attractive – sort of – and articulate – that's for sure – but she's a little too clinical to be interesting. Maybe she'll warm up over a glass of wine but I'm not counting on it. I suspect she's on the job all the time – taking mental notes, sorting and sifting through the file, honing her analysis. It's her eyebrows that give her away. Up and down, arched and flat, askew. I'll have to mention it to her – as one professional to another.

In any case, I'm glad we didn't decide to have dinner tonight. Today I have to recuperate. I went to see Louise last night – I had to – I've got enough guilt already. So I went to the restaurant and told her that I'm not doing her portrait. I wanted to give her the preliminary sketches but she told me to keep them – maybe I would change my mind. Look Alf, she said, if you lose something you have to find something. Otherwise you walk around with a hole in you. It's like me and my husband. When he left me I had to find something. So I did. You need to do the same. That's why you're here, right?

Not exactly.

I nodded my head. It seemed the easiest response. I had already told her about Julia in a round-about-not-quite-accurate sort of way. It was Wendy – not Julia. And she was my ex-wife – not my whatever-Julia-was. And she died in a car accident. Drowning in the Arctic would have been too much. So, I explained to Louise that I had come here for a break – to get away – to wander around a place I didn't know. To be alone. And to think. I wasn't up to doing portraits.

She shook her head and smiled. I'm sure you're up to it, Alf. But I understand. You're feeling shaky. Even if she was your ex she was still your ex and getting killed is no fun for anyone. But life goes on. So, take your time. Think about it. Keep the sketches and you can do the big one later – in a few days – or the next time you're in Montreal. It doesn't matter to me. I'm not going anywhere. I'll still be here next time you're in town.

I shrugged my shoulders and put the sketches away. Okay. I could always doodle on the other side of the paper. I started to leave but Louise held my arm. Not so fast, she said. You can't just walk away. I booked this evening for you. If we aren't going to draw we can at least go back to my place and talk. You can tell me about this Wendy woman. It'll be good for you to let it out.

That didn't sound like such a good idea to me. I was tired from all my walking and from meeting Sally and from fretting about Louise and Julia and life. I would rather go to the hotel and crash. But I wasn't going anywhere without my arm – she wasn't letting go – so I suggested a glass of wine at the jazz bar around the corner. Louise thought about it for half a second, kicked out the students who were working at the table in the corner and closed up the café. As we went out the door I promised myself – one glass and only one glass. And don't embarrass Alf again.

*

There was a good crowd at the bar but they were kind of young – mostly students – and I felt a bit out of place, especially with Louise sitting up close and leaning into me from time to time. She's big on running commentary – about the wine, about the crowd, about the band. I don't think she likes jazz.

The music was good – keyboard, double bass and guitar. The leader was a skinny blonde on the keyboard. She had tattoos up both arms and seemed to want to say something from time to time but left that to the guy on guitar. The bassist was standard issue – long beard, shaved head and eyes that were focused on the back of his skull. He played a couple of solos that I almost liked. The guitarist seemed the most normal of the crew – the one who did the banking. He had shaggy brown hair, a gaunt face, no piercings and a good voice. His guitar work wasn't fancy but he did the job.

We stayed for one set and by then I was toast. Louise took a cab home after a minor skirmish – a limp invitation that was easy to decline – and I walked back to the hotel with my sketches. It seemed a very long walk. I think Louise was truly disappointed about the portrait. She said she could see the picture hanging on the wall – behind the bar – watching over the place. I need all the help I can get, she said. Like in the old days. She seemed almost nostalgic. Weird. But she's an optimist. Later, she said, you'll do the portrait later. She could tell. She didn't know much but this she knew – that portrait was going to be hanging on her wall. For sure. I shrugged and waved as the cab pulled away. Bye-bye, Louise.

Of course, she was right. I'm a sucker for flattery. And I don't like to disappoint people. When I got back to the hotel I stayed up until four working on the immortalization of Louise. I did a quick rough sketch and then started on the real thing. It is not as big as she wants. I had already picked up a few medium size sheets – archival quality – but it's big enough for head and shoulders. She wanted her full body or at least the upper half – anything to show her boobs – but I don't want the distractions. Head and shoulders. That's all. She's got good hair and a great smile. I can make her look full without looking fat. Comfortable. At her best.

Louise, the Queen of Ease.

And so, the portrait is coming along very nicely if I say so myself. I've got her chin – and that is no joke. The eyes will be easy. Her ears may be a challenge – they aren't symmetric. And her nose tends to flare. I'll have to watch that. But for now, I've got her chin. And that is good. For some reason, I need to give her the portrait before I go back to Ottawa. Complete the circle, so to speak.

9

It is all very strange. The rational faculty surfaces, begins to flex its muscles and then immediately starts to batter itself black and blue. All is water. All is fire. The universe is numbers. There is no such thing as change.

Right.

What is it about humans? Why can't we be more like fish?

I am in the Presse Café at Milton and Parc – huge windows and huge plants and huge mirrors on the wall. The ceiling must be five metres high and the space and the light are wonderful. It was too windy to work outside and now that I'm in here I'm glad I came. The good spots by the windows are all taken but every spot is a good spot in this place. I've got a table by the south wall right across from the cash register and the pastry display. I get to see everyone who comes in and what they eat. What more do I need to know?

It's mostly students so far. Lots of notebooks – the battery powered kind – but some textbooks and novels and other arcana from the Gutenberg age. I've got the pre-Socratics open – blue as ever – and I've made it to Pythagoras. The void and the triad. Three dimensions. Space and life. Beginning, middle, end. I just read about the counter-earth – hidden behind the earth – on the other side of the central fire. The universe revolves around that core of heat and light – with the earth over here and the counter-earth over there – and we all go around – listening to the music of the spheres. Living and dying and being born again. Of course.

He was a traveller, Pythagoras – Egypt, Persia, India – finally settling in southern Italy by the sea. Crotona. A nice place and a hot spot for medicine but a little on the conservative side of things. He started a commune and was killed by the locals who weren't too keen on having hippies in their midst. I guess his high math scores didn't count. All the same, you have to give him his due. He had a solid focus on quality of life. Walk a lot – especially in the morning – alone – in silence. Be careful what you eat. Stay calm. Don't drink or talk too much. Live simply. And keep your eye on the metaphysical ball.

Hmm. That's a pretty one. She's got long red hair with a wave that's breaking into surf. Nice coat – dark green – and those are quite the boots. I wonder where she'll sit. There's a spot over here on my left she might like. Or straight ahead at the big table in the middle. Oh, it's a coffee to go. That's not right. In fact, it should be illegal. People need to relax. Take off their coats. Sit in full view.

Too bad. There she goes. Have a nice day.

Where was I? With Pythagoras by the sea – thinking deep thoughts. Right angle triangles and the square root of two. Never a dull moment. Well, maybe a few. I noticed there's a section on Hippocrates at the end of the book. I'm tempted to skip ahead and see how the medical and the metaphysical compare – who looks better after a few thousand years. First, do no harm. That's about all I know of Hippocrates. It's a good place to start. But there has got to be more.

Julia wasn't a fan of philosophy – not the academic kind. Stay away from anything based in the headache zone. And that includes William Blake on his off days. Monet was good. And Laozi. I think she liked Basho. Heraclitus might have been acceptable – she liked tension – creative or otherwise. Basically, she believed in the lyric life – open the door – float to the counter – order a coffee – chat for a moment – whisper to the plants on the way out. Tap into as much awareness as you can while you can. There's a finite amount of it and it shifts from place to place like the aurora borealis in the night sky. So, you have to go with the flow or you'll be left in the dark. That's what the Index is all about. If it starts to drop – move on.

*

I don't want to go back to the hotel but I should. I need to work on the portrait. I don't have that many days left and it has to be done and it has to be good. But I don't want to. It's pleasant here. Just enough of everything. Julia would have liked it – especially the plants and the windows – and the clocks on the wall showing the time in different cities. Location is temporary. Time is relative. Motion is what counts.

Maybe I'll have another coffee and a sandwich and relax for another hour or so. I'll do the no-mind thing. No sketching. No reading. No jotting. Just sitting. I used to be good at just sitting.

10

Sally didn't give me her number. We arranged to meet at the corner of Crescent and Sherbrooke with the idea of finding somewhere to eat. So, here I am. It didn't take as long to walk over as I thought it would and I'm a bit early. That's okay. It is beautiful out. There is a mild breeze coming down Sherbrooke that keeps the feel of the afternoon even as the light dies. As waiting goes, this is a good spot to do it. There are lots of people coming and going and most of them are dressed to impress – everything from silk suits to beaded blouses and feathered headbands. Capes and shawls. Even the cars seem to have upgraded. A lot of Mercedes and BMWs and brands I don't recognize but can guesstimate the price. Actually, I can't guesstimate the price. Cars like that are a mystery to me. So be it.

It's kind of amusing that we picked this spot – she picked it and I agreed. It's the place I am supposed to go before I leave – the Musée – and I still haven't been inside. Maybe Sally and I can take a quick look around. Or maybe I'll do a tour with Louise later. We'll see. I'm not making plans. And my expectations for tonight are set low. Go with the flow – as Alf would not say.

There are lots of art galleries clustered around here. The place across the street on Crescent has a spectacular display of glasswork. Sculpture, too. Mixed media set to topple. The twisted towers of wire and string I can live without but the glass pieces are worth looking at – other-world colours, web-like fractures and exotic surface effects – very cool. Some of the shapes are odd. Tilted. Turned. Too much or too little? Imbalanced? Maybe that's the point.

I wonder if Sally has a theory of art? Or of the artist? She didn't say what school of psychiatry she follows. Perhaps she's a renegade – most psychiatrists are in their own special way. It is a truly strange profession. Moats and turrets and retaining walls. I don't know how they carry all that weight but they do – and sometimes – almost by accident – they make sense.

I wonder what kind of car she drives?

"I have feelings, too."

It is a pretty woman with short brown hair. She looks to be in her early thirties and is standing beside an older man, grey hair, sunglasses. He is wearing a sports jacket and a shirt without a tie. She is in a sleek blue dress that seems too much for her. She has a black shawl over her shoulders. She notices me walking toward them and stops talking. I walk past them to a window with a large watercolour on display – a river and waterfall, large trees, no people. It is very pleasant.

"Have you been waiting long?"

The woman in the blue dress seems out of her depth, as if she had strayed onto a street where she doesn't belong. I wonder who the guy is. He looks like he has money. Maybe he's her boss and it's a depressing case of power and advantage. Or maybe he's her father and she's protesting because she said something that offended her mother and he has told her so and now she's defending herself. I wish I had my sketchbook. If I glance to the side I can see their reflection in the window. I could draw them while appearing to look at the painting. Subtle.

"Have you been waiting long?"

Someone nudges my elbow. I turn.

"Oh. Hi." It's Sally.

She looks at me and then at the watercolour in the window.

"Beautiful painting. You can feel the water falling, can't you?"

Yes. That's it. You can feel the water falling.

"Have you been waiting long?" she asks, again.

"I just got here." Sort of.

"Good. I hate being late."

She notices the woman in the blue dress who seems to be crying. The godfather is pretending it isn't happening. He is trying to usher her away.

Sally turns back to me. "And I *am* late."

If I tell her I have been waiting for fifteen minutes she will think I'm an early nerd, so I let that one pass. I doubt she would feel guilty anyway.

"Where should we go?" I ask.

"South."

She puts her hand on my elbow, guides me past the troubled couple and around the corner so that we are heading down Crescent.

After a moment she asks, "What was that all about?"

"Pardon?"

"The lady in blue. She was crying."

"I think they were having a mild disagreement."

"They should pick somewhere less public."

"Sometimes things get away from you."

She gives me a quick look.

"Not me," she says. She releases my arm. "And somehow I don't think they get away from you either."

My arm feels chilled by the sudden absence of her hand.

"I'll take that as a compliment but the truth is I've had my share of public embarrassment."

Sally looks at me again, this time more fully. Her eyebrows are perfect, as is her mouth – even when it is frowning.

"False modesty doesn't become you."

She is wearing tight black slacks, a red silk top and has a fine white cotton shawl draped over her shoulders. I am underdressed.

"It's not like I've been caught naked in the street," I say. "But I've had my days."

"Having and showing are two different things."

Fine. This is definitely one to lose.

"So, what do you feel like eating?" I ask.

"I wouldn't mind a glass of wine to start."

I thought we were going to have supper. I am starved.

"Sure, if you want. But you are going to have to lead the way. This is one street I haven't explored."

"It's a tourist trap." She puts her hand back on my arm. "You have good instincts."

We turn right at Maisonneuve, then right again at Bishop so we are now heading uphill, back toward Sherbrooke. Halfway up the block we stop at a red sports car with black leather seats and the top down. So, this is the kind of car that Sally drives.

*

If I had to pick one example that captured the oddness of my relationship with Julia I couldn't do it. But this comes close.

It was cool by the river. Dark. Quiet. Every now and then a car came past on the parkway – two bright rays of light that grew, spread and then disappeared. A crescent moon was rising. I was restless and had come down to the river to walk it off. I followed the path out to Kitchissippi Point and sat on a bench near a group of sleeping ducks, their heads tucked under their wings. It would have been comforting if it weren't for the nagging feeling that none of this was real.

Julia was in Japan. She was teaching in a place called Shiogama on the east coast of Honshu, north of Tokyo. She had been there a couple of months and I wasn't adjusting very well to her absence. I felt there was something she had wanted to tell me during her last visit. Had something changed? Had she met someone else? Was she thinking of staying in Japan? She never said. And so, the letters I wrote her were brief and cautious. The letters I received back were even briefer. Telegraphic. She was thinking things through. And sending me the rejects.

The faint roar of the Deschênes Rapids came across the water and against that sound there was the lapping of the waves against the shingle in the darkness. There were lights on the far shore but they were foreign and anonymous. Everything was distant except for the sounds of the shingle and the shadows and the breeze that came out of the night. This was my part of the world – close, quiet, whispering in the dark to the sleeping ducks. Julia's world was somewhere far away. An unknowable point of light.

It may have been an animal or a dream but something disturbed the ducks. First one and then several others stood up and began to flap their wings and quack in surprise and growing concern. I couldn't see anything other than the ducks – nothing to justify their alarm – so I took it as a signal that my quiet time was over. I headed home.

When I got back to my apartment there was a letter from Julia in my mailbox. I went up to the apartment, put the envelope on the kitchen table and made myself a cup of tea. I dried the dishes from supper as the tea cooled. I wiped the counter, took out the garbage, rearranged my shoes on the mat. Then I sat down with Julia's letter.

Hello you,

It is very early. The sun has begun to lighten the sky but it hasn't yet topped the horizon. In a few minutes I will go for my morning walk to watch the sun rise over the Pacific but I have to write this note first because I have a question for you, an important question that insists on becoming ink on paper before I bury it again. Questions can be like that, can't they? If only answers were so insistent.

The question I want to ask you is going to have to wait for a moment because I have to tell you about a dream first. It arrived this morning – the dream, not the question. The question has been hovering for months. This is not an evasion. Trust me.

In my dream I am walking in a marshy area at the edge of a large river –the Ottawa? – collecting reeds to make a basket. Why I want to make a basket, I don't know. But that is what I am doing. It is evening and the sun has disappeared below the line of trees on the far side of the river. The growing darkness makes it difficult for me to see, so I am moving very slowly through the water. It is getting deeper – up to my thighs. Suddenly there is a loud splashing and two ducks rise out of the reeds into the air.

76 Christopher A. Taylor

I am startled, step back and lose my balance. I turn and with my arm I hit something large that moves when I fall against it. It is a reed boat.

The boat is long and flat with an extended prow at one end. There is a slight depression in the middle with enough room for one person. I drop the reeds I have gathered onto the boat and then climb aboard. It seems made for lying down, so I do. It is very comfortable. Once I am settled the boat begins to move forward of its own, slipping out of the reeds into the river.

I lie quietly in the boat as it floats into the open water. I look briefly at the shoreline I have just left and I have the impression there is someone on the bank waving to me. I don't wave back. Instead, I watch for a moment then turn back to face the open water. The boat drifts toward the centre of the river then begins to move slowly upstream – against the current! As I move with the boat in the dark I hear the words "Finally, I am getting somewhere". And with those words, I wake up.

Odd, isn't it?

Finally, I am getting somewhere. As if all this time I have been in the same place. And even odder is the fact that as soon as I woke up from the dream I knew that it was you who was waving at me from the shore. Staying behind once again.

And now my question.

Will you come and visit me here? I know you would hate Tokyo but you would love the rest of Japan. You could visit the temples in Kyoto or go north to Hokkaido. Where I am now is so beautiful and magnificent at the same time. We could visit Matsushima – it isn't far – Basho called it the most beautiful place in Japan. If you came you would never want to leave. You should come.

Yes, you should come. My room is too small and it is against the rules to have guests, but I could find a cheap place for you to stay nearby. I would really like to have you here to see what I am seeing – the mountains and the hills and the ocean and the fishermen and the blossoms and birds and, above all else, the people. We could go for long walks by the ocean, take the ferry across to the Urato Islands or head back inland through the hills. We could drink tea for hours in a tea room or wander the streets being followed by the children who want to practice their English. We could talk all night. Or just sit and watch the stars.

You would see. Everything is different. You should come.

Please come.

Love -- Julia

I held the letter in front of me for a very long time, then put it down and took a sip of my tea.

11

"Were you born in Japan?"

"Vancouver. I came east to study. I liked it here and decided to stay. "

Sally is relaxing with the help of her glass of wine. The drive to the bistro was a little tense. I was too nervous to pay attention to the sights she was pointing out as the car slipped back and forth between lanes but I think we are on St. Denis. Or St. Laurent. Or St. Joseph. We seemed to take a lot of corners very quickly. And at least two pedestrians gave us the finger. I'm not sure we got here any faster but the time definitely didn't drag.

"I've never been to Japan," she says. "I'm not much of a traveller."

"Not even curious to see the country?"

"Oh, sure. Someday."

She waves her left hand in the air indicating an indefinite future.

"I don't speak much Japanese – just a little from my parents – hello, goodbye, thank you. It would be awkward walking through Tokyo with people thinking I'm Japanese but with me not understanding anything. They would think I was an idiot."

She puts her glass of wine to the side.

"But someday, yes, I plan to go. How about you?"

"Me?"

"Have you been to Japan?"

"No."

I am drinking the same wine as Sally – a French red with a name I don't recall. I pick up my glass and take a sip. She has almost finished her glass and I have hardly touched mine but that's okay. I'm not the one who is stressed out from listening to Westmount neurotics all day.

"I have a friend who lived in Japan for a while," I say.

Why did I say have? Had. I had a friend. Too late now.

"I've heard lots of stories but I've never been."

Sally's eyebrows rise and fall with the hope and the reality.

"Too bad," she says. "If you had gone you could have told me about it and saved me the trip." A smile. "If I had a friend living there I would definitely go. It's easier when you know people."

"Yeah, I guess so." Or maybe not.

"What was your friend doing in Japan?"

"Teaching English."

"Ah." Sally nods her head. "One of those."

I sit up slightly. This is Julia she is talking about.

"One of those?"

Sally laughs. "You know, the ESL warriors – have degree will travel."

I look at her askance.

"That makes it sound kind of frivolous."

"Isn't it? I mean – I'm sure your friend is rock solid – but, in general, these people are kind of flaky."

Sally picks up her glass and looks at the remaining wine. She takes a short sip.

"I need something to eat. Do you mind if I order some cheese?"

"Of course not."

I wave at the waiter who comes over, listens to the request and is soon back with sliced baguette, two small pieces of Quebec artisanal cheese and scattered black olives. He enquires about our wine but we both say no. The bistro has begun to fill up and it is getting noisy. This isn't a place for a proper meal.

"Does that offend you?" Sally asks, after she has eaten a piece of baguette and what looks like brie.

"Having cheese before supper? No. Why? Should it?"

"No," she says very slowly. She gives me a look. "My comment about the ESL crowd."

"That? Well ... yeah, I guess so."

"Why? It's not like I'm talking about you."

"True."

"They are like tourists – drifting from one place to another."

Sally eats an olive and puts the pit at the side of her plate.

"They stay longer than most tourists – get a better glimpse of a place –but they can never see what it is really like to live there. That takes years. Maybe even generations. They are outsiders. And that is all they ever will be. So, they keep drifting."

I am fighting not to overreact.

"Is that bad? Being an outsider?"

I sit up and lean forward slightly.

"They see different places, different people, different societies. What's wrong with that?"

"It's tourism. Voyeurism. It's adolescent."

Ouch. I am losing the fight to keep my emotions under control. At the same time I am surprised at how much her comments disturb me.

"Is that a professional opinion?" I ask. "Or just a casual observation?"

Sally smiles at my discomfort.

"I have known a few. It is a considered opinion."

She pauses for a second.

"I'm not putting anyone down. I'm not saying they are morally bankrupt, western white supremacists trying to impose their language and culture on other races. They aren't evil. They don't have a secret plan. Most of them go out of curiosity. Some go for the parties. And some of them wander the world looking for something they can never find. I think it is sad. Some very talented people waste their lives that way."

I try to wait a moment but I can't restrain myself.

"And who is to say whether it is a waste or not?"

Sally stares at me.

"We make judgments – you and I – when counselling patients – we make judgments all the time about what is bad and what is good, about what is wasting life and what isn't. Running from yourself – and that's what the long term ESL crowd is doing as they bounce from one country to the next – running from yourself fits in the first category. It qualifies as bad, as a waste of life."

I put some cheese and baguette in my mouth to keep the wrong words from coming out. Sally eats another piece of cheese then finishes her wine.

"Shall we go?" she asks.

12

I have a gift for misdirection. I wander with ease and grace. In other words, I get lost without difficulty and without panic. Julia was fond of pointing this out. She said it was because I didn't belong on the planet. I was an outcast from another world.

"An outlaw?" I asked.

"No," she smiled. "An outcast. Someone who has been banished – like the Greeks used to do with troublemakers."

Really? Me? A troublemaker? I took some pride in that comment. All the best Greeks got banished. It was a sign of an independent mind.

"Is that why you like to visit me? Because I'm in exile?"

She paused and smiled.

"Could be," she said. "Maybe I want to rescue you."

I laughed.

"Right. The maternal instinct meets The Twilight Zone."

She laughed as well and I could have kissed her right then but, instead, I waited as she settled back into her Julia calm. We were sitting on a bench in a park in Toronto where I was doing my PhD. I had a year to go and then I would be free to travel. If I wanted.

She took my hand.

"Or maybe," she said, "I want you to bring me home to your planet someday."

*

"Are you religious?"

Sally is having halibut with asparagus, beets and risotto. I have lamb, roast potatoes and a mix of vegetables, some of which I can't identify. We are sharing a bottle of white wine that, once again, Sally picked – something from New Zealand. The restaurant is intimate with dim lighting and wood panelling and a cellist playing in the far corner. The table next to us is empty.

I don't want to answer her question, so I don't.

"I knew a Buddhist once," I say.

I feel very tired. I shouldn't have had a scotch to start. In contrast, Sally seems anything but tired. She hasn't said another word about ESL. On the way here from the bistro – a short walk through a crowded street, down a back lane and back onto a main avenue – she talked about my drawing, complimenting and encouraging me. It didn't work. But the walk did us both good.

"And that's it?" she says. "You knew a Buddhist?"

"Two, actually." I pause. "You wouldn't happen to be a Buddhist, would you? That would make it three."

"No. Sorry. Can't help you there."

She picks up her wine but doesn't drink. She looks past me at the wall. It seems as if she is considering something important. An awkward question? A minor revelation?

"But I was asking about you," she says.

"I know."

"You are very guarded."

"As are you."

She puts down her wine, sits back in her chair and looks at me.

"I would say we are both aware."

She pauses and waits to see if I will say anything.

I don't. I'm fed up. I don't see why I should be the one talking so I smile and keep eating. Sally doesn't move. She remains sitting back in her chair with her cutlery down and her glass of wine out of reach. Her fish is going cold but that doesn't seem to matter.

"There's a line in the New Testament that fascinates me," she says.

I stop chewing. Okay. Go on.

"Jesus is in a boat with his disciples, crossing the Sea of Galilee. He falls asleep and, while he is asleep, a storm comes up. His disciples are terrified and they wake him up. When he realizes what the problem is he stands up, faces into the storm and he speaks to it. He talks to the storm and the wind drops, the sky clears and – and this is the line that I like – a great calm descends on the waters."

She pauses.

"I love that phrase – a great calm."

She sits forward, picks up her wine glass and takes a sip. Then she looks at me closely to see if I got it. Did I?

"His disciples are panicking but he stands up, faces into the wind and speaks to the storm." She puts down her glass of wine. "That is a magnificent piece of psychology."

*

We have finished our main course but not the wine. Neither of us wants dessert and I don't want any more wine. The waiter comes by, refills Sally's glass and at the motion of her hand, takes the bottle away. I order a decaf coffee.

"So, you have never been analysed?" she asks.

"I said I'm not religious."

It comes out before I have a chance to think. I am tired.

"That's a bit hostile."

"It was a joke." I try to keep the tone right. "But, you know, you ask a lot of questions – the probing kind."

"It comes with the profession."

She lifts her glass of wine, looks at it and then puts the glass down near the edge of the table. She waves at the waiter.

"You can always ask back," she says to me.

The waiter comes over and Sally explains that she has changed her mind and asks for a cappuccino. He leaves with her wineglass.

"Okay," I say with a thin smile. I will take up that invitation. "How old are you?"

"Talk about starting at the deep end," she says, blinking her eyes as if I had just shone a flashlight at her. "How old do you think I am?"

Always answer a question with a question. I make a show of looking at her from head to toe and back up, lingering on her hands, neck and eyes. It is only a show because I have already thought about her likely age several times.

"You look thirty-five," I say. "But I think you are forty."

"Right both times." She brings her hands together on the table, entwines her fingers and leans on her forearms. "I believe you are trying to flatter me."

The waiter brings my coffee and Sally's cappuccino.

"So, how old *are* you?"

Sally picks up her coffee spoon and gathers a bubble of foamed milk and shaved chocolate.

"I am forty-one," she says. "And a half."

"I was close," I say, pleased with myself. Of course, she could be lying.

"Yes, you were. Congratulations." She puts the spoonful of froth in her mouth and withdraws the spoon slowly. "But I already know you are a good observer. How is your intuition?"

"With respect to?"

She stirs her cappuccino. "Why am I here?"

I watch her stirring her cup, some of the foam dissolving into the liquid, the rest going around and around on the surface. This has been as bizarre an evening as any I can recall, so here goes.

"You want sex?"

She bursts out laughing and people turn to look. She slowly scans the other patrons and gives them a calming smile that says everything is under control; it was a very funny joke; too bad you missed it. As the people turn back to their own meals and conversation Sally puts down her coffee spoon, joins her hands above her cup of cappuccino.

"Has anyone ever told you that you have a face people trust?" she asks.

Diversion. I won't be distracted.

"Actually, yes, I have been told that." A long time ago. "But what does that have to do with why you are here?"

"It must be a problem for you – people trusting you so easily."

She looks me directly in the eye.

"It must get awkward at times."

I want my answer.

"Is that why you are here? Because you trust me? That hardly seems a reason."

"Happenstance," she says as she sits back.

"Pardon?"

"I am here because I believe in happenstance."

I am tired and I am not sure what she means so I keep my mouth shut.

"You are different," she says in a voice that recalls the smile she gave me on the train. "And I find difference intriguing. I noticed it on the train and again when I ran past you at Beaver Lake. You were sitting on a bench sketching and I did a second circuit around the lake just to be sure it was you. It was. Wasn't it?"

She doesn't wait for an answer.

"Then I walked past the café and saw you with your sketchbook again. Coming across you that third time I thought – happenstance. Here is somebody interesting. Meet him."

Beaver Lake? On the Mountain. The runner in the glasses and the baseball cap. Right. I saw but I did not observe, as they say. But she did. And she recognized me in the café. That's not what she said at the time. What is this all about?

"You have an air of detachment to you," she continues. "It's part of what makes you seem trustworthy. But there is something else. And I haven't quite figured it out. I am curious."

She picks up her cappuccino and takes a drink, then holds the cup by her lips as if to block any further words.

"That's it?" I say.

"Yes, that's it," she replies. "Chance and curiosity."

She lowers her cup, letting it hover just above the saucer.

"That's more than enough, isn't it?"

I shrug. What about sex?

"I am a professional," she says. "Like you, I'm a good listener and a good observer. I also trust my intuition. And all of my faculties tell me there is something interesting going on with you, something hidden. I am curious."

"There is always something hidden," I say dismissively. "Otherwise, you and I would starve."

"Not always," she says, sitting forward again. "Sometimes there is nothing – a great big nothing."

"Fine."

I have had enough. This is going nowhere. And I still have a question I want answered before I say goodbye.

"What I want to know," I say.

I stop and wait until her eyes meets mine. She raises an eyebrow.

Okay. Here I go.

"What I am curious about," Miss Happenstance, "Is ... why were you reading *The Art of War*?"

*

Alf says I'm not critical enough. By that he means that I don't analyse as much as he does. I agree with the observation but not the inference. I prefer to let things settle most of the time. Analysis can be aggressive. And aggression can drive off the timid spirits that hold the key. Or if you prefer, when you observe the finest elements of reality you change things. And when you analyse what you are observing you risk destroying it. So be careful. Or as Hippocrates put it – life is short, the Art is long, opportunity is fleeting, experience precarious, judgment difficult. That's how it's translated in the blue book – and that is fine as far it goes – but they missed the punch line: So be careful.

*

Sally has beautiful brown eyes.

"*The Art of War*?"

She gives me the blinking look again but I will not be put off.

"On the train you were reading *The Art of War*."

"Oh, yes," she says, as if remembering something from years ago.

"Well?"

I lean forward, rest my arms on the table and look at her directly. It is my turn. She looks back at me, still blinking, although more slowly.

"I will tell you," she says after a moment, "if you answer two simple questions."

For fuck's sake.

"Two?" Why am I bothering with this? "I asked one."

"They are simple," she says.

The blinking has stopped. She is smiling again and she doesn't wait for me to respond.

"Who is Alice?"

I can feel myself blushing. Serves me right. There is no point in being evasive. Get it over with and get back to her side of the bargain.

"You are," I say.

"I thought so." She smiles.

She waits for a moment but there is nothing to explain so I don't bother trying.

"And the second question?" I ask.

She sits and waits for my embarrassment to clear.

"Your friend in Japan. She invited you to visit."

I am too surprised to even shift in my chair. This is a statement not a question. She is asking me nothing. I try not to react but there is nothing to respond to anyway. The statement is true.

Sally leans forward and her hair slips from her shoulders. Her expression goes blank – like a stone. Softly, she asks, softly.

"Why didn't you go?"

December

1

It is a fine winter morning with a clear, brilliant sky. I am sitting at my desk looking out the window at a band of blue stretching above a broader band of red brick and windows. It is chilly in here but nothing compared to outside. As I walked to work this morning the snow gave that characteristic squeaky crunch and then, as if to emphasize the point, a few tiny flakes of snow drifted down out of the cloudless sky. That kind of cold.

I have two clients scheduled for this afternoon – one young, one older – but no one on the list this morning. I guess I could have stayed in bed but it's that limbo period between Christmas and New Year's and I need to move while the light is up. Walking is the universal cure, they say. Just ask Herzog. Or Hippocrates.

The younger client is a student – Heather – third year science at U of O. She wants to get into med school. Her grades are fine but she's started having panic attacks. She's losing weight, losing sleep. She's started smoking – which she hates – but she thinks the nicotine will help her concentrate. It's only a matter of time before she walks into a wall or melts down in front of a prof. For the moment we are talking about quality of life.

The older client is a vet – Afghanistan – named Martin. He's forty-eight but looks more like sixty. His problem, he says, is simple – he is lost. It's like he has stepped outside his life and is watching himself go through the motions. He's got no sense of direction, no motivation, no drives of any kind – not even sex. His wife thinks he's having an affair. That's a joke, he says. He doesn't give a shit about sex and that's just fine with him. He's tired of being dragged around the room by his penis. Let it sag. What he wants is to get some colour back into his life. He can do without the sex but he's not ready to die yet.

We've talked about the wars – he has seen more than one – but he says that's not the problem. War is war, he says. It's part of life – read your history. You don't join the military if you're afraid of war. No, it's not the war. And he's not depressed. He's not anxious. He's not confused. He's not paranoid or schizoid or delusional. He's not even sad. He's just lost.

It's early days – he started in November – just after I got back from Montreal. Based on what I've heard so far I don't think I'm facing a catastrophe. He's too solid, too coherent to be falling apart.

"I don't want to disappoint you but it sounds like a common enough problem."

He doesn't look like he's going to be disappointed.

"Is that right?"

"Yup." I smile. "It's called middle age."

Maybe.

"Great." He sits forward. "So what's the cure?"

"How about a long walk?"

*

My coffee is cold. It's the second cup to succumb to heat death this morning. I have been working on an article on hysterics and social media but I don't seem to be making much progress – on the article or on my coffee. I tried darts for a while but my hands were too cold for subtle work. So, I'm back to a critique of personal theatre on the World Wide Web.

I have a dozen pages down but things are moving very slowly. Usually the middle fills easily. It's the beginning and the end where the work lies but with this one I'm struggling. I've been working on it for well over a year – thinking, gathering – and the ideas have taken shape but I am having a hard time keeping a focus. There are obvious links with vanilla hysteria – demanding attention, rejecting attention, holding forth, holding aloof – but with social media there's a gap in space and time – a displacement of presence that seems important.

Post and wait. Read and respond. Withdraw the post. Withhold and wait. And wait. Re-post. Respond. Post something new. Or not. Wait. Are you there? Is anybody there? Another post. Are you listening? Waiting? Watching? What's going on? Did you read my post? Did you watch my video? Does anyone know what is going on?

The focus has shifted. It is no longer the hysteric storming into the room and demanding attention. Then storming out again. There's a gap that has taken hold and everything now revolves around that absence in the middle. Hysteric, family, friends, colleagues, complete strangers – they are all under the sway of that black hole of common attention. And, perhaps most interesting of all, while control has passed to that central emptiness no one even recognizes this fact. The syndrome is altered too subtly. It is, as Alf would say, very curious.

*

Alf had news at Christmas – Gillian is pregnant – due in July. I think that's what he said. July or August. Not September. And not June. Not that it matters to me. He called first thing Christmas morning – six-thirty my time. I told him I was already up. He wouldn't have cared either way. I got the impression he is hoping for a boy (they don't know yet) but Emily will be four in March and he thinks she'll do better with a little brother than a sister – less competitive – bring out the maternal instinct in her. That's the idea. Who knows? Jealousy strikes me as an equal opportunity destructor but I don't have kids. I don't even spend time with other people's kids. All I know is what I see in adults and they don't provide a lot of comfort. But I can't claim any special expertise. Neither can Alf but that never stops him.

He thinks I should visit once the baby is born. Actually, he wants me to visit before then. And again later. He says May might be good. I told him I would think about it but May isn't very likely. I have a feeling things are going to happen in a few months – I don't know what – but they are definitely going to – so I don't want to mess it up by not being here when they do.

"Sure, sure, Kit. Whatever you say. But, you know, I'm still waiting for your report on Montreal. Remember? Maybe you could bring it with you when you come in May. Or, better yet, send it along before then. I'm not going away, Kit. Not on this one."

"I didn't think you were, Alf."

"Good. So, stop avoiding the issue."

"I'm not avoiding anything, Alf."

"Sure, sure, Kit. But I sense a certain resistance here. A little wilful blindness. Head in the sand?"

"There's no sand here, Alf. It's snow and ice. And my head's free."

"Whatever, Kit. You know what I mean. You've got to deal with this sooner or later. You know that. I know that."

"Don't worry, Alf. I haven't forgotten."

"I'm not worried, Kit. You're the one who is worried. You just don't know it yet. But you will. Soon."

2

Sally drove me home from the restaurant that last evening. I would say I was nervous about the traffic – she had had too much wine for that lithe little body of hers – but nervousness wasn't in the air just then. I was tense in a hundred different ways but fear of meeting the tailgate of a truck at high speed was not one of them. She is an aggressive driver but she knows where she lives.

She stopped in front of my hotel.

"What's this place like?" she asked, glancing at the front entry.

"Cheap," I said. "And clean."

"Those are both positives."

I got out of the car. I had nothing to say.

"Thanks for the ride."

She smiled, waved her hand in a queen-like fashion and turned to drive away. She had her foot on the clutch when a sudden look of alarm came over her face.

"I almost forgot," she said, putting the car back into park.

She reached into the back and got her purse, dug around in it for a minute and then pulled something out. She leaned over and held it toward me. It was a CD.

"I brought this for you."

I took the CD from her without looking at it.

"I hope you like it," she said. "We are amateurs – but that just means we love what we are doing."

"Thanks," I said.

Sally looked at me standing stupidly at the curb with a CD in my hand.

"And, Kit."

"Yes?"

"Come back to Montreal sometime."

Sure. You bet.

She blinked and smiled.

"Soon."

*

I have Sally's CD playing right now. It's a mix of classical pieces – Bach, Beethoven, Chopin, Debussy – all very calm and soothing. The title on the cover says "Giocoso Souvenir" – whatever that means. On the back it lists the songs but there's no mention of the performers, let alone a description of who played what. I have wondered about that more than once. Was it modesty? Professional discretion? Was Sally Hatano her real name?

I guess I'll never know.

I went out for a sandwich at eleven-thirty. It's just past one right now and Heather is supposed to arrive at one-thirty. I hope she's on time. She's been late for her last two appointments and I don't like the trend, especially since I'm more forgiving than I should be. It's not good for either of us. She probably needs someone a little sterner than I am – more stringent on the cash and commitment side of things. I think she wants to be told to forget med school. And I suspect that's what she needs to do. Her dad's a doctor and she feels like she should be one too. Bad idea.

But I'm not telling her that directly. She needs to put the pieces together herself. So, we're talking about diversity and personal fulfilment and quality of life.

So be it.

I've got a free hour after Heather and then Martin at three-thirty. It has warmed up a bit and it is still sunny so maybe we'll do the walking cure. It seems to suit him. He tends to get uptight in the office and the words won't come. I don't mind silence – long inner journeys – but only some of the time. It all depends on the moment and the client. With Martin, right now, I think he needs to ramble aloud. We tried a walk by the river for the third session and it worked well. Since then we've walked at least part of each session. I've never done this before – walked this much with a client – but with Martin it seems to be the way to go. I wish I could do it with everyone.

*

Julia's mother sent me the letters I had written over the years. I didn't realize there were so many. They arrived in a box half way through November. I opened it right away to see what it was but it took another week before I could do more than that. I didn't want to read them – not after the first couple. Julia had marked them up with underlining, exclamations, notes and doodles. A few of them had sketches that looked vaguely like me – my nose was a prow and my ears were like side mirrors on a truck – not exactly photographic – but the basic resemblance was there. They were amusing – the sketches. Julia couldn't draw worth beans.

I've got the box at the apartment – in the den Julia used to call my monk's cell. The landlord calls it a second bedroom but that's a joke. I've got a desk in there and that's about all that fits. A small chair in the corner. A bookshelf. I sometimes sleep there – on the floor – when my mind won't settle. I like the rug and the feel of the hardwood underneath. It helps me believe I am somewhere else.

In fact, I slept there last night – on the floor, not somewhere else. I had supper with Angela and that was the beginning of it. We get together every month or so to chat about nothing – I think it helps her stay on course. She stopped sessions three years ago but she obviously needs ongoing contact and she can't afford proper sessions so we meet and eat. For me, it's part of the job. That's my not-stern-enough part showing up again. Not that I don't enjoy seeing her – she's a positive force in the universe – but sometimes she takes up a little too much oxygen. She does not know the meaning of quiet. But that's fine. I could always say no.

Unfortunately, the discussion at supper turned to Julia. She already knew the basics. I had given her a report on Montreal when we met in November and she had been thinking since then in her special Angela way – which meant she knew exactly where to land last night. I made my way through the meal without choking but afterwards I was restless. I walked through the streets for a while but it was too cold to stay out long so I came home and tried reading. I managed to fall asleep after a few pages of Lacan but there was a noise outside – maybe just the wind – and when I woke up I was even more restless than before. I got up and went to the den and took out the box with my letters to Julia. I don't know whether her mother read them. I hope not. I don't know what she thinks of me but I wouldn't want even the kindest mother to read the idiocies I wrote to Julia. Not that I was cruel. Or obscene. I was just stupid. There's no cure for stupidity.

Darts – and Sally playing on the stereo – and Angela asking pointed questions in replay of last night's supper – what more could anyone ask? Oh, I forgot – Heather is late again. That completes the circle.

Around and around we go.

Back in November I explained to Angela why I cancelled our October supper – I needed a break – I went to Montreal. And I gave her a sketch to prove it – the view from the top of the Mountain. I didn't mention Julia but, all the same, she asked about 'the rock lady'. That's her name for Julia. Explanation: I have a smooth stone I use as a paperweight on my desk and Angela zeroed in on it within five minutes of coming in the door for her first session – nice rock – where's it from? – who gave it to you? Julia, of course, and a brief description of our relationship followed. Really, doc? That is one nice rock. Don't lose it. Thanks. I appreciate that, Angela. I mean it, doc. Your friend knows how to pick a stone.

After that, Julia was the rock lady. And, despite the fact that Angela was the client and I was the psychologist, she became my big sister, prodding me about my love life from time to time. So, what's new? Any letters? I've got a feeling you're not telling me something, doc. Visitor coming, maybe? And, of course, when I got home that evening there would be a letter waiting for me from Julia. Seriously. It's that kind of thing that gets unnerving with Angela.

In November we sat down at the table and right away it was – long time, no see. Are you doing okay? You don't look so good. You've lost weight. I could stand to lose some weight, doc, but you don't need to shed any pounds. What's up? How come no Octoberfest?

So I told her about Montreal.

And without missing a beat she asked about Julia.

"This is about the rock lady, isn't it?"

I gave her a half smile.

"Gone."

The other half of the smile.

"You mean – dumped you gone? Or never coming back gone?"

I looked away.

Angela looked at me hard.

"Never coming back gone."

"She died, Angela."

She closed her eyes for half a second. Angela has wild curly hair and a round, round face. She is a round woman in all ways. She usually has a big round contagious smile that makes her look like the Laughing Buddha. But even when she's serious she still beams a rolling round warmth.

"I'm sorry, doc." A pause. "I had a feeling – back in September – but I didn't want to say anything. I knew it was more than just the geese flying."

I looked at Angela sitting as quietly as she ever gets. She knew it? How could she possibly have known it? Julia was alive. She was going north – not south like the geese. I hadn't said anything to her about Julia's visit. Of course, she knew Julia was visiting – she was Angela – but how could she possibly have known anything about what would happen next? And, if she did know, why didn't she say something?

I would have laughed – or shouted at her – but she was Angela. I tried to smile but I was having a hard time keeping my face together. That's when I gave her the sketch from the Mountain. It took her a moment to recognize the new direction but she's not stupid. She looked at the sketch, took the turn and went with it.

"You draw?" she said, holding the sketch up to the light.

"In Montreal I do."

"This is good, doc." She smiled. "Real good."

"Thanks."

She gave me a questioning look. "Only in Montreal?"

I laughed gently. "No. I draw here, too."

"Good."

She examined the sketch again.

"This is for me? To keep?"

Yes, Angela. I handed her the envelope I had brought the sketch in.

"For you – to keep."

"Thanks, doc."

She put the sketch in the envelope and the envelope in her bag. I tried not to wince at the compression. It was only a sketch.

Angela dropped her bag to the floor.

"Darts and drawing," she said. "You're full of surprises, doc."

A pause.

"That's two 'D' words. There has to be a third."

She leaned forward and lowered her voice.

"Don't tell me. You dance, right?"

No, Angela. I do not dance.

I smiled a big thank you for the joke.

"Drift, Angela. The missing word is drift."

*

So, I took a few letters out of the box. They are almost in chronological order but not quite – Julia wasn't neurotic about things like that. There is some muddling within the years but each year is held together by a big red elastic. I picked a few letters at random from the last two years and read them through. Then I picked out a few more from earlier years. I read them in reverse order – going back in time – then started at the beginning – chronologically – and read each letter one more time.

Hmmm. My handwriting hadn't changed much over the years but Julia's margin notes did. There were more of them and they were longer – dragging down the side of the page and across the bottom. And, there were more and more doodles – faces, birds, mountains, waves – a kid's scribbles – triangles and circles – stick figure people. They were amusing at first but then not so much. The tone changed as the years went on – the notes, the doodles. They went from silver dancing – spinning, rising – to light green tendrils – touching, holding – to dark green forests thickening into black.

I put the letters back in their proper year – almost chronologically – and closed the box and put it away in the closet. I wasn't any less restless than I had been before but it was later and I was more tired. I needed to move but there was no way I was going back out into the cold. So, I paced the rug until I was far enough away from where I started to feel safe. Then I lay down and fell asleep.

3

Heather is now officially a no-show. And I am officially not happy. I doubt she forgot but it is possible. Maybe she went skiing. Or skating on the canal. Or maybe she has an essay due in January and she has started freaking out about it. Whatever. She had an appointment. She should have called and cancelled.

I could see this coming but it still pisses me off. Sort of. Not really. It does – but not in a simple way. I don't care about the inconvenience. I was coming in anyway. Nothing would have changed if she had called and cancelled. No. What pisses me off is me, not her. I should have known enough to cancel the appointment myself. It would have broken the trend and we could have started the New Year with a clean slate. Instead, she has fizzled things out. Going, going, gone. She won't want to come back. And I will have dropped the ball. Again.

It was like that with Angela. In a way. On my side of the equation. Not that you can compare the two – Heather and Angela. They are about as different as people can be. Heather is a clenched fist, weeping. Angela is a slap in the face – with a smile.

I met Angela at a big craft show at Lansdowne Park. I was shopping for an anniversary present for Alf and Gem.

Angela had a small table she was sharing with a friend who made jewellery – pendants, pins and earrings fashioned from some type of coloured clay. I have a clear recollection of a pair of earrings with blue jays. They were fat and mischievous and perfect for a twelve year old. I complimented Angela on her work and she explained that she did the flowers, not the jewellery. I looked more closely at the flower arrangements. They were a confusion of stems, petals and leaves, without focus or order.

"It must be a lot of work," I said, trying to be tactful.

Angela laughed a little too loudly.

"It's just a hobby. Something I do to keep from going crazy. It's cheaper than bingo. For me, arranging the stuff is easy. It's picking and drying the flowers that takes time. I go all over the place trying to find good stuff. My swamp romp, I call it. It gets pretty wild but that's okay. I like a little hike every now and then. It helps keep me slim."

Angela smiled briefly at her joke – she is not slim – and then she went silent. It was an awkward moment. I didn't want to buy anything and my gaze wandered to the wood carvings of ducks and chipmunks at the next table. I was about to move on when Angela stopped me.

"Let me guess what you do," she said.

I stopped and turned toward her again. A big grin came across her face and I couldn't help but smile back.

"Good," she said.

She closed her eyes for a moment as if she was listening to something. I now know it was just an act but back then I waited patiently, curious.

"You're a shrink," she said, opening her eyes.

I raised my eyebrows in acknowledgement.

"A psychologist, actually. But 'shrink' is close enough. How did you know?"

She smiled and said it was a secret. Then she asked if I had a card. I checked my jacket pockets, then my wallet. Nothing. I apologized and muttered something about always forgetting. The truth was I had enough clients for the moment so I didn't feel the need to carry business cards.

I smiled and wished her luck, then started to move off but Angela asked me to wait a minute. She rummaged through her handbag, pulled out a pen and handed it to me together with one of her own business cards. The pen was cracked at the nib with an accumulated blob of blue ink at the tip. Her business card had her name, telephone number and the words "Floral Design and Inscription" printed in bold red script.

I wiped the blob of ink on the corner of the card, wrote my name and office number on the back and returned the card to her. She said thanks and dropped the card into her handbag without looking at it.

It was several weeks before I got a call. I didn't recognize her voice and she didn't give me her name. Instead, she described how we met and said she would like to drop by. I checked through my appointment book and set a time early the next week. When the day came and Angela arrived she said a loud "Hi" in the doorway and came into the room with the words "Am I late?" Before I could say anything, she said, "I don't think I'm late." She glanced over her shoulder at where I was looking – the clock over the door – and turned back with a big smile.

"Right on time."

"Yes," I said. "Right on time. That's a good start."

"Beginnings are easy," she said.

She took a quick survey of the office, staring for a moment at the dart board, and then sat down in one of the leather armchairs in the middle of the room. I got up and sat in the second chair.

"No couch?" she asked.

"No couch." I smiled. "Sometimes I sit here. Sometimes I sit at the desk. It all depends."

"On what?"

"On what seems to work best."

Angela looked around the room some more, lingered at the photograph of geese in flight hanging on the back wall and then began to study the layout of my desk.

"No flowers," she said, glancing at me. "You could use an arrangement to lighten things up."

"Maybe," I said.

"You need to be more definite, doc. Yes or no. And the answer is 'yes'. I'll bring something next time. You can buy it if you like it. Or we can trade – flowers for talk. How does that sound?"

Like sales patter.

"Okay. You bring something and I'll take a look."

Dead grass and withered flowers. I can hardly wait.

"Good."

She looked back at my desk and that was when she noticed the paperweight Julia gave me.

"Nice rock," she said.

*

I settled on a polished wooden bowl for Alf and Gem. Very simple, very elegant. I also sent a separate parcel with three smooth stones – one black, one white and one as close to red as I could find. One stone for each of Alf, Gem and Emily. I found them on the shore of the Ottawa River. They looked better when they were wet but there was nothing I could do about that. I guess I'll have to find another stone for the new baby. Green, maybe. I'll have to think about that. I don't want to make Emily jealous.

*

It became clear at our first meeting that Angela was hoping for a miracle. She went silent for a long moment when I told her sessions usually went on for months, often years. She did the math.

"You look like a nice guy to spend time with," she said. "But I can't afford to do this for months. You'll have to find a shortcut."

"There are no shortcuts."

"There are always shortcuts," she said. "They aren't pretty most of the time – but that's okay. I'm not here for the scenery. And I'm not afraid of some shit on the path. I've seen my share of shit so a bit more won't do me any harm."

"I can't promise you anything."

"I'm not asking for promises. I'm asking for results."

My mind told me to stop while there was still time. This woman would be a disaster as a client – nothing but shouting, swearing and bounced cheques.

Then she smiled that Laughing Buddha smile.

"Loosen up," she said. "I know you can do it."

No way. I shook my head and smiled back.

"All I can do is provide perspective. You have to do the work. And you have to accept that fact."

"I'm not afraid of work. But I want results. If I am going to pay you all that money, I want results."

"I can't promise anything."

"Why not?"

"Because it depends on you."

Angela looked at her feet and said nothing.

"If you aren't comfortable with this," I said, "then you shouldn't do it. At a minimum, you should think about it some more."

Angela looked up.

"I don't have the time," she said.

I waited but I knew she was stuck on the money. She was a waitress at a small restaurant not known for gourmet dining and big tips. She didn't have money to waste.

"Why don't we try six sessions," I said, "and then see where we are."

Angela did the math again.

"Six sessions?" A pause. "Can we stop sooner?"

"You can stop anytime. But what I'm saying is – don't count on anything less than six sessions. And even then you have to ..."

She held up her hand to stop me.

"Okay," she said. "I get the point. Rome wasn't built in a day. We'll do six."

*

Maybe I could find a blue stone. That would be good if the baby were a boy. Stereotyping, I know, but so what? I can deal with the social pressure. The problem is finding a blue stone in the first place. I don't mean now – everything's buried under ice and snow right now. In the spring. But even then blue stones aren't exactly plentiful in the Ottawa River. I might have to buy one somewhere – but that wouldn't be right. It's got to be from the river like the other three. Definitely. So, it may have to be green.

*

After Angela left I sat staring out the window passing Julia's stone back and forth from hand to hand. It was warm and smooth and fit my palm perfectly. Yes, it was a nice rock. I put the stone down, got up, walked over to the window and looked outside. It was late in the afternoon. There was plenty of traffic and the sidewalks were busy. A kid on a bike was trying to navigate between the pedestrians. I went back to my desk, took the darts from the desk drawer and went over to the toe line. Twenty. Twenty. Triple twenty.

After half an hour of tossing darts and inventing names for Angela's problem, I went to the Bridgehead down the street for a sandwich. I sat at the counter by the window and watched the people passing by. No one seemed worth noticing. They all looked boring and bored. When I finished eating I went back to the office and read and napped until after nine. I still didn't want to go home but neither did I want to stay in the office all night. So, I packed up and went for a walk by the river.

*

Another red stone. That would be the easiest. But it would have to be a good match. Or very different. Alf and Gem could let Emily decide which one she wanted. The baby would never know.

*

It was cool by the water. The headlights of the cars on the parkway streamed past and a crescent moon was rising. There was no one else out walking. A group of runners passed me and then a guy on his bike with his dog keeping pace beside him. A pair of runners going the other way. I walked along the path as far as Kitchissippi Point. There were a few cars parked in the dark – teenagers probably. I made my way to the far side and sat on a bench near a flock of sleeping ducks, their heads tucked under their wings.

The faint roar of the Deschênes Rapids came across the water and against that sound there was the soft lapping of the waves against the shingle. I seldom came down to the river when it was dark. Everything seemed alien – even the sound of the waves and the shadows and the breeze that came out of the night. I sat for half an hour listening to nothing, thinking about my session with Angela and the dream she found so troublesome.

In her dream Angela is collecting flowers by a river when she suddenly feels sleepy and lies down on the embankment for a rest. She immediately falls asleep but at the same time she can see herself lying in the grass and she thinks – you're getting old, sweetheart; you aren't going to live forever, you know. She watches herself breathing for a moment and then somehow she is awake, standing up again. She picks up her basket of flowers and walks to the river edge, slip/slides down the riverbank and into the water. She doesn't know why she has done this – her basket is full – she should be going home. Instead, she wades out into the river, sets her basket gently on top of the water and lets it go.

As the basket floats away from her she notices a sudden movement underwater. She looks down and sees a large fish swim past. She freezes. It is enormous – longer than her arm – and it has come so close she could have reached out and touched it. The fish swims further out into the river and then arcs slowly in front of her again, even closer this time. Angela bends down and lifts the fish from the water, cradling it with both arms. Its skin is a rainbow of colours – blue, green, purple, orange and red. It is sleek and huge and beautiful – a marvel. She holds it in front of her, not knowing what to do.

"I have had that dream a dozen times in the last year," Angela said.

She got up and walked over to the window, looked down at the street and then directly across at the karate studio that faces my office. There wouldn't have been a karate class at that time of day but there might have been one of the instructors practising; at least, that seemed likely given the way Angela was staring and making small movements with her hands.

"It is always the same," she said.

She looked down at the far side of the street and then she pressed her cheek against the glass to try to look at the sidewalk on our side. She watched the traffic on the road for a moment then turned her attention indoors.

"It is always the same," she said. "Picking flowers, falling asleep, walking into the river. And, I always end up standing waist deep in water with that fish in my arms."

She paused for a second. Then she looked at me.

"That fish," she said. "I've got to get rid of it before it dies and starts to rot."

*

I could always send two or three stones – red, green, grey – and tell Alf to let Emily choose one for the baby. They could throw out the rest. That might work.

*

I stayed by the river until I started to yawn. It must have been getting close to midnight and the traffic had settled to almost nothing – a bus every ten minutes or so, a car or two now and then. The ducks started to move around so I took that as a cue, stood up, quacked at the ducks and headed home.

When I got back to the apartment I checked the mailbox on my way in and there was a letter from Julia waiting for me. Somehow I knew there would be. Angela's questions about the rock lady had made me think about Julia and thinking about Julia had made me wonder. She was in Japan teaching – again – but she didn't seem to be settling in the way she usually did. Her letters had become shorter, more difficult, cryptic. It had been a few weeks since the last one arrived and when Angela asked where the rock lady was I hesitated. For all I knew she had quit her job and moved on without telling me. But this letter was from Japan. I went up to my apartment, put the envelope on the kitchen table and made myself a cup of green tea.

> *Hello you,*
>
> *It is very early. The sun has begun to lighten the sky but it hasn't yet topped the horizon. In a few minutes I will go for my morning walk to watch the sun rise over the Pacific but I have to write this note first because I have a question for you, an important question that insists on becoming ink on paper before I bury it again. Questions can be like that, can't they? If only answers were so insistent.*
>
> *The question I want to ask you is going to have to wait for a moment because I have to tell you about a dream first. It arrived this morning – the dream, not the question. The question has been hovering for months. This is not an evasion. Trust me.*
>
> *In my dream I am walking in a marshy area at the edge of a large river – the Ottawa?*

– collecting reeds to make a basket. Why I want to make a basket, I don't know. But that is what I am doing. It is evening and the sun has disappeared below the line of trees on the far side of the river. The growing darkness makes it difficult for me to see, so I am moving very slowly through the water. It is getting deeper – up to my thighs. Suddenly there is a loud splashing and two ducks rise out of the reeds into the air. I am startled, step back and lose my balance. I turn and with my arm I hit something large that moves when I fall against it. It is a reed boat.

The boat is long and flat with an extended prow at one end. There is a slight depression in the middle with enough room for one person. I drop the reeds I have gathered onto the boat and then climb aboard. It seems made for lying down, so I do. It is very comfortable. Once I am settled the boat begins to move forward of its own, slipping out of the reeds into the river.

I lie quietly in the boat as it floats into the open water. I look briefly at the shoreline I have just left and I have the impression there is someone on the bank waving to me. I don't wave back. Instead, I watch for a moment then turn back to face the open water. The boat drifts toward the centre of the river then begins to move slowly upstream – against the current! As I move with the boat in the dark I hear the words "Finally, I am getting somewhere". And with those words, I wake up.

Odd, isn't it?

Finally, I am getting somewhere. As if all this time I have been in the same place. And even odder is the fact that as soon as I woke up from the dream I knew that it was you who was waving at me from the shore. Staying behind once again.

And now my question.

Will you come and visit me here? I know you would hate Tokyo but you would love the rest of Japan. You could visit the temples in Kyoto or go north to Hokkaido. Where I am now is so beautiful and magnificent at the same time. We could visit Matsushima – it isn't far – Basho called it the most beautiful place in Japan. If you came you would never want to leave. You should come.

Yes, you should come. My room is too small and it is against the rules to have guests, but I could find a cheap place for you to stay nearby. I would really like to have you here to see what I am seeing – the mountains and the hills and the ocean and the fishermen and the blossoms and birds and, above all else, the people. We could go for long walks by the ocean, take the ferry across to the Urato Islands or head back inland through the hills. We could drink tea for hours in a tea room or wander the streets being followed by the children who want to practice their English. We could talk all night. Or just sit and watch the stars.

You would see. Everything is different. You should come.

Please come.

Love -- Julia

I held the letter in front of me for a very long time, then put it down and took a sip of my tea.

4

Martin will arrive in forty-seven minutes. That is one thing I can count on. I can also count on my mind circling like a wasp unless I find it something to do. I'm too tired to play darts and too stupid to work. I suppose I could go for a quick walk to wake myself up but my fingers are telling me to forget it.

I need to sketch.

*

When Alf went back to Scotland and made peace with Gem I expected a photograph. I had never seen a picture of Gem and I dropped a few not too subtle hints that putting a face to a name would be nice. Alf was either dense or difficult. He ignored my hints. I didn't want to insist – just in case he had a reason – so in my ludicrous way I imagined every type of face and figure for Gem based on what I knew about Alf – who is an odd character made mostly of bones – and what I thought a female clarinettist might look like. I tried all the search engines on the Internet and came up with some impressive guidance.

As a clarinettist she would have rounded, maybe even hunched shoulders from practising all the time. And she would have to be short – since Alf was short. And she would have to be thin – since Alf was thin – unless of course she was fat – since Alf was thin. She was Scottish so her hair would have to be curly – unless it was just wavy or maybe even straight – and probably red or black but maybe brown (not blonde). Her complexion would be fair, her eyes green or grey or blue (not brown). Her features would be sharp – except her cheeks which would be rounded (and rosy). Her breasts would be large – since Alf was infantile. And her feet would be small – for no particular reason.

In other words, I had a pretty good idea of what she looked like even before Alf sent me a picture a few years later, along with a wedding invitation. Of course, I was right. The photo showed Gem and Alf standing in front of what looked to be a public garden. There was an iron gate and a stone wall and lots of bushes barely visible in the background. Gem was the same height as Alf. She was wearing a large green hat that covered her head completely – so her hair had to be short – unless it was tied back in a ponytail. The shadow from the brim of her hat obscured her face so it was difficult to tell much about her features other than she had a rounded chin and a small smiling mouth. It must have been cold because they were both wearing winter coats. Alf had on a ski jacket and Gem was wearing a knee length grey wool coat that managed to obscure every curve in her body. She didn't look thin and she couldn't have been obese but the full range in between was available.

When I got the wedding invitation I studied the photo and smiled a lot. Then I called to say congratulations. Gem answered and I almost hung up – I thought I had the wrong number. I knew Alf and Gem were living together but it never occurred to me that Gem might answer the telephone. I was calling Alf, so I expected Alf to answer.

"Who is calling?" she asked.

"This is Kit – from Canada." I didn't see any harm in letting the woman know my name. Canada was a big place. I could still hang up. "I was calling for ..."

"Kit! Hello, Kit. It's Gillian. I'm so glad to finally hear your voice. I should have known it was you from the accent. You sound closer than Canada. And taller than Alf described you. You've got a pleasant voice – like a bass clarinet. No wonder Alfie likes you."

She paused to catch her breath but I was too over-whelmed to jump in.

"Just a moment, Kit. Alfie's trying to get the cat to come back inside. It's raining and she's hiding under the steps."

The phone clunked against something solid – a desk or table top – and there was the sound of footsteps across a wooden floor, then a door opening. I could feel the fresh, damp Scottish air. Gem's voice carried across the room.

"Alfie – it's Kit from Canada on the telephone."

There were more words, more footsteps and the sound of Gem calling the cat; then the door closed and I could tell that Gem had come in as well.

"Kit," said Alf. "How are you?"

"I'm great. I just got the invitation. Congratulations."

"Thanks."

"And best wishes to Gem. I've been wondering when you two would get married. It's great."

"Yeah. We're excited."

"In June."

"Yeah. Gem wants a June wedding. You know how it goes."

Actually, I didn't. But I had heard rumours.

"Sounds great. It gives you time to plan."

"Yeah. That's Gem's job – and her mom. I'm standing as far back as I can."

I laughed. "Good idea."

"You know me, Kit. All that ritual – it's just another attachment."

Sure, Alf.

"Whatever. It's great, Alf. I'm really happy for you and Gem."

"Thanks." A pause. "You know, Kit, you should stay for a while when you come. You could use our place while we go on our honeymoon. Look after the cat. It would make a cheap holiday. Edinburgh is beautiful in June."

"Sounds good."

But I'm not sure about the cat.

"Terrific," said Alf. "And when we get back I'll give you a mini-tour – show you the Highlands."

Hills with sheep.

"I've always wanted to see the Highlands."

"Good." Alf said something to Gem I couldn't quite make out. "We'll count on you being here – house sitting – after the wedding."

"Right."

I hadn't seen Alf in years. And I had never seen Gem – not in person. It was a great idea. Edinburgh was supposed to be beautiful – the Castle and all that. And the Highlands – well, they might be interesting. I could go to Glasgow. And, maybe Aberdeen or Inverness. Plus, if I stayed at Alf's place part of the time it wouldn't break the bank. Maybe Julia would come. Hmmm. Alf could meet Julia and Julia could meet Alf. That would be interesting.

It was a great idea.

Of course, I didn't go.

*

I'm sketching Gem – from memory – which means from what I remember of the wedding photos. Alf wasn't happy that I didn't go. He griped a lot about getting someone to look after the cat – I had doubts about that cat – but Gem sent me photos anyway with a long cheery thank you note for the gift I sent – cutlery. She has beautiful handwriting – fountain pen – black ink – fancy paper – very calligraphic. I wonder if she took lessons. She and Angela might get along. Or not. In any case, I was grateful for the photos. I keep them handy in my desk drawer at home – in the den – but it's been a while since I've taken them out.

Gem looks exactly as I knew she would – smiling, happy and easy to draw – but Alf looks older and none too comfortable in a tux. Don't worry, Alf, it won't take long and then you can get back into your jeans – which I am sure he did. He is not a man for formalities or constraints. I wonder what he looks like now.

In my sketch I've got Gem waving a clarinet at Alf. She's soft and round and he's hard and pointed. It's just a cartoon but it's who they are in my imagination. Alf is taking notes while holding up his left hand as if asking Gem to wait. And she is pretending to listen – a look of attention on her face – just before she does what she intended to do all along. They are, I think, an excellent match.

*

Okay, so now what? The sketch of Alf and Gem is all very fine but it doesn't solve the problem of the wasp. It's not the kind you can kill. You have to distract it. Over and over again.

*

Last night at supper Angela asked if I had any drawings of Julia. She had been thinking about the sketch of the

Mountain I had given her in November. I should have known better.

"Do you?"

I waffled.

"I know what she looks like, doc."

"I know you know, Angela."

"So ...?"

I didn't want to answer because if I did there would only be more questions.

"Look doc, now that I know you can draw I was wondering if you ever did a picture of the rock lady. You know, she sits, you draw. That kind of thing."

A pause.

"Is that such a tough question?"

Actually, yes. It is.

I ate some of my soup. But she was not giving up.

"There's nothing in your office. Right? I guess that would be kind of personal. Not professional."

Correct.

"So, what about at home?"

Let it go, Angela.

"I mean, you can draw pretty good. It only makes sense."

A pause.

"Is this bothering you, doc?" She leaned closer. "Because if it is, you know, I'll stop – once you tell me."

Thanks, Angela. I knew I could count on you.

"No. I don't," I said. Julia never sat for me.

She leaned back.

"Why not?"

That, my dear, is an excellent question.

"I guess it never occurred to me."

"Didn't she ask?"

Hmmm. How could she ask? She didn't know.

"I guess it never occurred to her either."

Angela began to eat her soup which had been sitting patiently in her bowl going cold while she interrogated me.

"You know, doc," she said, her spoon in mid-air. "That's pretty weird."

*

Maybe I should send Alf and Gem four new stones for the bowl. They could put the first three in the garden. Or in the sea. The Firth of Forth. Wherever. It would be a completely new configuration – the new family – four new shapes and colours – not just an add-on pebble. That might be better psychologically for everyone.

5

It is two forty-nine. Eleven minutes until Martin arrives.

I've put away my pencil and sketchbook. It's not a bad cartoon – I like the expression on Gem's face – but the pencil didn't quite do the job. There are too many lines leading nowhere. It gets like that sometimes – fraying at the edges – that's what erasers are for – but I can't be bothered with this one. It's recycling material. I should have played darts instead. There's no waste, no trace with darts. They fly through the air without a sound. When you take them out of the board everything closes up nicely again. It's all in the moment. Hmm. That's something to think about.

What I should really think about is ending my suppers with Angela. It's too much. I don't owe her anything. She did eight sessions and then the money ran out. Thanks, doc. You've been a big help. I knew you could do the job. We should keep in touch. I'll give you a call sometime. Maybe supper. How's that sound?

Bad idea.

I didn't do the job. We talked about her family – her wandering father and pious mother, her fortune-teller grandmother. Angela said she was a witch – the grandmother. She had a reputation – lots of fear mixed with respect – and more. We sailed through Angela's marriage, her divorce and her leaving town. Her time in Toronto and then Peterborough and then here. Her waitressing job. Her flowers and her calligraphy business. But mostly we talked about me. Was I married? Did I like my job? What did the rock lady do? How did we get together? What did I think of this town? Did I plan to stay? Did I really think this shrink stuff did any good?

With anyone else I would have steered things differently – my life is not a topic for discussion – but with Angela it was as if focusing on me drained her dream of its energy. She smiled more, snapped less. Her anxiety began to lift. She wasn't calm – that wasn't in her genes – but her edge took a different shape. It stopped cutting inward. And so I decided that focusing on my life wasn't an avoidance. It was the way she was working things out.

But it was annoying. Tiring, delicate and annoying. Eventually, near the end of her fifth session when she had been asking about my childhood and I was getting more than fed up, I came back at her.

"We aren't here to talk about my childhood, Angela. You came here because of your dream. Remember? So, now that you have had five sessions, tell me – what do you think about your dream – now, today, at this instant."

My voice was a little loud. My tone a little nasty. I was more than a little fed up. Not very professional.

Angela shrugged and looked away.

"Hey, doc, it's just a dream. I've cooked fish before. I'll cook this one, too."

And then Julia came for a visit.

It was week six of Angela's sessions. There was no heads-up, no warning of any kind. She just showed up at the office one day before lunch.

"I told them my father died. It wasn't a lie."

Her father had died two years before.

"They said to take my time."

A pause.

"I can go back in a week or two."

After the funeral, of course.

"Or longer."

A look.

"There's no rush."

Turn away. A pause.

"The other teachers are happy to get the extra hours."

Right.

It was a wide open door.

*

"Where did you get these?"

I was putting Julia's stuff in the bedroom. She had gone directly to the kitchen and made herself a cup of tea before settling in the living room on the sofa. The flower arrangement from Angela was occupying most of the rest of the room. Just kidding. It was on the coffee table but it was kind of large and impossible to miss. Or ignore.

I guess Angela figured I needed extra help so she made me an extra big one. Spend some time with the flowers, she said when she brought the arrangement to my office. That was her second visit and I insisted on giving her a discount on the session. She didn't fuss about it for long. Instead, she told me to talk to them – the flowers. Other people did. Customers at the restaurant. They'd buy an arrangement and a few weeks later they'd be having lunch and mention how pleased they were. At least half of them would explain how they found themselves sitting beside the flowers talking. It sounded crazy to Angela but she knew enough not to insult paying customers. They smiled or laughed, feeling embarrassed, but they said it anyway.

"Who am I to call them on it?" Angela said. "If they say it helps then it helps."

A pause.

"Maybe you should try it, doc."

I smiled but didn't say anything.

"Think of it like prayer," Angela said.

Pardon?

"You don't have to look at me like that, doc."

Why not?

"I'm not saying you pray *to* them – it's just a bunch of dead flowers for crying out loud. You pray *with* them – like a rosary. The flowers are there and you pray with them."

Right. Okay. Not 'to' but 'with'. Like a rosary. Got it. And let's skip whether they've been blessed or not. That's just a detail. I get the basic concept and that's what's important. You pray with them – count the petals or something – like a rosary. Okay. What I don't get is the theological part.

"Angela," I said. "Why would I want to pray?"

She looked at me as if I had just spit on my hand and rubbed it all over my face. She had put the arrangement on the small table beside her chair when she came in. She glanced at it and then back at me.

"Everybody prays, doc."

Not me.

She reached over, tugged at one of the flowers, turned it slightly and then stuck it back down.

"Praying is just talking, trying to work things out."

She gave me a hard look.

"What do you think you are doing with people all day?"

*

I brought them home and put them in the den. They would have been a distraction at the office. It was a very big and very odd arrangement – a tight cluster in the middle with bunches of grasses and leaves and feathery things sprouting on the sides. I kept them in the den for a few days but moved them into the living room after I found myself sitting at the desk talking to a bulrush. The power of suggestion, I guess. When I came into the living room Julia was standing in front of the flower arrangement looking at it with awe. Other words might also apply.

"Where did you get this?"

She had a puzzled look on her face. I wasn't the kind of guy to buy flowers. Especially not something like Angela's over-sized, wild reaching, strangely hypnotic dried flower arrangement.

"A client gave it to me."

"Really?"

Julia walked around the table and, hence, around the arrangement.

"A new one," I said. "I just got it a few weeks ago."

I think it may still be growing.

"Female?" she asked.

I don't think it has a sex. But Angela is definitely ...

"Yes, as a matter of fact."

"Young?"

Julia, Julia, Julia.

"You know I can't talk about my clients."

She took a sip of her tea.

"Is she a friend, too?" A pause. "I mean, in addition to being a client."

Good grief, Julia. It's just a bunch of dead flowers.

Think of it as early stage compost.

"She's a client. She's had six sessions. That's about all I can tell you."

Julia reached out and lifted a flower that was dangling awkwardly. I thought maybe she was going to crush it.

Instead, she pushed it more firmly into the centre and let the head slump gently as she let go.

"Early days, you mean."

"Early. Late." I tried a smile. "You know how it goes."

"Only what you tell me."

I walked over to where she was standing and put my arm around her waist.

"She doesn't have much money. This was a partial payment for a session."

Julia glanced at me.

"Oh, that's sweet. How else does she pay her bills?"

She shifted slightly and my arm fell away.

"Stop it, Julia." This was Angela we were talking about. "Believe me – you are being ridiculous."

"Not as ridiculous as this," she said, gesturing at the arrangement.

Hey. This is not ridiculous. This is Angela.

Julia took another sip of her tea and then poked at a bulrush rising in the centre of the arrangement.

"Nice touch."

She made it wobble back and forth.

"Very phallic."

*

At the beginning of her seventh session Angela asked about the rock lady – of course. She said she had seen her on the street as she was coming into the office.

Pardon?

"Kind of skinny. Long brown hair. Pale blue top. Blue jeans. Sandals."

Sounds right.

"She was standing around like she was waiting for someone. Are you supposed to meet her once we're done?

We can quit early, if you want – as long as I get a refund – pro-rated – is that what you call it?"

I looked toward the window. What was Julia doing outside?

"That's alright. We can take our time. She knows I'm working."

And how did Angela know it was Julia?

"You sure, doc? I don't mind."

I smiled.

"She's been here before," I said. "She'll find something to do."

"If you say so. I just thought I should offer – cuz, you know, we're almost done."

Done? You just got here.

"Are we?"

Angela smiled a little smile and rocked lightly in her chair.

"Sure, doc."

She stood up and walked to the window. The smile was gone. She looked down at the street, then back at me.

"Is she staying long? Here? In Ottawa?"

I don't know.

"A few days."

"Is that all?"

The volume was up and she was looking at me like I was joking.

"Maybe a week. I don't know."

Angela paused and then looked outside again. She looked both ways down the street and then across at the karate studio. Her hands started, then stopped.

"She came all the way from Japan for a few days?"

She was talking directly at the window.

Welcome to Julia.

"Quality time," I said with a half laugh.

Angela turned and looked at the dart board and then at Julia's paperweight which had somehow found its way into my hand. She walked back to her chair and sat down.

"That's a long way to come for a few days, doc."

6

The day is brilliant. The snow is crisp. The air is clear. Martin keeps slapping his hands together because of the cold but it's more theatre than anything else. He likes the vigour and the sound – the gloved thud of his palms meeting. We are walking quickly as we head toward the river. When we get to the pathway we'll slow down but for now it's swift strides and slapping hands. No talking. Not yet.

*

"Do you think I'm sexy?"

It was Angela's final session, although I didn't know it at the time, and the answer was – no, she was not sexy. Sympathetic? Definitely. Intriguing? Maybe. She could even be called appealing – with that captivating smile of hers. But sexy? No, I don't think so.

"Why do you ask?"

"I used to be pretty hot," she said as if she hadn't heard me. "I had beautiful hair. I still do. But back in high school my body – it was worth looking at, too."

Alright. Was this going somewhere? Perhaps.

"And?" I asked.

"And then I got fat. But I wasn't always fat. I had curves. My hair was beautiful. The other girls would have died to have hair like mine."

"Okay."

Angela had been looking directly at me, as if challenging me. She took a deep breath and looked to the side. I focussed on my notepad.

"One day I was combing out my hair after a shower. I had left the bathroom door open because of the steam and I was standing in front of the mirror with a towel wrapped around me. I was sixteen. My boobs had come in – all the way. I had a good body. And I knew it."

Angela glanced at me and smiled.

"Hard to believe, eh? But it's true. I was standing there in the bathroom, combing my hair, feeling proud of myself. I liked my hips and legs. I liked my boobs. I liked my face. And, I especially liked my hair. It was beautiful. I was standing there combing out my beautiful hair feeling nothing but happy. And then my grandmother came down the hall."

Angela paused. I waited. There was definitely something going on here.

"She came down the hall, stopped in the bathroom doorway and looked at me. I saw her in the mirror – all steamy and dripping – but I ignored her. I was sixteen and I tried to hide it but she still scared the shit out of me."

Angela paused again.

"I could handle everyone else but not her. She was a dried up old lady – nothing but alligator skin and white hair – but she scared the shit out me. And I hated that. So, I looked straight ahead and kept combing."

A pause.

"After a minute she stepped into the bathroom and stood behind me – right up close. I tried to ignore her but I can tell you it wasn't easy with her wheezing at my neck.

I tried ... but I couldn't take it. I stopped combing. That's what she was waiting for. Right away she reached up and took hold of my hair. She didn't pull it or anything. She just held a few strands out to the side, as if showing them to me in the mirror. When she knew I was looking she said, 'All this beautiful hair – it won't do you any good when it comes time to swim upstream.'"

Angela stopped. She looked at me and then out the window.

I waited a minute, two, three.

"And?" I asked.

Angela looked back at me.

"And nothing." She made a tight face. "I didn't say anything and neither did she."

She shifted in her chair.

"That was it – one stupid sentence. She let go of my hair and walked back down the hall."

And?

Angela shifted in her chair again. She crossed her legs, uncrossed them, leaned forward, sat back, then stood up and walked over to the dart board. She stepped back a few steps, stood there for a moment and then started throwing invisible darts at the board.

"You know, doc." She looked my way. "She could have been a little clearer."

*

Martin has slowed to his standard pace. He's a good walker but my natural pace is faster than his. I guess he likes to think harder than me when he walks.

"It's strange where you find it."

He is underway and I am letting him talk.

"Take Mao. He was a politico, really, but he knew how to fight a war. I guess that's not surprising. Politics is just war made small. Everything is war one way or another. War is the king of all – that's Heraclitus – you can't put your foot in the same river twice – that guy. Everything is change. And change comes from strife. And strife is war."

He glances at me.

"Have you read him?"

"Heraclitus? Not really."

Actually, I did glance at him recently. Along with all those other dead Greeks. But I'd rather hear what you have to say.

"I know his name. The river thing."

So keep talking.

"You should read him. He didn't say much but what he said is worth looking at."

Okay.

"Mao, too. But not so much. He was a politico. Sun Tzu – he's the guy. Mao on guerrilla war is just Sun Tzu reheated. But that's not the point."

Okay.

"The point is – it's the same idea – over and over. The Bhagavad Gita. Norse Myths. The Chinese yin and yang. Everywhere you look – it's creative destruction."

A pause.

"Do you know what I mean?"

Nope. But let me guess.

"Polarities?"

Martin looks my way.

"More than that."

He whacks the branch of a pine near the path and sets off a shower of snow. It sparkles in the sun.

"War is king," he says. "It's not just a phase. It's not some primitive instinct we'll get over – like fish learning to breathe air."

A pause.

"It's not something we'll grow out of." A pause. "It's how we grow."

Now that's catchy. You could sell it as a slogan to the arms industry.

Martin slows down even more. He's wearing a bomber jacket and a wool toque. It's minus thirty. I don't know how he does it. Me, I'm going to freeze if we keep walking at this pace. So, I stop.

"All these celebrity moments." He stops and turns toward me. "Let's end poverty. Let's end war." He slaps his hands together in mock applause. "They make me laugh."

I nod, stomp my feet and then start walking again. Faster. Martin is keeping pace beside me. He's still working on his lecture.

"You might as well say you don't want to exhale."

Okay.

"If all you do is breathe in, sooner or later you'll explode."

Right.

"You can't force it – either way. That's what Mao got wrong. He knew the old had to go – that's just nature. But he fucked up. He tried to engineer what can't be engineered."

He glances at me. He's wearing sunglasses. Aviator.

"Life isn't a lab. You can't set up the equipment, turn on the burner and let it rip. It has to develop on its own. Mao was wrong. What was the Cultural Revolution? A lot of dead bodies and broken souls. Not good enough."

Broken souls? I'll have to remember that.

"So where's this leading?" I ask. "What does this have to do with you?"

It's freezing out here. I'm freezing out here. So, let's skip the history lesson. We are supposed to be talking about you.

"Me?"

Yeah, you.

There is a long silence. I keep up the pace but I am never going to get warm this way. And it is beginning to look like Martin is never going to answer. We have reached Island Park and the Champlain Bridge. It's a natural place to turn around so I stop. Martin goes ahead a bit and then comes back to where I am standing.

"People don't understand," he says. "You've got the war – the troops in the field. And you've got the folks back home. They don't see the connection. They think the war is one thing – out there – and what they are doing – back here – is something else."

A pause.

"They think they aren't part of it. But that's wrong. And it's a problem."

We start walking again – west now – facing the sun. The reflection on the snow is brilliant. Sparkling. Painful. I wish I had sunglasses.

Martin picks up the conversation again.

"You remember Zhou Enlai?"

"Sort of."

"Mao's guy – when Nixon went to China."

Right. Zhou Enlai.

"Well, some smartass reporter asked him about the French Revolution. What did it mean? How important was it?"

A pause.

"Zhou said it was too soon to tell."

Hmm.

"People thought it was a joke."

Martin slaps his hands together. He adjusts his toque. Is he getting cold?

"It was no joke. He was giving us a lesson but nobody got it because people in the West have no perspective. It's pathetic."

It's freezing out here and the sunlight is burning a hole in my eyeballs. Get to the fucking point.

"What does this have to do with you?" I don't let him answer. "This is all very interesting, Martin, but you are losing me. I don't see the connection. I don't get what Zhou Enlai or creative destruction or Heraclitus has to do with you – with your life – with why you came to see me."

It is definitely the cold. I shouldn't have snapped like that but it is fucking freezing out here and we are wasting our time in addition to freezing our balls off. Martin is lecturing, not talking. It's the kind of bullshit he spouted his first few sessions. It's all avoidance. I don't know what's gone wrong but if it's going to be like this I'd rather be back in the office with a cup of hot coffee in my hands. This is a waste of everybody's time.

We are coming up to Westboro Beach – hang left, take the underpass and homeward we go – but Martin has broken away and is already heading down toward the snow covered beach. The river is frozen close to shore but the water's open further out. Blue and white and silver. He has picked up the pace and he's slapping his hands together again. He is down to what must be the shoreline and he is still going. Hands slapping, head down, he's on the ice and still walking – out toward the open water.

*

That day – not today but *that* day – after Angela told me about her grandmother and the bathroom and her hair – I went for a walk by the river – down to Westboro Beach and then further west along the path to a spot that's sheltered from the traffic. It's a place where I can think.

She said – that's it, doc. I'm done like dinner. No more sessions.

She said – I knew you were the guy when you came up to the booth at the craft show. The minute you opened your mouth I knew – this guy – he's going to fix it for you. One way or another. He's going to do it.

She said – I knew you would. And you did.

Did what?

Fix it?

When the session ended and she left, I tossed darts for a while. Maybe if I went around the clock and ended with a bull's eye I would figure out what she meant, what she thought it was I did.

Twenty down to one and then a bull's eye. One. Two. Three.

It didn't work. It was more complicated than darts. It wasn't skill. It wasn't luck. It was something else. What was it?

I didn't have a clue. So, I locked up and headed outside.

It was a warm and bright day. There were lots of people on the street. I made my way down to the river and walked out to the sheltered spot I liked – a secluded area set well back from the parkway and the walking path. There's a small beach of pebbles and sand and a large log at the head of the beach. A big willow leans out over the river, its leaves almost touching the water. Very calm. Very serene. But I was too stressed for sitting. Or even leaning against the tree.

What had the old lady meant? It was a warning. Just you wait little girl with your big tits and flowing hair. It won't always be like this. Life won't always be so easy. It was the kind of thing old people say because they are old and can't even remember what it's like to be young. Why did Angela take her so seriously? She was just a senile old woman. She was pious. She was cranky. She was a pain in the neck.

I didn't get it.

What did she do to Angela?

It was almost like a curse.

And what had I done?

I hadn't done anything.

I skipped stones for a while and then stood there, halfway up the beach, watching the waves come in. The wind was rising and the water clear and the sunlight brilliant on the slow breaking waves. I was standing quietly, looking out at the water, one last stone in my hand, when Julia showed up. She was in a peach and green sundress I had never seen before. Bare feet. I didn't hear her approach. I guess I was too wrapped up thinking about Angela and her grandmother. Or maybe just drifting into outer space. Julia was beside me saying hello before I clued in I was no longer alone.

"Beautiful," she said. "How was your afternoon?"

I smiled at her.

"Challenging."

"Good. We don't want you getting bored."

No chance of that.

"And yours?"

"Quiet."

That's okay. We don't want you getting anxious.

"Angela says hello."

A raised eyebrow.

"Who's Angela?"

"The flower lady."

Two raised eyebrows. And then none.

"I thought you couldn't talk about her."

"I couldn't. But she stopped being a client about an hour ago and she said to say hello."

In fact, she insisted. She said, doc, say hello to the rock lady for me. Tell her what a good job you did. Tell her I think you're tops – a little dense sometimes – but still tops.

"Hello, Angela."

Julia stepped toward the water.

"How does she know me about me?"

"Angela knows about everything."

Julia looked back at me. "Of course."

"I'm serious."

She ignored my bait and took another few steps toward the water.

"But she's happy now? Thanks to Herr Doktor?"

"She says so. In fact, she said to tell you what a good job I did. She was having anxiety attacks and now they're gone. But it's got nothing to do with me."

Julia laughed and shook her head.

"You don't get it, do you?" she said.

She was standing by the edge of the water, looking across the river.

"No, I guess don't," I said, slightly irritated. I didn't get much of anything these days.

She turned around and came up to where I was standing. She faced me directly and took my hand, squeezed it lightly then put my hand to her head. She held it there, pressed against the long hair at the back of her neck.

"What do you think," she asked. "Blessing or curse?"

"What?"

She looked at me until I began to feel small and sad. She didn't smile or frown or give any sign of judgment or disappointment. I was a child being given a lesson.

She gripped my hand more firmly, then moved it forward to her mouth and let my fingers touch her lips before lowering my hand to the air in front of her chin.

"Blessing or curse?" she asked.

I didn't know what to say.

She reached up and straightened my fingers with her other hand and then lowered my open palm and pressed it against her breast. I could feel the softness of her flesh, the firmness of her nipple.

"Blessing or curse?"

I couldn't say a thing.

She dropped my hand, walked to the edge of the water and in a single smooth motion pulled the flowered shift she was wearing over her head. She was naked and stood there for half a second smiling at me.

"Blessing or curse?" she asked.

I heard the water rising against the stony shore.

What was going on? What was she doing?

Julia turned and walked into the water until she disappeared.

7

"Let me tell you something."

I don't know if I can hear this, Martin.

He has gone out toward the edge of the ice and now has come back to where I am standing – a safe distance from the open water. I am listening to him but I am listening even more closely to the ice. I have no intention of ending up in that water.

He has gone silent after his opening statement. I wait for him to continue but he stares at me from behind the two black lenses of his sunglasses – or that is how it feels. I can't see his eyes so I don't know where he is looking. What I *do* know is he is angry. And I am the target of that anger.

He turns his head and starts to walk away from Westboro Beach, further upstream, still well out from the shore. I am keeping beside him but not too close. He is on the water side and keeps drifting further out onto the ice, toward the open water. The ice is thick but I don't want to test whether it can hold the two of us. To my left is the shoreline, the trees leaning out over the frozen river. The shadows of the trees are getting longer, stretching further out onto the ice. In between, the sunlight glitters on the snow.

"Have you ever killed someone, Doctor Gillespie?"

He is speaking loudly, not quite shouting. Doctor Gillespie. He usually calls me Kit.

"No, Martin. I have never killed anyone."

"Are you sure?"

I have been watching him from the corner of my eye. Now I look at him. He looks back, directly at me, his aviator glasses like insect eyes. His toque. His bomber jacket. He is not slapping his hands.

"I am sure."

We have stopped walking.

"Has anyone ever tried to kill you?"

Why would someone try to kill me?

"Not that I'm aware of."

Martin starts walking again, drifting closer to the open water.

"That's the question, isn't it, Doctor Gillespie?" He pauses. "Not that I'm aware of."

He has lowered his voice, forcing me to come closer if I want to be able to hear him. I move further out from the shore but the distance between us grows as he continues to drift closer to the water. I am not going to the edge of the ice.

"What are any of us aware of? Isn't that the question, Doctor Gillespie?"

He slaps his hands together, stops, looks at me then walks directly toward the dark blue open water. I hear a crack. He must hear it as well but he keeps walking. Another crack – louder – he slows. I don't think he wants to go into that water any more than I do.

"Let me be a little clearer," he says.

He stops and turns toward me. He is only a few steps from the edge of the ice. This cannot be safe.

"I think," he says "you need to try a little harder, Doctor Gillespie."

He is speaking softly. If I move closer to him, so I can hear, the ice may break. If I can't hear him I can't respond. And he may get even more frustrated, more hostile.

I take a step forward. Then another. That's it. I am not going any closer.

"You don't have to be in a war to kill people," he says.

"I realize that, Martin. You can have an accident. You can hit somebody with a car. You can hold up a bank and shoot the teller."

Martin slaps his hands together. Twice.

"Very good, Doctor Gillespie." He smiles. "Those are all possibilities."

He goes silent. Spreads his arms wide. The smile disappears.

"Or you can just fail to pay attention," he says.

He drops his arms.

"You can fail to be aware."

Without looking behind him, he steps backwards towards the edge of the ice. There is a sound, a cracking. He brings his feet together, as if standing at attention. Another sound. He doesn't move.

"Sometimes you can kill someone just by not being aware."

A loud crack. Then another.

The ice tilts.

The water rises.

The sunlight sparkles on the waves.

Move, Martin, move.

April

1

"What's so big about Montreal?"

Angela has finished her dessert – tiramisu – not worth
the calories but better than nothing – and I have just cancelled our next supper. She isn't pleased. We bumped up
the frequency to every two weeks back in January. It was
her idea and it's been okay. I was paying before and part
of the two week deal was we would start splitting the bill.
I think the winter was getting to her although she didn't
put it that way. The way she put it was – you look like shit,
doc; we should get together more often; I don't think you're
eating your greens. Which wasn't true. But I didn't have
the energy to refuse so it's spinach salad every two weeks. I
don't mind. When there isn't spinach I have a regular salad,
mixed greens, beets, whatever. I don't much care about
things like that. But Angela does.

In addition to upping the frequency of our suppers,
she brought me a new flower arrangement – a small one
for the office – free of charge. I've got it on the credenza
behind my desk and it has settled in just fine. It knows its
place. The old one – the big one at the apartment – she took
it back for a refresh – no charge, again. The bulrushes are
gone and a lot of the side chatter has disappeared. It's still
big but not enormous. I've got it on the bookshelf in the

den and it seems comfortable there. No trouble so far. I come in and keep an eye on it when I need to.

Tonight I skipped dessert and went straight to coffee. Angela usually has tea but she is clearly in a mood and my cancelling our next supper hasn't helped. She decided to splurge on dessert despite her perpetual diet. I guess she could tell something was up. Or maybe it's just the change of season. Spring? Easter? I don't know. She's been pretty good for the last few months – ever since we started meeting more often. She got a little anxious in the fall and that was a strain. She puts it all on me, of course. She's worried about me – blah, blah, blah – but little bits of her own life slip through every now and then and that gives me a glimpse of what's actually bothering her. I think it's her work but I'm not sure. She talks a lot about the people she meets – their moods, their weight, the colour of their hair. Her grandmother seems to have faded from view. Right now – at this moment – Montreal has taken centre stage and she is looking at me with that I'm-not-your-mother-but-you-need-one look.

"Have you got a woman there?" she says. "Or what?"

I smile. It's not my fault your tiramisu was second rate.

"Two, actually."

And the older one reminds me a bit of you except she's slimmer and nicer to me. But you've got the better smile – for what it's worth. In any case, it's the other one I'm going to see. We have something to discuss. And then we'll see where things go. I don't have any expectations. And she definitely doesn't since she doesn't even know I'm coming.

"Two? Are you serious?"

Painfully.

"You're asking for trouble, doc."

No. I've already got trouble. That's why I'm going to Montreal.

"Don't worry, Angela. I'm not a kid."

"I wasn't a kid when I dated two guys and I can tell you it was a mistake."

Two at once? Angela. Shame on you.

She sits back.

"What? You don't think I could find two guys to date me? I've got assets, you know."

Don't get all insulted.

"After I left the jerk I got my act together. I shed some flab, toned my butt. I wasn't eighteen anymore but I wasn't the gorgon lady either."

Okay. Okay.

"Look, Angela ..."

She waves her hands in the air.

"Listen, doc. I'm not trying to claim a prize. It was the stupidest thing I ever did. Worse than marrying the jerk in the first place. I don't need you to tell me. I had to move to Peterborough to get away from that mess. That's what I'm trying to tell you – watch out. One is trouble, two is an apocalypse."

She looks like she's going to say something more but stops and reaches down for her purse instead.

"My treat this time," she says.

"No way." We agreed to split the bill. That's the deal.

"Look, doc. If you're going to be paying for two women in Montreal you need to save your pennies. I just sold a big arrangement to a woman from Toronto. She paid me two hundred bucks. Can you believe it?"

"Congratulations." I give her a look. "Why didn't you tell me earlier?"

"You seemed a little preoccupied."

Hmm.

"From Toronto?" That's a long way to come flower shopping.

"Yeah. Her sister's a regular at the restaurant and she gave her an arrangement for Christmas. She liked it and ordered another one – a big one. She came up last weekend to pick it up. Two hundred bucks."

A pause.

"I wanted maybe seventy-five. Good thing I kept my mouth shut. She didn't even ask – just took a look at the arrangement and wrote me a cheque for two hundred. I hope that's enough, she said. I didn't look at the amount. I figured her sister would have told her a decent price. I stuck the cheque in my pocket and said thanks."

I hope it doesn't bounce.

"It felt kind of weird afterwards."

She looks at the wall, then out the window.

"Two hundred bucks is way too much. But it's her money. She drives an Audi and dresses like Yorkville. So I guess she can afford it."

Another pause.

"She did not look like a happy gal."

She waves at the waitress to pick up the bill then looks at me.

"So, what's wrong, doc? Why Montreal?"

*

It's late and I'm tired and I should go to bed but I want to get more done. I'm sorting through Julia's letters, building piles – the bored, the urgent and the incomprehensible. I've got a fourth pile – the indeterminate – and it's the largest by far but it's only temporary. Everything has to go into one of three permanent piles sooner or later. That's the plan.

I want to bring a few to show Sally and see what she thinks. Or maybe not. We'll see how things go when I get there. It all depends on whether her head is tilting or her eyes blinking. In any case, I won't tell her about my categories. The whole point is to get an unbiased view from someone with solid judgment. We'll see. It doesn't really matter what she says or doesn't say. I need a reason to do this and Sally gives me a reason. That is good enough. It is time to move forward. The baby is coming and I have to decide. Angela didn't seem to get that part but that's okay. It's good to have something Angela doesn't get – but that's not the point. The point is going through the letters. It's something I have to do. And I am doing it. And there is one thing that doing it makes very clear – Julia was a very strange woman.

As if I didn't know that already. I thought about bringing Sally some of my letters to Julia – to round out the context – but I don't have the stomach to look through them. There's only so much stupidity I can take in a day. Besides, Sally can ask questions if she has them. She isn't shy. And, double besides, the point isn't me. It's Julia.

Looking through her letters – it is odd – everything has a different tone, a different edge, a different inclination. Of course, none of that is true. The paper hasn't changed. The ink hasn't changed. The words haven't changed. She wrote what she wrote. And I read what I read. But everything seems different now. The fact is – I'm engaged in some hard core revisionism. What you see is what you want to see – or don't want to see – except at another level you do want to see it – if only to settle things once and for all. Get it out there in the open. Once you accept the worst there's no need to fret anymore. What's done is done. So, get on with life.

I expect Sally will agree. And if she doesn't she will let me know. I think I can trust her on that. What I can't trust is my judgement on anything involving Julia. I can't even choose which pile to put a letter in. Take this one. It's from about a year ago – May or April – a few months before her last visit. It doesn't have a date. There's no hello. No Dear Kit. No Herr Doktor. No anything. It just starts.

Why don't you write? This is my third letter without getting one back. I know I said I am leaving, but not tomorrow. So why haven't you written? Is there something wrong? If there is I want to know. As much as I may laugh at the funny little life you lead I do want to know what's going on.

I can see that smile of yours. Stop it!! This isn't funny. I have been thinking about you a lot lately. I don't know why but that goofy face of yours keeps coming up in my mind. I probably shouldn't say this but I have a feeling something bad has happened. Is that why you haven't written?

Don't laugh. I have a reason. It may sound silly but listen anyway.

Last week I was walking down the street doing nothing. I was feeling anxious – not about you. I was thinking about my class and things like that. It doesn't matter. What matters is that as I was walking along I got a weird feeling you were around somewhere, hiding, waiting to surprise me. I knew you weren't but I kept looking around, thinking "Kit's here. Somewhere." I walked around the block and then circled it in the opposite direction thinking maybe I had missed you. It was silly but I had to see if you were there even though I knew you couldn't be.

It was creepy. I got really anxious and stopped walking. I closed my eyes and did some slow breathing. I calmed down and eventually everything slipped back to normal. I was here, alone, back in reality. And I had a terrible feeling that something had happened to you. I knew I was being silly so I tried to ignore it but the feeling wouldn't go away. I kept seeing your face, feeling like you were nearby. And then I remembered you haven't written. I started to fixate on that fact – no letters. Why? There must be a reason. And then, of course, I realized you couldn't write because something had happened. You were in the hospital or lost somewhere. And I was getting this strange, horrible feeling because that is what you were sending me instead of letters. It was all you could do.

Are you alright?

*

I should go to bed. The light is dim and I'm finding it hard to read. I could swear the lamp flickered a moment ago. Either that or I nodded off. I heard a voice and then the lamp and then nothing.

This den is too small. Not enough oxygen. She used to sleep here when she was pissed at me. In the beginning I gave her the bedroom but she said she didn't want to sleep there alone. She tried the living room but it was too open. She was used to smaller spaces – they made her feel like she was travelling – so she slept here. And I didn't sleep at all.

I have to get a better lamp. It's so dim in here I can barely read. I'm going to go blind. For the last half hour I've been drifting – reading the same few sentences over and over – getting nowhere – zoning in and out – then waking up to find myself staring at Angela's flowers. The stems. The shadows. The awkwardness. There's nothing else to look at so I end up looking at the rug, then the bookshelf and then the flowers. The petals. The leaves. The dried ferns. The grasses.

I should go to bed.

*

At the end of her first session Angela spent a long time sitting in her chair, looking past me, saying nothing. It took a while before I figured out she was looking at the black and white photograph on the wall behind me. It was a picture of geese flying at dusk over a marshland at the edge of Hudson's Bay – a gift from Julia.

Angela seemed to be lost in thought, staring at the geese, so I cleared my throat. The session was over. It was time for her to leave. At the sound of my cough she stood up without looking at me and walked around the desk to the back wall. She stepped right up to the photograph and stood there counting the geese, pointing them out with her finger. One, two, three. There were seven.

"This is from the rock lady," she said, still looking at the geese. It wasn't a question.

"Yes," I said. How did you know?

She stepped back and fixed her gaze on the photograph, taking it all in.

"They're flying south," she said. "Coming this way."

I guess so. They're migrating. It's fall.

She stood looking at the picture for another minute, then turned and walked to the front of the desk. Without a word she picked up the stone Julia had given me and squeezed it tightly in her hand. She looked at the photograph yet again.

"Nice picture."

She kept looking at the photograph and started passing Julia's stone from hand to hand, feeling its smoothness. She did this for a little while, stopped, then held the rock up to look at it.

"Nice rock."

She squeezed the stone tightly one more time then put it back on my desk.

"You know something?" she said, looking at me for the first time since she started her little fixation with the geese.

"What?" What is I should know, Angela?

She looked back at the photograph.

"You are one strange guy, doc."

2

It was raining when I came to work this morning. Puddles everywhere and that dreary feeling that takes the place of a missing sun. The buds on the trees are starting – shades of red and green – but that isn't enough on a morning like this. I had an appointment at nine so I came in early to play some darts. Of course, the rain stopped shortly after I got here but that's okay. I was dry and warm by the time my client showed up. He's a retired diplomat, a distinguished looking man with silver hair and a solid jaw. He speaks carefully but with ease – smooth – like a river running steady and strong above a rapids. He gives you the impression that it may be possible to avoid the rocks and the rapids altogether if everyone remains as calm as he is. But deep down you know that isn't so.

His problem is simple. He makes lists for everything – primarily chores (fix the faucet, replace the broken pane of glass) but also household items in need of replenishing (toilet paper, paper towels, hand soap) and then there are the social appointments, birthdays, political promises (pending and broken), neighbourhood misdemeanours and so on. It is driving his wife crazy. It isn't doing much for his own state of mind either. He knows it isn't normal. And he knows it's because of his retirement. He knows what the problem is but he can't get it under control. He gets up in the morning and he can't stop himself. Even before getting in the shower he checks his list for the day, adds anything that occurred to him in the night – assuming he didn't get up in the night to write it down – which he often does. He has tried to stop. He's made rules about when he can check the lists – but rules are for breaking – especially rules he has made himself. It is too hard. He can't do it. He finds it all very embarrassing.

We talked about ways of putting more structure into his day so he wouldn't need the lists. We talked about his hobbies and places he could volunteer. I asked about his postings and suggested he write down some anecdotes from his life – where he had been, people he had met, little incidents – nothing confidential, obviously. I said it would be more interesting than adding items to his lists. Plus, it would help me get a better idea of who he is and what might be the best way to work through his problem. He thought it was a good idea but he emphasized that he wasn't a writer. And I emphasized that I wasn't a critic. We both laughed. He's an intelligent man.

I'm sure everything will go fine.

I called Sally after my appointment. It took her a moment to place me. Or that's how she played it.

"Oh, yes, I remember – the psychologist from Ottawa – on the train – Kit. That's your name, isn't it? Of course – you just told me – but I remember. I gave you a CD when you left, didn't I? Do you like it?"

"Very pleasant." Positively existential. "That's why I called. I'd like to do some follow-up."

A pause.

"Music?"

Um, sure. Dancing perhaps?

"No. Professional."

A very long silence.

"You mean a consultation?"

Um, well. Do you have any other profession?

"I guess we could call it that."

*

I don't know why I think this is a good idea. The woman is a ninja – but that is exactly what I need – someone who will slit my throat at the least bit of nonsense. It is time to stop the nonsense.

Alf has tried. He's shoved me again and again – but he's a friend and he can't help. He's already got enough to think about. He's got a family. He's got a life. The baby's coming. Besides, he's carrying too much baggage. In fact, he is part of the baggage – an old leather satchel filled with notes that are very, very curious.

You have to have seen it coming, Kit. There have to have been signs. Think about what she said, what you said, what you did. This is too big to ignore. It's not going to go away. You have to work it through. Because what you have told me so far doesn't make any sense.

Thanks, Alf.

*

It took twenty minutes of darts for me to calm down after talking to Sally. Once I'd hit the bulls-eye a dozen times I started sorting through Julia's letters. I brought a bunch in with me this morning – a handful pulled at random. No more nonsense. I've decided to send a package to Sally and that means I have to focus. I want to send all the important letters and a cover note and maybe a sketch of Julia. I didn't mention it to Sally but she'll understand. It makes more sense for her to have the stuff in advance instead of my bringing it with me and her having to rush through it. It's all billable time – assuming she has the time. And I suspect she'll make it if she doesn't. She sounded curious. I want to send the package by Thursday which means I've got today and tomorrow to put it all together. I want her to have it before the weekend – next day delivery. That'll be expensive but that's just too bad. No more nonsense.

So far, I have three keepers and a bunch of she-doesn't-need-to-see-this. Only one indeterminate. It's still three categories – I've just changed the names – and eliminated one. The point is – it's getting done. I've got a dozen letters left to go through from the ones I brought with me so I am doing okay. I'm doing fine. I'm totally copasetic. But this isn't easy.

Right now, I've got a probable keeper in front of me. Five years ago. She was in China. She hated China. All the little emperors. The raging fuck-you-I'm-first on the rise. It made the West look communist. She was glad to be coming home.

> *Hello you,*
>
> *I am shedding again. I don't know how I accumulate so much junk. I buy art (carvings and scrolls and pottery) but when it comes time to leave everything turns into junk. So I'm gifting again. It makes people laugh when I show up with my surprises. Some of the stuff no one wants – there's too much of that this time – so I am giving it out as prizes to my students. They have no choice but to accept.*
>
> *I'll be so happy to get out of this place. And I've promised myself never to come back. I know, I*

know – never say never – but this is as close to never as I will ever get. Watching this cancer grow is something I can do without. I used to think all change was good one way or another. Painful sometimes but good all the same. I'm not so sure about that anymore. The energy is rising but the index is going down. That's what I see happening here. I could be wrong but I doubt it. Not that it matters what I think except to me. I have to follow the flow the way I see it flowing. It's all I can do. And that means getting out of here asap because I definitely do not see it flowing this way.

Where is it going? I don't know. But I have to get out of here. Soon.

It is only days. That's how I'm counting. Days, not weeks, even though it is weeks. It isn't months. Not really. Anything less than six is weeks, not months. And anything less than four is days, not weeks. So, it is days. Twenty-six to be precise. Less than that by the time you get this. By then it will be close to hours, if not minutes. Are you ready?

I am ready, almost. I get the feeling something will be different this time. Do you feel like that? I don't know why but I do. Maybe it's because we are getting old. But, no, that's not right. I am getting old. You never change. Why is that? I thought the traveller was supposed to be the one who stayed young. I fly away at the speed of life and when I get back you are so much older than me. Isn't that the way it goes? But that's the sci fi version. And this is real life.

I don't feel young anymore. Or look it. But you — you look like you always did. Smiling Kit — the kid with magnetic resonance — the one who never needs to travel. All you have to do is stand on one foot and spin — hooking into the earth's magnetic field — the sun's magnetic field — the North Star — the Milky Way — and beyond — always aligned. That's you, Kit. Always aligned. I don't know how you do it. Someday I hope to find out. And that is why I have to return.

Maybe that's what will be different this time. I'll arrive and instead of Smiling Kit I'll find Kit the Old: greying hair, wobbly jowls, slumped shoulders, pot belly and a stoop. Is that how you are now?

No. You never change.

Shit. I would like to start over. Try it all again from the beginning.

What do you think?

I am coming, soon, with all my sojourning love,

Your Old and Lonely Julia

3

Black leather pants. Tight red top.

I recognize the smile.

She points me toward a chair and I sit down, look around. Mahogany desk. Persian rug. Tiffany lamp. She obviously has a wealthier client base than I do. Westmount versus Westboro. No contest.

Nice painting.

"Is that a Borduas?"

Sally glances at the painting and smiles lightly.

"Yes. Do you like it?"

"Very pleasant."

And very expensive. I couldn't afford that if I sold a kidney. Both kidneys.

"It was a gift," she says. "Pleasant is a good word for it. Calming is another."

She picks up a pen but doesn't write anything. She has a pale green pad of paper in front of her – legal size. I guess she takes long notes.

"I got your package," she says, motioning with the pen to a billows lying on her desk. "Thank you for sending it so quickly. That was helpful."

That was the idea.

"And thank you," I say, "for making time to see me."

It is ten past nine, Sunday morning. I came on the train yesterday and I am staying at the same place as last time. It is cheap. I booked in for a week but I might leave tomorrow if things get ugly.

"I know you must be busy."

I glance at the billows. There is a lot of paper in there and not all of it is from me. Layers of green – legal size.

"Plus," I look back at Sally. "My request is a bit unusual."

Sally tilts her head and straightens again. A smile flickers.

"I didn't have any plans for today." She brings her hands together. "And, of course, you knew the magic formula."

"Did I?"

"Don't pretend," she says.

She leans forward and rests her arms on the desk.

"You know I love a challenge."

*

"Have you been back to Montreal since October?"

"No."

Sally shifts in her chair and crosses her legs. She has moved around to my side of the desk. We are sitting at an angle to each other so she can both reach the desk and face me easily.

"Gone anywhere else?" she asks.

Like where? Paris? Peru? Iraq? Iran?

"No." I have clients to see. Bills to pay.

Head tilt.

"Just Ottawa?"

That's right. All work and no play.

"Just Ottawa."

Sally straightens and sits back. She brings her hands together, making a triangle, the vertex at her chin. She glances at the billows then looks back at me. She tilts her hands slightly toward me. She should have been a choreographer.

"So, why now?"

She collapses the triangle, her hands coming to rest on her lap.

"Pardon?"

She sits forward slightly.

"Why did you decide to come here now?"

I don't get it.

"To see you." Of course.

"I understand that." She waves her hand at nothing. "But it's been six months and when you called it sounded urgent. So, I'm wondering if there was a trigger. Did something happen? Why now?"

Oh. I get it.

"Right. Good question. Did something happen?"

I don't know. I don't think so.

"Nothing specific. I mean, I've been thinking a lot about Julia – who she was – why she travelled – things like that."

I look at Sally. She is still waiting.

"But, basically, it comes down to how she died. I've been thinking about how she died."

Sally sits up, her elbows on the armrests of her chair.

"Yes?"

I guess I said the magic word.

"Well, like I said in my letter..."

I motion toward the billows. My cover letter is buried in there somewhere – sunk among Julia's letters and Sally's green notes and the one lone sketch of Julia's face that I sent along. The letter's in there somewhere. Eight pages of preliminary context. I thought I would list a few quick points to give her a roadmap. A paragraph would probably do. Two at most. I wrote eight pages.

"She drowned up north. She wasn't the kind of person to take stupid risks. She knew what she was doing. It makes no sense. So, I wonder."

"What exactly do you wonder?" Sally asks.

I told you in my letter.

"About what happened." Of course.

"Kit. You are a psychologist. You know what this," she moves her hand in a slow horizontal circle, "is all about."

She sits back.

"Listen to my question."

She fixes her dark brown eyes on me.

"What exactly do you wonder?"

*

I haven't told Sally about Alf yet. Maybe I should. Sooner or later he and Gem and the baby are going to come up. If I tell her now I might not have to spend time answering stupid questions. I could just list his.

*

"This isn't a social visit, Kit. I am charging you for this."

Lighten up. I didn't come here to be spanked.

"I understand the economics of the relationship."

I get poorer and you get richer.

Sally looks past me, toward the door. Is she expecting someone? It's nine-thirty and we have barely started. There can't be anyone else coming already.

"Good. Then don't waste your time," she says. "Or mine."

It must be all the wood and the sheers on the windows – the filtered light – because it is beginning to feel like a funeral parlour in here.

"I'm sorry."

I straighten. I was slouching. Maybe she doesn't like my slouching. I won't do it again.

"I'm not trying to be difficult but what exactly is the problem?"

She gives me a look, then reaches into the billows and pulls out some pages. They are stapled together. She holds them up for me to see.

"This is the letter you sent with your package."

Okay. I didn't staple it. I guess I should have. Sorry.

"Did you read it over before you sent it?" she asks.

Read it over? Why? Are there typos?

"Yes." Of course I read it over.

She glances at the first page of the letter then back at me.

"More than once?"

Okay. There are definitely typos.

"I can't remember. Maybe not. Why?"

She puts the letter on top of the billows. She brings her hands together and faces me like a grade school teacher.

"That letter, Kit, is why you are here today."

Pardon? I think you have the order wrong. The letter is here because I am here. I called you up, made an appointment and sent the package. That's the way it went.

"I'm not sure I understand. You agreed to meet me. So I sent the package with the letter."

Sally crosses her arms.

"I agreed to see you for an hour on Monday. That's what I said on the phone. Remember?"

Sure. I remember.

"When I got your package and read your letter – after that – that's when I called you back and suggested you come today. Correct?"

Okay. Sure. Monday. Sunday. Technical point. Very anal. I'm beginning to have my doubts about your technique.

"Correct?"

Why are you so pissed off?

"Correct."

Happy now?

Obviously not. She doesn't relax. Her arms are still crossed and her face like stone. There must be more.

"And why do you think I did that?" she asks.

How am I supposed to know? Because Monday filled up? Because the letter was filled with typos? Because it's dim and quiet in here on a Sunday morning and you wanted to have slow endless sex on your Persian rug?

I shrug. "Because you like a challenge?"

She freezes.

Wrong answer?

"Whatever Julia may have been," I say. "She was a challenge."

A pause. This isn't working. When in doubt, dig deeper.

"She still is a challenge for me. That's why I'm here. I need help."

Sally uncrosses her arms, lets them slip to her side. She leans forward slightly. She speaks softly.

"You don't seem to get it, Kit."

Thanks. That's what Julia said. Repeatedly.

"Get what?"

What is it I am supposed to get – for fuck's sake?

"This isn't about Julia."

Really? Who is it about? Angela? Louise? You?

"Sorry?"

Sally sits back and crosses her arms again.

Please don't do the Freeze Queen again. It's disturbing.

"Kit, this isn't about Julia."

Those dark eyes weighing on me.

"This is about you."

4

Sally pauses the recorder. I'm not sure why. Isn't this part important?

"You have a vivid memory, Kit."

Vivid? You mean like I'm making things up?

"I keep a journal," I say. "I did some prep work."

She frowns for an instant then looks at the door again.

Why do you keep looking over there? Is that how you re-focus? Send the disruptive bits out into the hall? Whatever you may think you are doing, it is a distracting habit. You should get it under control.

"How long ago was it?" she asks.

Julia's visit?

"Three years." More or less.

She nods. She has her green pad on her lap and she makes a note, then looks up at me. The tilting head has returned.

"How did she look then?"

"Pardon?"

"When she showed up at your office – was there any difference in the way she looked? Her clothes? Her hair? Her general manner?"

Hmm.

"Not really."

She puts her writing pad on the billows, stands up and goes behind her desk. She opens one of the drawers and takes out a set of pencils and a sketch pad. They both look new. She returns to the front of the desk and hands me the pad and pencils before sitting down.

"Draw her," she says. "As she was then."

I glance at her. She has her stone face on again. She watches as I pry open the flat tin box and look at the neat array of glossy, new pencils. I smile lightly. Every pencil has been sharpened. I can't help it. I'm impressed.

"You sent me one sketch of her," she says. "I'd like another. Draw her as she was that day when she showed up at your office."

That day? I hesitate for a second then take out a 2B, close the container and flip open the sketch pad. Do I remember what she looked like?

She had her big backpack with her – enough clothes for a long visit. She was wearing runners and jeans and a t-shirt, probably. Definitely. And her hair – it was tied back in a ponytail. She was very thin. I think she had lost weight. She looked very tired. And her smile kept breaking.

*

She wanted to live by the sea. I don't know why she ever thought Ottawa would work. Maybe she didn't. Maybe she was just trying to make a point. It's a possibility but I doubt it.

She lasted six months. After that she lined up another contract and she was gone. Travelling again. It was almost like it never happened. Except the next time she came for a visit she seemed much older. Her energy was lower. It was like she had hoped she could settle down and recuperate. But she couldn't. I don't know. It was a strange time.

She needed something to do. She said she had come to stay but she couldn't find anything to do. A part-time job for a while at a gift shop but it didn't last. She refused to teach. That part I really didn't understand. She said if she wanted to teach she would travel. She didn't want to travel. So she wouldn't teach. Association, I guess. But it would have made things easier for her if she had taught. It would have kept her busy.

*

"Do you want to take a break?"

It is almost noon. My sketch is done and set aside. We didn't talk about the drawing. Sally took a quick look and put the sketchpad on top of the billows. She thanked me for sending the first sketch in the package. It always helps to put a face to a name, she said. A photo would have been good but a sketch was a pleasant surprise. I didn't tell her I don't have any photos. I didn't want to spoil the mood. She is being much nicer now. Nothing like a minor victory to smooth the way.

"How long are you planning to go for?" I ask.

I had figured an hour or two on Sunday and then maybe a few hours over the rest of the week. That should do it. She stands up and moves to her place behind the desk. She does a quick survey of the office, sits down and waits a minute before facing me. It is much brighter in the room than when I first arrived. The sun is coming in full through the sheers on the south windows. It is very pleasant. I wish I could afford a place like this.

"I planned on going all day," she says.

All day? Won't that be kind of tiring? On the other hand, if we go all day I could leave tomorrow. Or Tuesday if

I want to have a visit with Louise. I would save on hotel and meals. That would be a plus.

"Sure," I say. "If you want. But I can stay through the week if you want to split things up. A few hours today. An hour a day for the rest of the week. Whatever you think best."

She puts her elbows on the desk and forms the triangle, hands at her chin. This is a protective gesture. Okay. What's up?

"I think we should take a break now and then go for the rest of the day."

A pause. She is watching me.

"I have cleared my week of appointments so we can start again tomorrow morning and go every day this week if we have to. Nine to six. I can pick you up at your hotel at eight-thirty. I can drive you back, too, if you wish. Or you can walk. That will be up to you."

She looks at me as if expecting an answer about walking home but I am stuck at the beginning – the part about the week being cleared.

You cancelled all your appointments?

For me?

Are you crazy? You expect me to pay for a solid week of consultations – every hour, every day. I never agreed to that.

"Sally ..."

Where to start?

She is watching me. Her eyes don't move.

"Isn't that ... isn't this kind of ... unconventional? I mean, I have never heard of all day sessions, day after day, for an entire week."

She doesn't smile. She doesn't frown. She just looks at me with her stone face.

"It's not unheard of. I think in your case, based on your letter and what I have heard this morning, it is the right approach."

The letter again. What the fuck did I say in that stupid letter? Forget it. I don't care. You can have all the suspicions you want about the psychological significance of my typos but the bottom line is – I can't afford to pay for an entire week.

"Sally ..."

"We may not have to go for the full week," she says. "We'll stop earlier if we can. And if more work is necessary we will figure that out on Saturday."

Saturday? You must be joking.

"But the fee?"

I am trying not to look shell-shocked but I know I'm not doing a very good job. Seven full days, eight hours a day – that's fifty-six hours – at Sally's rate that's over ten thousand dollars – this is not what I agreed to.

"I will charge you for today," she says. "Eight hours. The rest of the week ... let's call it personal research."

The triangle descends and she rests her hands on the desk. A flicker of a smile lightens her face.

"Or if you prefer," she says. "You can think of it as you and I going on a little trip together."

5

It's a bright day, a little cool and there's a breeze from the west. It is good to get outside. It would be great if I could go for a long walk but I'm hungry and I have to keep up my strength. All this talking is wearing me down. Sally has gone off somewhere. She insisted we split up for lunch so she gave me an hour and pointed me in this direction. Not even a goodbye kiss.

I found this place on Greene. I think it's a chain but it's good enough for now. I've got a coffee and a panini and a seat near the front where I can watch the people go by except I don't feel like doing even that at the moment. My mind is spinning from this morning's adventure. And there is still the afternoon to go.

When I get home I'll have to do some research on this all day stuff. It sounds more like torture than therapy to me. Maybe that's the point. I suppose I should view it as a learning experience – from a professional perspective. In any case, it's clear that something has captured Sally's imagination. I suspect she has a view on Julia but there is no way she is going to tell me at this stage. And that's fine. She has to go through the process with her stone face on. And leather pants. That part I don't get. Does she wear that kind of outfit for all her clients? I hope not. Maybe she wants to make sure I pay attention. I don't know. I guess I'll see what she wears for the rest of the week.

*

"You must have dealt with clients who were having a breakdown."

Sally is behind the desk. I am in my chair. It isn't a question so I don't respond. Julia was having a breakdown. That's the suggestion. I suppose it's possible. She didn't seem that way the last time I saw her. She was sad. That's true. The old woman had died. But the baby had been born. She was going up north to visit the baby and her parents. She wasn't upbeat. But she wasn't breaking down either.

"Have you?" she asks.

Now, that is a question.

"Yes," I say. "A few."

Three or four, I think. It's kind of a fuzzy concept so there are others who might qualify. But definitely four.

"And what have you done?"

Sally is leaning forward, her arms on the desk. She looks interested.

"It all depends on the client. If the breakdown comes on suddenly there may be no alternative but hospitalization – which I am not keen on – but it may be necessary. If you see it coming then you can try to work through it. Increasing the length or the number of sessions is an obvious approach."

Sally sits back.

"That's a general answer to a specific question."

Is it?

"Your question was general."

"No. My question was specific – what have you done when you have had a client in breakdown. You responded by speaking in generalities."

Too bad. Fuck you.

"Did you want case histories?" I ask. "That might take some time to work up."

She waves her hand.

"We aren't here to discuss technique."

No? Okay. In that case I won't mention my impression of yours.

"My main point," she says. "The point I want to make at this stage is that there are always going to be clients that we – you or me or any particular therapist – may not be able to help. It could be a personality mismatch – someone else would be able to do the job but not you or me. Or it could be a situation where the psychic damage is too deep – the problem will never be fixed – and the most you can hope for is to stop things from getting worse."

Sure. I get that.

"Do you agree?"

Yes, but I have a question – what did you have for lunch? Why are you back to the spit and snarl routine?

"Do you?"

She is leaning forward again. And the stone face is heating up.

"Sorry, I thought I said yes."

"Kit, we need to have some clarity here. So, if I ask a question, please respond."

"Okay." Sheesh, what a grouch.

A pause. She sits back, lets the sunlight settle. A long open silence.

"I compared your two sketches of Julia over lunch."

She doesn't move and her expression remains the same.

"When did you do the first one?"

"About ten years ago." Maybe twelve.

She shifts in her chair.

"She looks much younger. Fresh. Happy."

She was. It was a good time.

"Thanks. I think it's my best sketch of her. That's why I picked it."

Sally leans forward and rests her arms on the desk.

"The one you did just now – she's older, tired, uncertain."

Yup.

She stands up and comes around to my side of the desk. She waits a moment and then sits down in her chair. She smiles.

Is this a good thing?

She reaches for the sketchpad and pencils, hands them to me.

"I'd like you to draw Julia the way she was in September – before she went up north."

I take the pad and pencils, flip the sketchpad open. The drawing I had done earlier is gone.

"But first, I have a question."

Sally pauses to make sure she has my attention.

"You said she stayed six months, correct?"

I look up. "Yes." July to January. More or less.

Sally's smile is gone.

"During those six months." She is watching me closely. "When she was living with you, did you ever take a trip? I mean together. Did the two of you ever go anywhere together?"

She leans back in the chair, stone faced, waiting.

Did we go anywhere? The answer is easy. No victory there.

I start to sketch.

"I don't think she considered it a special mission. But she wasn't a kid anymore. Things don't last forever – she recognized that – so if she wanted to see Johnny and his wife and the baby then she should do it while she had the chance. It was as simple as that. She went north for a visit. That's all."

Sally looks at me but says nothing. The recorder is still going so I guess that means I am supposed to keep talking but right now I don't have anything more to say. I am doing what she asked but that doesn't seem to be making her any happier. She's made a few notes but mostly she's been watching, listening, stone-faced. I suppose it might be worse if she were smiling.

I put the last few touches on the sketch and that's it. Julia in September. It's good enough. That's how she looked. Tired. Sad. Looking past me towards the north. I hand the sketchpad to Sally.

Sally looks at the drawing briefly and puts the pad on the desk. The pencils are sitting on the table beside me. Does she want them? I'll let her ask.

She doesn't ask. She lets the silence draw out for a minute, two, three, then she stands up. She looks like she going to stretch, touch her toes. Her body is tense and she seems to be rising slightly on her toes then she relaxes. She picks up the sketchpad and puts it on top of the billows, straightens the billows and then goes around to the back of the desk. She sits down. Am I going to get another lecture?

*

Did I do enough? I don't know. She was the one who decided to stay. I was living my life – the way I liked it. She knew that. She was living the way she liked to live – travelling

– until she decided to stay with me. That was her decision, not mine. I take no responsibility for it.

Why did she try to settle down? I don't know. I didn't ask her. I figured we would see how it worked. That's what was important. Reasons are just words. Not that words aren't important. But with something like that words don't carry much weight. You do it. Or you don't. Talking only gets in the way.

I did enough. It wasn't a test. There wasn't a goal. She was trying it out. And she didn't like it. So she left. It's as simple as that.

On and on. She had to move. It's the way she was.

It's not the way I am.

It's as simple as that.

*

"I think that's enough for today."

It's five to six.

"Would you like a ride to the hotel?"

With you? After today?

"I'll walk, thanks."

She smiles.

"I think that's a good idea. It's been a long day."

No kidding.

I stand up. Sally raises her hand.

"Wait a minute."

She reaches over to the billows and takes out some pages – white – from the top of the pile. They are stapled together. She flips through the pages quickly, as if triple checking her work, and then hands them to me.

"Take this home and read it."

Homework? Good grief.

I glance at the first page. It is a photocopy of my cover letter. There are faint marks in the right margin – just vertical lines, sometimes double lines – barely visible. She must have made them before she realized she would want to make a copy for me.

"Bring that with you tomorrow," she says.

She is watching me closely.

"We may want to go through it together."

6

Of all the places I have never been I am beginning to think I should have kept Montreal at the top of the list. Four sketches of Julia in one day – that's three too many. Especially with Sally sitting stone-faced and me talking while I sketch because I have nothing better to do with my mouth. On and on. And on and on. Are those your guts on the floor? Hmm. I guess so.

I should take up smoking.

I understand what she is doing. She is testing. She has to test. I am paying her to test. Testing and exploring. Now she has five sketches of Julia – from beginning to end – and running commentary on four of the five. It makes sense. I'd even call it efficient. But, from my side of the pencil it's all give and no take. I'm waiting for the feedback. I know it takes time but I'm going to need some kind of response soon or I'll start sketching Sally and then where will we be?

Here comes the pizza. I think I need another beer.

*

It's getting dark and the streetlamps have come on. The lighting is bright in here. It makes for an aquarium feeling with the people passing by on the sidewalk outside. I thought about going to the café for supper – have a little visit with Louise and a glass of wine and do some serious fish-watching – but I am too tired to face that wall of welcome. I need quiet. I need to relax. I need to think. So instead I am sitting in the back corner of this steel and plastic pizza joint – everything bright and barren – with half a beer getting warm and a slice of pizza getting cold. And – most important of all – my sketchbook.

I've got my back to the wall and I'm doing sketches of Sally in the nude on her Persian rug – various poses. It is all very artistic. I have to vent this stuff somehow. The leather pants and the stone face. She knows what she is doing. Tomorrow it will be a long skirt – grey or black – and a tight sweater – probably red but maybe black – or maybe even multi-coloured fluffy stuff – cashmere and angora – but not too fluffy. Little Kitten Sally? I don't think so.

But who knows? She is full of surprises – like the sketchpad and the pencil set. Good idea. I have to give her that. And the billows filled with notes – green paper so it stands out. The pages could be empty for all I know but they have served their purpose – take me seriously they say. And I do. At the same time she needs to keep me off balance. So maybe tomorrow it will be tiger leotards and a black sports bra. Hmm. It gives me something to think about in the middle of the night.

*

This place is quiet. There are a few students and that's about it. Sunday night, I guess. The pizza isn't bad. The beer is bottles. The lighting is almost too good. I could use a personal dimmer in my corner now that I've finished sketching. I brought my other book with me – *The Master of Go* – but I don't feel like reading. I got about a third of the way into it on the train ride down. I don't know if I'll get much further. Not tonight, anyway. I still have to do my homework for tomorrow.

I do wonder about that woman. What is she after? What makes her tick? She's not doing it for the money – that's for sure. And there's nothing very interesting about me. I'm a half-empty-glass. She must see that. It's what makes me a decent therapist – easy-to-talk-to and boring-to-be-with. Just ask Julia – well, no, fine – read her letters. She makes it pretty clear. Repeatedly.

So, there has to be something else. And it has to be on Sally's side of the equation because my side has nothing but zeroes rolling around making clunking sounds. I'm easy to figure out. But Sally – what exactly is driving her? Curiosity? Loneliness? Sadism?

What is her neurosis?

What is her need?

*

Sally,

I thought it would be a good idea for you to see some of Julia's letters before our first session. We wrote to each other for years so I have a boxful and I picked out a few to show you her different sides and moods. I tried to be balanced but obviously you are getting what I think shows what she was like. In an ideal world you would read all the letters and avoid having me as a filter but wherever we live it is not an ideal world. When I come down to Montreal I can answer any questions you may have about the letters – where she was, what she was doing.

Or you can send me an email ahead of time if you want. Whatever you prefer.

As you know, Julia taught ESL and travelled – with emphasis on the travel part. I think it is fair to say that travelling was her life. Her father was in the army so her family moved around a lot when she was young and she got used to that way of being. She said one time there was nowhere that felt like home. But it was more than that. I think the simplest way to explain it is she had a fear of getting bored.

No one likes to be bored but most of us can put up with it a little better than Julia. She had an almost pathological fear of stasis. That's a bit strong I know but that is what it was like. She was quick. And curious. But she was also – or could be – impatient. Not that she was ADD or hysterical or anything like that. On the surface she was calm – very calm – like a therapist is supposed to be. Composed would be a good word for it.

Calm. Composed. She was so calm and composed it could be disturbing. At times, it made me feel inferior. I don't know why. She could be critical about the way I lived – my sedentary life – you'll see lots of that in the letters – but that wasn't what unsettled me. A frontal attack is easy to deal with – one way or another. It was something else that bothered me.

Julia had a theory. I don't think she took it seriously but sometimes I wasn't so sure. She said everything is finite. There is a finite amount of oil in the ground and a finite number of stars in the sky and a finite amount of matter and energy in the universe. So that meant, she said, there was a finite amount of awareness in the cosmos. There was one big lump at the Beginning – she called it God – and over time it spread out across space – thinning, shifting – spreading from place to place. Sort of like the background radiation physicists talk about.

According to Julia, awareness was subject to a basic law of conservation – just like mass and energy – which meant that if one person was gaining awareness then another, somewhere else, must be losing it. As she described it, the grand total of awareness shifted like the aurora borealis in the summer sky, lighting up the consciousness of one being after another. In her view, this theory explained everything from reincarnation to business cycles to serial monogamy.

The amount of awareness at any place at any time is what Julia called the Index. It was a barometer for consciousness. It went up and down like the weather and everything else followed in due course. If the Index started going down where you were that meant awareness was leaving for somewhere else. And that meant it was time to move on unless you wanted to end up in the food court eating poutine with a shopping mall mind. Or worse.

Travelling, she said on more than one occasion, kept her riding the wave of awareness. It kept her high on the Index. I know it sounds adolescent but that's how she talked. Index is going down, Kit. Time to travel. And off she would go. Now to be accurate – and fair – she didn't talk that way as much as she got older. The Index kind of faded from view over the years. But she kept travelling. She kept leaving for one place or another. She just couldn't settle down.

I don't know whether, in the later years, it was still a fear of boredom or whether it had become such an ingrained habit that she couldn't live any other way. We never really talked about it. If I tried to bring it up she flipped the conversation to focus on my stuck-in-the-mud life. She refused to accept the idea that there was anything peculiar about her nomadic ways. It was my stay-in-one-place life that was peculiar. It was the one thing that made her lose her composure. She would get so frustrated at the fact that I refused to travel. It didn't matter what I said. It didn't matter that I was happy where I was. It didn't matter that for millennia people used to die where they were born and no one accused them of wasting their lives. It didn't matter that travel is a fool's paradise. It didn't matter that we were different. She wanted me to change.

I didn't see a reason to change.

I don't know how many times I tried to let go. I knew we were too different to be happy but she refused to accept that fact. We met in university and started going out in second year. At the end of third year we broke up. Except we didn't really. What we did was move into a strange form of distance where we lived together-apart until she died.

Julia wanted to be attached and separate at the same time. That's the only way I can describe it. She wanted her freedom – freedom to travel, freedom to come and go according to her own schedule, according to how she felt about the Index, about the weather, about me. She insisted on her freedom. She was independent. She was a traveller. But she kept on coming back.

Why did I put up with it? I don't really know. Because she was smart. She was interesting. She always had something to say – not in a bad way. She wasn't a motor mouth. She was very bright – top of her class – she could have done a lot of different things with her life if she wanted. At the beginning I thought she should do grad work. She would have made a great academic – she liked to teach and she liked to think – but she didn't want it. She was a wanderer. She was independent. She refused to accept what the world said she should accept. She was different.

Example. She refused to use email. She wrote letters. Period. No email, no social media. Totally analog. Strange, isn't it? A world traveller stuck on the postal service. Why? I don't know. It's a small thing. I don't want to blow it out of proportion. And I'm not complaining – it was kind of nice to get letters – she used different kinds of paper and inks and pens and brushes. She did little pictures – she couldn't draw worth beans but that made it all the better. They were fun – as was the paper and the pens and the brushes. Sometimes she used sticks or leaf stems. Everything had a mood. I could picture her in a shop picking out some fancy paper or ink – or in a garden looking for a suitable twig to draw with. It was lyrical. That doesn't come across very well in the photocopies but you should still be able to get the basic idea.

Alf thought the letters were a ploy, a way of keeping the relationship alive. He thought there was something about it being both idiosyncratic and anachronistic. She was denying categorization and defying time. It was another way for her to demonstrate that she was separate and special. Maybe. I don't know. Alf has lots of theories. About everything. He's a psychologist – specializing in addiction. And a Buddhist.

Anyway, that is just an example. She did things her way. And she didn't care what anyone else thought or said or did. It's not that she was arrogant. She was just willing to let things flow one way while she went the other. She had no desire to convert anyone. No one except me.

That may have been the problem. I think she had my conversion as a life goal. She had to get me to accept that I was not quite what I should be. I needed to move – to circulate – like she did. And I wouldn't. And, in the end, that drove her crazy.

That may be it. I'm not sure. She said I wasn't paying attention – which didn't make any sense. I have a successful practice – good enough for me. I don't make a ton of money but I have lots of freedom. I have time to write papers. I have time to read. I have time to walk and wander around town. I don't like to be rushed or squeezed. Pace is important to me. She knew that. Not that she liked to be rushed. We were the same that way. But she was restless. And I am not.

It came down to that, I guess. That pea under her mattress – if you know what I mean. She couldn't get comfortable. And so she wanted me to be uncomfortable, too. But I am hard to move. Which isn't the same thing as not paying attention. I just don't see any reason to jump up and run away every time things get a little quiet. I think people have to be able to listen as well as talk. Silence is important.

That's unfair to Julia. She wasn't a yacker or a fusser. She liked peace and quiet as much as I do. That's one of the reasons we got along. We both liked quiet and solitude – the solitude of two, especially. We both liked to watch crowds but we never joined them. Separation was important. Distance. Because without distance you could be trapped in the noise.

Commitment. I suppose that's one way of looking at it. We both steered away from commitment to any group – to any collective – to anything institutional. Which is not the same as saying we were indifferent. Julia was committed to her students. And she was committed to her mother. She was committed to awareness – to seeing the world – what was out there – in all its diversity. I know she kept a journal and I expected her to write a book someday. She wasn't frivolous. But she refused to let herself become trapped by any type of group or school or ideology – whether it was teaching, politics, art or whatever.

She brought me things. Souvenirs, you could call them. Little pieces of art or artifacts – found items – anything that could jog her memory of a place, a person, an event. She would present it to me and tell me the story that went with it. After that whenever I looked at that piece of glass or stone or carving a particular story would come to mind. It was very clever. It was her way of hooking me into her travels, her life, her experiences. It worked. If she had been away for a few months and I hadn't received a letter in a while, recalling those stories made me want to travel – almost.

My apartment is littered with that stuff. That's a harsh word – littered – but that's how it feels sometimes. Much of the time. She didn't have a place of her own where she could keep things. There was her mother's place but she said she didn't like leaving anything there. It was too upsetting for her mother. I never really understood that. Besides, she said, this is my home – isn't it? She meant my apartment – not Ottawa. She made that clear. Where you are – that's my home. That was a dream. The first time she said it I told her the airport was her home. She got insulted so I didn't make that mistake again.

Coming home. That's what she called it. She'd write that she would be coming home in a month and that meant she would be coming to stay with me for a while. I got used to the phrase even though it made me uncomfortable. It wasn't her home. It was my home filled with fragments from her travels.

I think I'm hitting a theme. She wanted to change me. And one of the ways she tried to do that was by changing where I lived – turning it into a storage closet for her memories. Eventually, they would become my memories. And I would be different. Changed. That's what she wanted. I know that.

But I didn't change. She did. She gave up on the Index. She kept travelling but she got quieter, less energetic over the years. I think she wanted to settle down. She tried once. She came and stayed with me for six months. She even got a job. She worked retail – at Ten Thousand Villages – but it didn't last. She couldn't take *the quiet times – trapped inside the store. Plus, it was a little too much of an organization. She liked what they were doing but she didn't want to be a booster. Not for anyone. So, she quit. And left. I was on my own again.*

What I think you need to understand is that she never let circumstances get the better of her. She was used to improvising. She was quick. I know I have said that already but it's important. She was hard to catch off guard. In all the years I spent with her I don't know if I ever succeeded – not that I was trying. It wasn't that kind of relationship. We weren't competitive. We were too different to be competitive. But sometimes she would get on one of her rolls – her rants – not that she really ranted. She was too calm to rant. She lectured. And that's when I might try to trip her up. No one likes to be lectured. Not even me. I am a good listener. But I finished school a long time ago.

You know she drowned. I told you that in October. She was up north visiting friends who had a new baby. She got up early and took a kayak out on the water. Alone. She liked to watch the sunrise – wherever she was – so this was nothing unusual. But she went too far – far out into open water. It wasn't safe to do that alone – especially that time of year. Some bad weather came in and she capsized. There was no one to help. They eventually found her but she had been dead for more than a day by then.

Alf thinks she did it on purpose – took the risk, tested fate. I don't know. How can I know? I wasn't there. And I haven't talked to anyone who was there. Her mother had the body cremated before I even knew Julia had died. I think she holds me responsible although I don't know why. Julia did what she wanted. Period. Her mother knew that better than anyone. What I know is that Julia didn't take foolish risks. I do not understand how this could have happened.

She said I wasn't paying attention – that I had stopped paying attention. I don't think that was true. Maybe it is. I don't know. I'm human. I make mistakes – with clients, with myself and with her. I had a client tell me I wasn't paying attention recently. We had a difficult session. And he challenged me. I think it may be true. I am more easily distracted since her death – but that's to be expected. She was here. And then she was gone. It was a shock. But that's no excuse.

I need to pay attention. Otherwise it will be difficult to go forward. There's the baby, of course. That is something. But I need to clear this up, figure it out. She would want me to. She would insist. Pay attention, she would say. The Index is going down. Move, Kit. You have to move.

And so, this is where you come in. If you can look through the letters before I arrive we can discuss them. I can tell you whatever else you want to know about her – what I know to tell, that is. Given her life – her travels – there is a lot I don't and can't know. But I will share with you whatever I do know. And maybe you will be able to help me figure this out.

I am including a copy of a sketch I did of Julia about ten years ago. I thought it might be helpful. She didn't change much over the years.

Call or email if you have any questions.

Thank you for agreeing to help me with this.

Kit Gillespie

7

"Did you have any other relationships?"

The leather is gone but there's no long skirt. Instead, she's wearing black slacks and a purple knit top with a shawl collar. It's a very mellow outfit. Attractive but not in-your-face sexy. Hmm.

She is in the chair on my side of the desk. It's a grey day and the office is dim compared to yesterday. Chilly. I walked to her office this morning since I couldn't face the prospect of talking to her while she drove – too stressful. I think she was disappointed but that's too bad. The fresh air was a better way to wake up. And now she is waiting for my response. An eyebrow is beginning to lift – slowly, slowly. I'll let it arch a little more before I respond. Up. Up. There. That's good.

"What exactly do you mean by a relationship?"

I need to know what I am being asked about. Don't I?

I don't want to waste anyone's time. Do I?

The eyebrow drops. I don't think she liked that response. Her hands just went into the triangle formation. That means she is getting uptight.

"What do *you* consider a relationship?"

Right. Answer a question with a question. On and on. Until the sun burns out.

"It's your question, not mine," I say. "But I assume you want to know whether I had sex with anyone other than Julia? Is that correct?"

She smiles.

"If that's how you want to think about it, then that will do."

This is Day Two so don't bother with the mock deference. I've seen where it leads.

"Okay," I say. "I just don't want to waste time answering the wrong question."

Before she can react I continue.

"As far as sex is concerned, the answer is yes. I did have sex with other women."

Three, to be exact. But who is counting?

She's put on her stone face again. Does that mean I'm winning?

"That's a start," she says. "Now, let's consider emotions."

She shifts in her chair and adjusts her shawl collar.

"Did you have any relationships with a strong emotional element?"

A pause.

"And, if you did, how did they affect your relationship with Julia."

She sits back. Her hands are on her lap again. She seems calmer now that she has got to her real question. Emotions. Why didn't she start there? Maybe she thinks she did. Or maybe she thought it best to cast the net wide and see what came up. Does it matter? Not at the moment.

It's my turn. Where should I start?

"I'm not promiscuous – if that's what you are asking. I had one longer term relationship – a woman I saw off and on for several years. She was divorced and wanted companionship but she wasn't looking for anything permanent. We got along well."

"What happened with her?"

Caught your attention, have I?

"She moved to the States."

You look disappointed. Sorry.

"Do you keep in touch?"

"No." She was starting a new life. But that's none of your business.

"And did Julia know about her? Or any of the other women?"

There was only one other. The third one doesn't count. She was a tourist who was in town looking for a fling. I got flung. It was okay.

"Julia knew who I was."

Sally lets that slide.

"And the other women, did they know about Julia?"

"It depended on the circumstances."

Sally looks toward the door without saying anything. Is she doing the clearing house process? Or inviting in new ideas?

She shifts her gaze from the door to the window to the desk to the billows. She brings her hands together and leans toward me.

"Were these clients?" she asks.

Ouch. That is nasty.

Stay calm. She is trying to put you off balance. She is setting you up for a sucker punch. Stay calm. It is grey in here. It is cold outside. She is wearing wool for a reason. But she isn't comfortable in it. She keeps adjusting her shawl collar. She doesn't want to be talking about this. She doesn't like her outfit. She should have stuck with the severe look. But she didn't. Why? She's not sure what to do. She is conflicted. She is starting to slip. Be careful. If she falls, you will have to catch her.

Calm, calm, calm.

"I don't fuck my clients."

Do you?

*

We are taking an early break – it's only ten – and I am walking around Westmount Park while Sally does whatever it is she needs to do. She is definitely in an odd state. Is it an act? A tactic? Is she trying to regain position? Maybe she's having second thoughts. Or maybe she's just giving me time to cool down after that nasty little exchange. She was out of bounds and she knew it. Didn't she? Maybe not. The first rule is there are no rules except what works. Did that work? I don't think so. And maybe that's why she needs a break. Or maybe not. I have to be careful. She is subtle.

How much does she plan? And how much does she surf? She definitely prepares. But that's never enough. Preparation is a necessary but not a sufficient condition. This dance isn't easy. She knows that. I know that. And I know that I am an especially difficult case since I think we are doing one thing and she thinks we are doing something else. And the reality is we are doing something neither of us fully understands because it changes as we go – except we both know that that is what is happening – or we should – and so, isn't life wonderfully complicated?

I know what I want. Except I also know that that is only half true. Pray for what you want – that's what Angela says. And that way you'll find out if you really want it. That's what her flowers are for – discernment, not miracles. You don't pray to get something. You pray to sift through the possibilities, clear out the distractions and gain focus. There are no miracles in this life. Only possibilities.

This is a very pleasant park. Big. Convoluted. Varied. Fantastic trees. I could picture living around here. A walk through the park every morning. A walk up the Mountain on weekends. Coffee and croissant midmorning every day. A whole city to explore – slowly, randomly. Lots of sketching. Lots of thinking. Sounds good.

I'm sitting by the water – a little stream-come-pond that provides a place for kids to throw sticks at the ducks. There's a bit of sun trying to break through the clouds but without much success. It is still chilly. The crocuses are up. The daffodils are rising. This is the kind of place Julia might have liked. Or maybe not. She got so unpredictable in the end. I could never know.

Got? She was always unpredictable. Always. Sometimes it was just plain contrariness. Whatever I said, she said the opposite. It was childish. But sometimes it was more subtle. She would talk about how the weather affects people or the different character of time – seasons, hours of the day – but no matter how smooth the veneer there was always a sliver of you-must-be-kidding sticking out somewhere. I couldn't take it seriously. And so she pushed it even more. Stretched it even more. And I would walk away.

And then there was the weeping. Christ that was hard to take. Why are you crying? No reason. I'm crying because I'm crying. I don't need a reason to cry. It doesn't mean anything. It's just crying. Sometimes my body just wants to cry. Really? Okay. Right. Then you won't mind if I shout for the sake of shouting. My body wants to shout. Give it a break!

What the fuck did she want? Security and freedom and attachment and detachment and constant sun through the rain. A place by the sea that didn't exist because the sea wasn't the sea it was a state of mind. And that state of mind changed from day to day, from hour to hour, from one blink of the sun to the next. She wanted a life on the move that wasn't lonely. She wanted a relationship that didn't require commitment. She wanted to be connected and untethered at the same time. She wanted everything. Well, who doesn't? But the rest of us are adults. We don't expect to actually get it. We know life doesn't work that way. This is a world we live in, not a novel or a movie or a TV show. Christ. Why couldn't she grow up?

It should be easier now – with her gone. I should be able to untangle this mess and move on – but I can't. I am still holding on. That's the problem. I need to let go. However it happened – for whatever reason – she is gone – and I need to let go. But I can't. I can't let it slide. I need to know something that I will never know – that I can never know. She drowned – by accident or on purpose – there is no way to know. She did something stupid and she died. That's all there is to it. That's the reality. Accept it. Let go. It was not my fault.

*

I should head back to Sally's. She said half an hour and it has been forty minutes – but I'm not paying by the hour anymore so what do I care?

It's pleasant here. The trees. The water. The ducks. The air. Why would I go back to that dim office with the veiled windows, dark wood, muted floors and masked assassin? I can think here. In there I can barely breathe.

I wonder if Louise ever comes to this end of town. Probably not. Alien territory. People are like that – big cities, small neighbourhoods. We are villagers at heart. Once we settle-in we don't want to stray too far.

I like this place – this park – this pond – the ducks –
the way they land – feet first. If only I could learn to do that.

8

Well, well, well. The purple top is gone. She's changed into a red silk blouse with a black bolero vest – red and gold embroidery swirling on the front. Very sleek. Very Spanish-Japanese. I have to admit I like it. But the slacks are the same. No. I take that back. They are still black but this pair is tighter – some kind of stretch material that likes curves. And the boots. She's taller. Hmm. It takes some nerve to switch outfits at intermission like that. Not that I'm complaining. Should I comment? Or leave it to her?

I'll leave it to her.

She is standing by the window. I think she was watching for me. I am half an hour late but she hasn't said anything so far. She steps toward the desk and motions to her vest and blouse with a sweep of her hand.

"I spilled my coffee." Crooked smile. "Sometimes I can be such a klutz."

Right. If I were a Freudian I would say you lost your grip. But I'm not, so I won't. I'll just smile back and nod agreeably.

"I went for a walk through the park," I say. "Very pleasant."

"Isn't it?"

Yes. I had a hard time leaving. And, by the way, I think I get points for letting the quick change pass so easily.

"I run there sometimes."

Do you? When?

She picks up her pad of paper and pauses. Is that a signal for me to sit down?

"I prefer the Mountain for a real workout," she says. "But the park is good for a quick run when I need to clear my head."

Another nod and smile. I'm racking up agreeability points like crazy. I sit down and Sally comes around to my side of the desk. Those boots definitely have an effect. Much taller. The whole outfit. I like it. The embroidery on the vest – what's it supposed to be? There's a bird in there among the swirls – on either side – rising – or is it a dragon?

"It's a phoenix," she says.

I guess I was staring.

"It's quite something." And those are flames, right?

"Thank you."

"I'm glad you spilled your coffee."

She laughs. "I'm not. That poor sweater has suffered too much. I'm always spilling things on it. Must be Freudian."

I knew it. But I am not going there.

"It's a nice sweater but that vest is really something."

Boy. Are we being civil or what? A whole lot of repair going on.

"I'm glad you like it," she says. "I think it turned out well."

Turned out well?

"You did it?"

A crooked smile again. Is that a blush? Too much spotlight.

"My mother taught me. She was exceptional."

A pause.

"I don't do much sewing anymore. The embroidery ... it's very time consuming."

She stays standing, turns a bit, lets me have a good look – at everything – and then sits down. Or that's the way it feels. She is on display. And I am looking. That's the way it feels. She knows what she's doing. Do I know what I'm doing? Or being done to?

It's genetic. Neither of us had to learn this.

So, what's next? I assume the social time is over. Yup. She reaches into the billows and takes out two white pages stapled together. She hands them to me then turns on the recorder.

"I'm interested in this."

One glance and I know which letter it is. The original was on pale blue paper – two small sheets – with swift letters in red ink that would not win a calligraphy prize. It was one of Julia's telegrams – mostly punctuation. The photocopy doesn't show the drama of the red ink. It doesn't need to.

Herr Doktor,

Are you copasetic? Conclusive? Deranged?

I am spinning. Ready to move. More than ready. Underway.

Only four weeks left and it's Number 1 for Take-off!!!

Destination?? ((((Unknown)))))

Plans under development ~ ~ ~ ~ ~ ~ >

Could be time for the Antarctic???

Or Paraguay??

What do you think?

Never been to Tahiti - - - that's not right!!

Or Samoa??

Anywhere but here.

The Index is down.

Dimness dimming dimmer.

Circulation is the Key!!

Bad money chases out good. Never forget that.

So stay ahead of the game.

Lift!

Do not fall.

J

*

What do I make of this?
  Welcome to my world.

*

"Not in the beginning. Later."

It seems like a long time but it's only been a minute. Sally is halfway to a stone face and I am sitting quietly, trying to recall if there was ever a time when Julia wasn't difficult.

Not in the beginning. Not like that. It was different in the beginning.

"She changed."

We all change. So what? Answer the question intelligently, please.

"She had her moods when we first met but that was different. It was only in the last few years – five? seven? – that's when she started to get ... I don't know ... frantic, I guess."

Frantic is a bit strong. But maybe not.

"And what did you think?"

Thinking wasn't my first response.

"I thought she was struggling."

An eyebrow goes up.

"With?"

How should I know?

"Her life, I guess."

What else do people struggle with?

"Her travelling. Getting old. Her relationship with me."

Sally shifts. Her head tilts.

"And what did you do?"

What could I do?

"I listened. I wrote back. I talked to her."

She blinks.

"I tried to calm her down. If it was a letter – like that one – I ignored it. I mean, what could I say to that kind of thing? Instead, I would write her a long letter with lots of news and questions and stories. Distractions."

Get it?

"If she was visiting – if she went off the edge while she was with me – crying or ranting or just giving me that long numb silence – well, I couldn't just ignore it so I would try to talk about it, try to find out what was bothering her."

"And how would she respond?"

"Poorly. I didn't understand anything. I was making a big deal about nothing. I had gone stupid from staying in one place for too long. I wasn't the Kit she used to know.

Then she would hide in the den or go for a walk or tell me to leave her alone."

Sally sits back.

"How often was she like this? In the last few years."

Always.

"I don't know."

Another head tilt.

"I mean, I don't know what she was like when she was away. She could have been off balance and I wouldn't have known it. You've seen her letters. They are all over the place."

She straightens her vest.

I know you aren't happy but I am trying. This isn't easy.

"Letters like this one," she says. "How often? Once a year? Twice a year? Every month?"

Be patient. I'm thinking.

"There were no other letters quite like that one. But there were plenty that had outbursts in them – a couple of sentences – maybe more."

Sally thinks for a moment, makes a note, looks up.

"And the others? Why didn't you include them in the package?"

All of them?

"I did include some. I didn't think it was necessary to include them all. Everyone gets like that sometimes..."

"Do they?"

Don't interrupt.

"Everyone gets frustrated or excited or anxious. So, the occasional outburst doesn't strike me as significant. But that letter – it was over the top – so I thought you should see it."

Sally blinks.

"Can you give me some idea of how often?"

Okay, okay.

"Over the last few years ..." Hmm. "I'd say she blew up at least once every visit."

I look around the room. That's about right. At least once per visit. Often twice. They weren't always separate events. When does one blow up end and another begin? And when is it one long, continuous blow up from beginning to end?

"And the letters?"

The letters. Hmm.

I like that painting by Borduas. But I don't like this office. The dark wood. The sheers. It's stifling. Why does she keep it this way?

"The letters are tougher." Definitely. "I'd say – probably twice a year there was something that would make me shake my head. More often in the last couple of years."

Sally goes full stone face and lets it drop.

9

Alf says the key to understanding any human behavior is to figure out what is being avoided. Okay. But how does that relate to the other idea – the one where everything is based on attachment?

Avoidance? Attachment? Which is it?

He had an answer, of course. It just didn't make a lot of sense. I tried to get him to explain but after an extended bout of get-serious-Alf I gave up. He's stubborn and verbose and I have only so much patience. I try not to waste it jabbing at Alfisms. There are too many of them. They come and go like food poisoning – a week later you've forgotten all about it – but this one – this special spin on avoidance and attachment – it I remember.

When it comes to Julia, he said, try to calculate the center of gravity. Is she avoiding travel by her attachment to you; or avoiding you by her attachment to travel? Think about it, he said.

And think about it is what I have done.

10

"Did you bring your sketchbook?"

"To Montreal?"

She blinks.

Okay. Stupid question. But I'm getting hungry. It's quarter past one. Are you punishing me for taking such a long time at the park? That hardly seems fair. You are the one who called the break, not me. And you are the one who did a complete change of clothes. That must have taken some time. And then you put on that waiting-by-the-window act. For all I know, you got back to the office two minutes before I arrived. So, don't get all self-righteous about this. Okay?

But, no, I didn't bring my sketchbook with me this morning. And, yes, I did bring my sketchbook to Montreal. Sorry for putting us both through that little detour. I lose ten agreeability points.

"Yes."

Straight face. Pure business.

"Could you bring it with you tomorrow? Show me what you've been sketching recently?"

"Sure." I guess.

Or maybe not. I was hoping we could finish today. But I suppose one more day won't kill me. I've already paid, right?

She seems satisfied. Not quite a smile but her eyes are brighter.

"Good. I think that may be helpful."

I doubt it. In fact, I know it won't be. There is no way I am showing you what I was sketching last night. Or for the last few weeks, either. I suspect my memory is about to fail – sometime tomorrow morning – just as I am getting dressed to come here. You won't be happy but we'll worry about that later. In the meantime, how about lunch?

She makes a note, then looks up.

"I need five minutes to make a call."

What?

She puts her pad on the desk, turns off the recorder and looks at me.

"Do you want to take a quick walk around the block?"

I still can't say anything. She must be kidding. I don't want a five minute walk around the block. I want lunch.

She stands up.

"Five minutes – no more. Please."

*

Opening doors. Closing doors. Walking in circles. Or squares. Or circles becoming squares. Concrete. Reality. Fresh air in April slipping back toward March. Wrong direction. Sun, not grey. Lean forward, not back. Wind's coming up. It's chilly out here. It should be warm. Flowers coming. Buds coming. When is lunch coming? Once around. Twice around. How many times can you cover the same ground? Well? That's an old one, idiot. It is never the same ground twice.

*

Enough is enough. Seven minutes exactly. I'll make it ten.

*

"I don't know how many times I tried to let go."

Sally is holding my letter. She lets the words sit there, the silence growing. Time, time, time. I am not going to give in. Play your game. Fuck lunch. We are all adults here.

"What does that mean?" she asks.

I have my copy of the letter in my hand. And there aren't any typos. It's a long letter. Too long. I said too much. Maybe that's her point. I know I said what she just read out – but where? It's a long letter. I definitely said too much. But here it is – about half way through.

> I don't know how many times I tried to let go. I knew we were too different to be happy but she refused to accept that fact.

What does that mean?

It means what it says. I don't know how many times I tried to let go but she kept hanging on. She refused to accept that we didn't fit. She insisted on living her life the way she wanted to live it – and that included me as part of it – no matter what I said or did. Or wanted. That's what it means. Get it?

"I guess you could say ..."

There's a knock at the door. Sally turns off the recorder and goes to the door. She speaks briefly to whoever is there then comes back with two bags. She sets them on a side table against the wall and opens them up. Sandwiches and coffee. Croissants, to be exact. And cookies.

Lunch.

The telephone call. Very clever. And here I thought she was sneaking a snack while I was circling the block, trying to starve me into submission. Well, well. Surprise, surprise. Maybe the coffee's drugged.

There are three croissants – roast beef, salmon and roasted vegetables with goat cheese. The coffee is one medium, one dark. The cookies look like chocolate chip. It all looks very good. And she says I get first choice of everything. Be polite. Be gracious. Sadistic ladies first.

Well, well. This woman. Surprise, surprise.

There is no such thing as control.

11

So, I've bought a new sketchbook and I've been sketching like crazy for the last hour. I'm at the coffee shop at Milton and Parc – the place with the big windows – but it's dark outside so all that glass doesn't make any difference to me right now. The high ceilings do, though. So much space – open and airy. It's great. I could live here – set up a cot in the back and go out for walks twice a day for my health. The food is good. The light is good. The air is good. And the coffee. Why not?

I'll have to think about it. But the big question right now is how many ducks and geese are believable? I've got five pages worth. I started with some faces, people sitting, people walking – quick sketch material – nothing detailed – but everything needs to be done well enough or she'll catch on. I've got a few trees overhanging the water. And that's where the ducks and geese come in. But really, I'm not a duck and goose kind of guy. I have two sketches of ducks landing – that's okay – but the geese gliding along in the water? Who cares? A couple is enough. How about a hand holding a stone? More water? A kayak?

Okay. A kayak. She's got me. I need to do a few of Julia – her face? Her hair? A sketch of her standing by the river – the very last time I saw her. Long hair hanging down, arms in the air, stretching to the sky. Her smile. Her nose. A face in the water? No, I don't think so. A train scene – coming into Montreal – suitably wobbled. And a couple of Sally in her office on Sunday. A side view of her face? Something safe. Maybe.

*

The peg that stands up will be hammered down.

That was one of her favourite sayings. Not that she believed in it as a rule for social cohesion. Schools of fish. But she took it as a basic rule for personal behaviour. The adept doesn't show herself. Not if she wants to keep her freedom. Not if she wants to survive.

Don't make yourself a target, Kit. Pay attention. All the time.

I understood that part. My profile was and is about as low as it gets. She should have been proud of me. But no such luck. Instead, it was just another way for her to be unhappy.

It's like you're not there anymore, Kit.

What was that supposed to mean? I am staying invisible like you told me to. And, in any case, you were the one who wasn't there. Or here. Or anywhere. Always on the move. A travelling phantom. An illusion. That's what you became – always a memory, never a presence. So, if I wasn't there, well, so what? Who were you to talk?

There was no pleasing her.

*

I like this one. I've got Sally bending over to pick up her pen. She dropped it on the first day – when she was sitting in the chair in front of the desk. The image stuck with me

– her hair hanging down, the curve of her back. She'll like it. It's done as a quick sketch. Very believable. Flattering. Elegant. Not obscene.

I'm getting tired but I need to do a couple more to finish up. How about Heraclitus? That would give her something to think about. An old man by a stream, looking down at the water. No dipping toes. He's just looking – a puzzled expression on his face. And then, maybe, another duck.

*

Woman. Tree. Crow. Horse. River. Water. Old man. Duck, duck, duck.

*

Home sweet home.

It's past midnight and my personal art party is finally over. It has been a very long evening. I may sleep. I hope not to dream. I need to be in decent shape in the morning for Sally. No alcohol tonight but too much coffee and all that drawing has got my mind circling. No matter what I put down it is going to be revealing but I keep thinking about certain images. Julia by the river. Sally by the window. The mind is a mysterious place. It never asks your permission before landing you in the middle of a jungle – or a desert – or the arctic. Pay attention. That's the minimum luggage you have to bring with you. But you don't always have time to pack. Sometimes I think it's better not to go at all.

Good night, Sally. Good night, Julia.

Good night ladies, good night.

12

"Do you mind if I pace?"

I made the mistake of mentioning the coffee shop at Milton and Parc. Sally's never been. A neighbourhood girl, I guess. So, that led to a discussion of islands on the island – the village mentality and insularity and that led to – Louise. Big mistake.

"Are you nervous?"

Me? With you – the Ninja of Westmount? Are you kidding?

"I'm just not awake. I wake up by walking."

I'm already up and pacing. I stop by the window, pivot and face her.

"I assume you would prefer me awake."

She smiles. Today she has a long skirt – charcoal grey – and a long sleeved black top with a V-neck. Jewellery – a necklace – silver chain with a red stone. And a bracelet – silver with the same red stone. She seems comfortable with what she's wearing.

"Can you draw walking?" she asks.

Walking, running, standing on my head.

"Is that the assignment for this morning?"

I don't think I have much drawing left in me. I gave her my sketchbook when I came in. She fanned the pages then set it aside. It felt like she was carbon dating the sketches and they came up young. So, now I'm supposed to do more?

"Could you draw Louise?"

What's she got to do with this?

"I suppose so. Why?"

"Let's call it context."

As in, who else might I be fucking? None of your business.

Calm, calm, calm.

There is no such thing as control.

Okay. Let's see. I am not going to sketch Louise standing up. In fact, I am not going to sketch Louise at all. There's no reason why she should get sucked into this little circus. Sally can dream all she wants but Louise has no relevance to what we are talking about. The therapeutic value is zero. Professional opinion. So, who should I do instead?

Christiane, of course.

*

"She's young."

Sally studies the sketch for a while. It's a pretty good likeness. I heightened the harshness – spikey, tense, vibrating. It's fair to Christiane. And it is about as far from Louise as you can get.

"Youth is relative," I say. So there.

She's got me sitting again – settled, constrained – which is obviously what she prefers. I suppose it works better for the recorder but I have a feeling I'm going to be antsy today. Doing that new sketchbook last night was a mistake. Too many images. And mentioning Louise was another. That's two. Third one coming soon.

"True," she says. "But she looks in her twenties."

"Late twenties." I didn't ask. "Maybe thirty."

So what? If twenty-eight is young what do you call a six year old?

She closes the sketchpad and puts it on the desk. She looks toward the door, then at the window, then back at the door. End of topic, right?

"Have you seen Louise since you've been here?"

Okay, wrong. Same topic, zeroing in.

"Not yet."

"So you plan to?"

Pretty smooth. Hardly a ripple in that question.

"Maybe. It depends on how things go here."

She tilts her head.

You need an explanation?

"This is pretty tiring." Wouldn't you say? "Maybe when we're done. If I have time."

That's about it. When we are done. When I am through with this and I have what I came for – if I have what I came for – then maybe if I'm not too wiped out and if I have the time and if I feel like it and if it seems like the right thing to do – and not like mistake number three – then maybe I will go visit Louise. Probably. Maybe. Got that? Okay?

She goes stone face and lets it drop.

*

"Do you feel any responsibility for Julia's lifestyle?" she asks.

Being dead? Is that called a 'lifestyle' in Montreal?

"Sorry? I don't know what you mean."

"The fact that she never settled down." Sally blinks. "Do you feel responsible for that?"

Explain please.

"Why would that be my responsibility?"

"I am just asking."

Oh, of course. Random question. I'll give a random answer.

"She was an adult."

Consequently it was not my responsibility to determine her lifestyle.

And by the way. "You make it sound like it was a problem."

"Wasn't it?"

"She lived the way she wanted to."

"Was it that simple? Didn't you want her to stay with you?"

"Sure." Maybe. Sometimes.

"But that didn't work out."

"No."

"And she wanted you to travel with her."

"Yes." Sometimes. Maybe. I could never be sure if she really meant it.

"But you didn't."

"No." Is this little summation leading somewhere?

"So neither of you got your wish."

"Right." No ruby slippers. No magic wishbone. No genie in the lamp.

"And you don't feel any responsibility for that failure?"

"Why do you call it a failure?" It didn't happen. That's all.

"What would you call it?"

I'll tell you what I would call it you stone-faced dragon.

"I would call it the best proof there is of the central fact about our relationship – we didn't fit. We were a mistake."

That is what my letter is all about.

Aren't you paying attention?

"I'm not saying we didn't get along. What I am saying is there is a reason we didn't settle down, get married, have kids – all that jazz."

Are you listening?

Sally is looking at the window. Is she still thinking about the sketch of Louise? Let it go. Sex is a small thing with a big voice and a lot of lint around the edges. It doesn't matter one way or another. It is not relevant to what we are talking about. Don't you get that?

"We had the kind of relationship that made sense given who we were. It was tangential. We kept each other in sight and brushed against each other now and then. Every attempt to make it more fell apart. Call it centrifugal force. I don't know. It was what it was. And nothing more."

Why do you keep staring at the window? There are sheers. You can't see outside. What's there to look at over there? Are you ignoring me? Is this a ploy?

I do not believe there is all that much to think about on this point. The issue isn't us – Julia and me – whether we could have settled down or not. It is Julia.

Was she depressed? Was she suicidal? Or did she just make a stupid mistake on that particular day?

That is the question. Not whether our relationship could or should have been different.

"We didn't fit. I knew that. She knew that."

Are you listening?

"We would have been better off simply cutting the connection."

Do you understand?

Stop staring at the window. I am talking to you.

"But she wouldn't let go."

That was the problem. She wouldn't let go.

You've read the letters. You can see that she wouldn't let go.

Can't you?

*

There's the window. And there's the door. And there's the lamp on the desk and the art on the walls and the rug on the floor. There are chairs. And a couch. Side tables. Air between the walls.

It's a nice place in a rigid sort of way but what you really need here, Sally, is a dartboard. Maybe that would help you relax, loosen up, melt the stone.

A game of darts. Would you be able to aim and flow? Let it fly? Or would you be too uptight, too focused on trying to control? Guidance. That's the most we can hope for. There is no such thing as control.

I think, Sally, you are trying too hard. You seem to believe that silence is a tool you can use to pry open places that want to stay closed. And maybe it is. But that's not why we are here. Not for me, at least.

I know why I'm here – and it's not to break down for you. So, give up on that. I am a patient man. I can wait. Remember – I live and work alone.

And don't forget that silence flows both ways. You are as exposed to this as I am. No one controls what's empty. Either one of us could fall through.

*

"Tell me about Alf."

Thank you.

"What would you like to know?"

Sally crosses her legs and leans forward with her arms resting on her knees. She is a very compact woman. That pose – all the angles – tight and snug – secure, protected. I would like to draw it.

"Where does he live? What does he do?"

Start with the basics. Good idea.

"Alf lives in Edinburgh." I think I told you that before.

"He's a psychologist. He specializes in addiction."

Is that enough?

She sits back a little, adjusts her balance. I liked the other position better.

"Edinburgh?"

Yes, Edinburgh. You seem surprised.

"When is the last time you saw him?" she asks.

Saw him? Face to face? Breathing?

"Years ago."

Eyebrows up. Both of them.

"In Edinburgh?" she asks.

Are you kidding?

"No. In Toronto."

Sally pauses. Her gaze drops to my feet. She looks and she looks. You could call it staring – like she did with the window but this time it's my feet. Why? Is there something wrong with my shoes?

"You haven't seen him since university?" she asks.

"That's right." It's not like I can pop over to Edinburgh to have a coffee and a chat.

She gives up on my shoes and focuses on my hands for a moment before shifting to my face. An improvement, I hope.

"I got the impression it was a more recent friendship," she says, looking directly at me.

What does that mean?

"It's an old friendship," I say. "But we still talk now and then." And email.

"But you have never gone to visit?" she says.

"No." Almost. The wedding was an almost. But no.

"I see."

She looks at the window and then at the door.

And the silence starts up again.

*

Alf would say you are playing on my opacity. You shine a light. Look at the reflection. Show it to me in a mirror. And then wait.

He has tried that method – a few times – but in a moment of incredible frankness for Alf he admitted he wasn't any good with silence. He prefers to keep things moving and watch for something to spill out.

I know he's right about himself. And he may be right about you. Not that he's actually said that stuff about you – he's a little distant right now – but I know he would if he were here – watching from the corner – assuming he could sit and just watch. Which is doubtful. But if he could – and if he did – then that's what he would say. You are playing on my opacity. And he might be right.

In any case, the question is not what Alf would or would not say. The question is what I do about the zero decibel zone you have set up again. Long, empty and inviting. You want to draw me out. And I want you to focus on my question, not yours – whatever your question may be – which is another question, so to speak. But I am better at this than Alf. When it comes to an empty mind it's a natural for me. So, let us go then, you and I, and wait in silence together.

*

"What's this about a baby?"

That took a while. Half an hour? Forty minutes? Whatever. All I know is I won. I told you I know how to wait. Number one at doing nothing. But what's this about a baby? What baby?

She can see I don't know what she's talking about so she's getting back at me by letting me wonder. Will I admit I don't know? Or will I let the silence do the work for me again? It's my turn to speak. She asked the question. I should be polite. There are rules. Even here.

She doesn't wait.

"In your letter you mention a baby."

Is she losing patience?

Okay.

"Where?"

Sally takes the letter out of the billows and flips to the last page. No hesitation. She hands me the letter and points to the paragraph. I read it once, twice.

> *I need to pay attention. Otherwise it will be difficult to go forward. There's the baby, of course. That is something. But I need to clear this up, figure it out. She would want me to. She would insist. Pay attention, she would say. The Index is going down. Move, Kit. You have to move.*

Okay. Right. There's a baby in there. No doubt about it. And it kind of comes out of left field, doesn't it? Hmm.

"Gem is pregnant."

Sally sits back. She seems puzzled.

"Gem?" she asks.

"Alf's wife." Sorry. "It's a nickname. Her real name is Gillian."

Meredith McCaul.

An eyebrow rises, then slowly settles again. She seems relieved. Why? What was she thinking?

"Is this her first child?"

She is sitting up straight, elbows on her armrests, hands together, fingertips touching. I have her attention.

"Second. They have a daughter, Emily."

And, no, I didn't go to Edinburgh when Emily was born. Not to the wedding. Not when Emily was born. But this time, maybe. Probably. We shall see.

Her fingers flex as she pushes her hands together, the tops of her palms touching. She is staring at my feet again. Her face is tight. Her eyes almost closed.

Be careful. You'll get wrinkles doing that, you know. On your hands. And your face – around your eyes. It's not helping the corners of your mouth either. Lighten up. It's only a baby. You were one once.

She looks up.

"When is she due?"

She tilts her head, drops her hands.

"Sometime this summer. July, I think."

She does the math. Three months from now. Maybe four.

Head straightens. Face turns to stone.

"And what does the baby have to do with you going forward?"

I look at the paragraph again. To be honest, I'm not sure. But I'm sure I knew when I wrote it. It's in the future. The future is forward. Something like that.

"Alf wants me to visit."

Actually he wants me to visit in May. But that's not on. Later. Maybe.

She nods. Of course. That makes sense.

"Are you going? Once the baby's born?"

Of course. I've never been to Edinburgh. That's not right.

Or maybe not. It's a long way. Expensive.

And who knows what might happen between now and then.

"We'll see."

*

It has been a long morning. In fact, it's not morning anymore. It's almost one-thirty. We had a break just before eleven and I was well behaved. I did a quick walk to the park, out past the ducks and back to Sally's without dawdling. Fifteen minutes on the nose. Well, maybe seventeen minutes. Definitely not twenty.

I was good. So, why am I being punished? It's past lunchtime. And I am hungry. Is this a habit with you? If so, get over it. Either call a break for lunch or order the sandwiches. One or the other. I need to eat. Is that so hard to understand?

Or have you ordered them already? During the break? Hmm. Is that the game? Are you seeing if you can make me ask? I won't ask. No way. I would rather pass out, fall to the floor and wither to a stick figure like something out of Kafka. How would you like that?

Is that what you want? Would that make you happy?

*

"That's all for today."

Pardon? I was drifting. What time is it?

It's not even two. We're quitting? For the day?

She is watching me. I shouldn't have looked at my watch. I was thinking about high school. People. What they might be doing now. Not sitting here, that's for sure.

What does my face show? Surprise? Relief? Disappointment? We are quitting? But I want those croissants again. And a cookie. I'm not going back to that second-rate bistro after putting up with this torture session.

And what about my question? You haven't answered my question. What were those long blank spaces about if all they do is lead to this – quitting early? Half this session's been nothing but silence. What's the point?

There's been too-much-empty and too-little-full today.

That's a professional opinion.

"I need a long run," she says. "And some time with my guitar."

Oh. You need a break. This is about you, is it?

"Sure," I say. "I could use a long walk."

She smiles.

"Do you mind if I hold on to the sketchbook for tonight?"

Hmm.

That is a difficult question. Be careful.

"I feel kind of naked walking around without it."

Frown. Look thoughtful.

"But I guess it's okay. Twenty-four hours without sketching isn't going to kill me."

And I have another at the hotel if I get desperate.

She leans toward me.

"If you would rather not."

Don't look so concerned. I don't believe you. Those worry wrinkles are bullshit. I can tell. Should I call your bluff?

"No, it's okay." I wave my hand in the air dismissively. "I'll manage."

A pause. Does she believe me?

"I'll buy some paper if I go into withdrawal."

Sally smiles. She isn't going to push it.

"Good. Thank you."

She stands up and goes to the window, pulls aside the sheers.

"It looks like it might clear," she says.

I get up and walk to the window beside her. Not too close.

"A good afternoon to play hooky," I say.

She turns and smiles. Pretty.

"No one," she says, "wants to be too good."

13

There she is – hanging on the wall behind the bar – keeping watch.

"Alf!"

And here she is – all in black – coming at me, closing in. As full as ever.

"I knew you would be back!"

Funny, I didn't. But that's how it goes with me. Always the last to know.

"Hi, Louise."

She is hugging me, squeezing me against her breasts. The French-style two-cheek-kiss. Another hug. Squeeze and release.

"When did you arrive? How long are you here for? Did you bring your paints?"

She stands back and gives me a pose.

"I'm ready to model," she says.

She turns and motions to the sketch on the wall with a sweep of her arm.

"You see – I've got it up there where I told you. Looks great, doesn't it?"

I smile. It's not a bad drawing. I put some effort into it. It is definitely Louise – the way Louise wants to be.

"Sit down. I'll get you a glass of wine. What do you want to eat?"

She heads behind the bar while I look around. The fish are still there – sedate as ever. And there's a new plant – some kind of cactus. That's fitting. There's an open table by the window and that's where I'm going. I don't want to be trapped in the back.

I sit down and glance back at Louise who is pouring the wine. It looks like she's lost weight. Hmm. She's doing fine. That's obvious. I turn and look out the window. It is about three-thirty and the traffic is light for Sherbrooke – more pedestrians than cars. The sun is out and everything looks alive. The people are smiling. The air is warmer. Winter is finally fading from view. And I have the distinct feeling that I made a mistake coming here.

There's a rumbling on my right. Louise is singing – no words, just wobbling notes in a rolling near-soprano that dips and soars. Here she comes. She has definitely lost some weight. And her hair looks different – softer, cleaner. She looks good. Happy. I wonder if she's got a new boyfriend. I hope so.

She puts my very full glass of wine on the table and sits down opposite me.

"So, you couldn't resist Montreal, right?"

She is beaming. Her eyes wide. It is nice to be welcome.

"How long are you here for? Where are you staying? Is this business? Or pleasure?"

One question at a time.

"Both," I say. "I have some meetings but I've left myself some free time – to visit you, of course."

I glance at the wine but stop myself. I should have something to eat first or I'll end up drunk, sleepy and I-wish-I-hadn't-done-that.

"Good." She looks at the wine. "You didn't want red? That's what you had before."

I wave my hand.

"Red is great but I missed lunch so I need to have something to eat. I don't want to fall asleep on you."

"Not here," she says with a laugh. "Wait a second."

She gets up, gives me a big wink and heads to the kitchen. I glance out the window but before I can settle she is back with a plate of assorted cheese and a basket of sliced baguette.

"This will get you started," she says.

Big smile. Hand on my shoulder.

"You need to keep up your strength."

I start to say something but she is already gone.

*

It is an odd thing – déjà vu. I know I have been here before and so the familiarity makes sense. But the sensation I am getting right now is beyond that echoing of people and place. I have the feeling that these thoughts have come through my mind before – in this place, with these people around – and I have a foggy intimation of where things are heading – like the plot of a book you read years ago and can't quite remember except you know there are bad things ahead.

Louise has stopped by to check on me a few times. Some people have come in so she has had to deal with them, as well. After the cheese she brought a small salad and there is something major in the works. She says it's a surprise. I'm sure it will be good but I hope she doesn't go over the top. I'm already getting full and I want to take a long walk after I'm done here. I need the exercise and the open space.

Looking out the window is getting more interesting. The sunshine has brought out some spring hats – big brims, bright colours. No one wants to be slush and ice twelve months a year. But, on the other hand, not everybody wants to be on display. Louise loves the stage but not Julia. And Sally? She wants to be seen but not known. There is a difference. Display is not revelation. Except that at some level it still is. Whatever you choose reveals something.

I think I need another glass of wine.

*

If it weren't for a flicker in the way she holds herself, I would say Sally is a natural. She floats. Almost. But only almost. She's got this glimmer of stiffness in her. Not rigid. Not awkward. But a little too stern for comfort. Like the world needs to be held off – not far – just a fingertip.

Julia wasn't like that. She said once – six or seven years ago – she said she had been watching pelicans diving for fish and she felt herself tumbling – like when you see someone trip and you feel your gut rise as if you were falling with them – except this was a pelican diving for fish. She felt herself falling as the bird dropped toward the water. Tumbling. In free fall.

Her life, she said, was like that. Open. Falling. Unsupported.

It was a weird thing for her to say. And I still don't get it.

Along with everything else.

*

Here comes the main course. Louise looks pleased. There's a bed of rice with steamed vegetables on the side. On the rice there's steak, salmon and grilled chicken. A small piece of each. It looks like a cream sauce with dill on the salmon. The beef has a very light gravy. And the chicken? Are those jalapeno peppers? I guess I'll find out.

"Looks fantastic, Louise." I mean it.

She sits down.

"It should be good. I've got a new chef."

She leans forward and lowers her voice.

"She is unbelievable. Business is up. Tips are way up. But I have to be careful or she'll want a raise. Next month maybe. I don't want to lose her. But I don't want her getting a swelled head, either."

A pause.

"Managing is a pain in the ass, you know. But I love this business."

I give her a big smile.

"It agrees with you. You're looking great."

She sits back and crosses her arms. Her breasts rise and the cleavage expands. She looks at me sideways.

"Are you flirting with me, Alf?"

No. That's the wine.

Don't worry. I'll get it under control.

"I'm just being honest. You look good, the place looks good, the food looks good. Everything is coming together."

She drops her arms and leans forward again. The cleavage is still there.

"You're right. Life is good." She pauses. "You know, it's funny but things started to get better just after your visit. I mean, life wasn't bad but it was slow. After you came things picked up. Maybe it's the picture."

She glances at the sketch hanging behind the bar.

"Everybody loves it. I give everyone your name – credit where credit's due. You've got a lot of fans in Montreal. You should move here. I could get you customers like that." She snaps her fingers. "You could have a nice life doing portraits. Life here is better – the food, the air – the women." She gives me a wink.

Someone has just come in. Two men and a woman. Middle aged. Middle income. Louise stands up and says bonjour/hello to the newcomers. She looks back at me.

"I'm serious, Alf. You should think about it."

She takes a step away, then stops and faces me again.

"The French aren't like the English," she says. "We respect art."

*

Definitely jalapeno peppers. Everything was delicious – great chef – but it was too much – especially after the cheese and the baguette and the salad and the wine. I ate the meat and the vegetables but left most of the rice. I hope Louise isn't planning dessert. All I need now is a coffee. And a very long walk up the Mountain.

I wonder if Sally went for her run. Play the guitar and go for a run – that's what she said. If I head out soon I might see her on the Mountain. You never know. Or was that just a diversion? Maybe she's still in her office, reading through her notes, listening to the sessions, flipping through the sketchbook and the letters. Analyzing.

Maybe. Maybe not. She's hard to figure out. What's her plan? She must have a strategy worked out but I can't see it yet. A lot of clever tactics but no overarching method or framework. No apparent goal. And that's the question – the big question – why is she doing this? It doesn't make any sense. There has to be more to it.

Louise is busy with the other customers. And I am done. I don't need or want dessert. I need to move on. I keep looking at the aquarium and it's depressing me – round and round they go. Hour after hour. Day after day. That's no life – not even for a fish. Don't they get bored circling that tank? Don't they miss the sea?

I need to get outside. I don't want dessert. I don't want coffee. And I don't want to sit here sinking in that water. If Julia were here it would be different. We could sit and talk and watch the people. We could watch the fish. We could sit and do nothing. But she isn't. And she never will be.

I need to go.

Now.

*

"What's the matter, Alf? Where are you going?"

There's sixty bucks on the table. That should cover the meal. If not, too bad. I didn't ask for a feast, just lunch.

"Are you okay?"

She's at my side, hand on my arm.

"I've got to go Louise."

I turn and face her, freeing my arm at the same time.

"Is something wrong?" she says. "You look terrible. Was it the chicken? The wine?"

It was the aquarium. I don't expect you to understand.

"Everything was great, Louise. Fantastic. I'm fine. I just have to go. I didn't realize it was so late. I'm supposed to meet someone and I'm late. I'm sorry but I have to run."

She's upset. She doesn't believe me.

"Is it something I said? You can't leave like this. We didn't even get a chance to talk."

That's not my fault.

"It was nothing you said. It's my fault. I'm late. I'll be back. Don't worry. But I've got to go now."

Not good enough. I know.

"You look great, Louise. I'm really happy things are going so well. And I'm really sorry to have to leave like this. The meal was fantastic. We can have a real visit tomorrow. Or Thursday. We'll talk about Montreal and food and art. But I've got to go now."

Is it sinking in? She's dropped her hand to her side.

"Alf."

She's giving up. Good. Now don't start to cry.

I lean forward, give her a hug, whisper in her ear.

"My name's not Alf." Are you listening? "It's Kit."

And I don't live in Toronto. Got that?

I give her a kiss on the cheek. And step back, looking her in the eye.

"We can talk about this later."

Or never.

"But right now – I really have to go."

14

"Let's start with the sketchbook."

Sure.

"When did you start drawing?"

In that book? Are you serious?

She can see I'm confused.

"I know you told me before but I want to double check. Was this something you did when you were a child?"

Oh. Right. Not that book. Okay.

"I don't know. I guess I always liked to draw. I took art in high school."

Is that good enough?

"And you kept it up as a hobby?"

Today she is wearing a knee length skirt – black, of course – and a short sleeve red and white and black print top – an abstract quasi-floral design that's a little hard on the eyes. I guess she doesn't want me to stare. It is warmer today and sunny. Feels like spring. I had a good walk over here this morning. She's wearing black flats with nylons. Sensible shoes. Maybe we could go for a walk in the park later. Expand her technique.

"I guess you could say that."

You could call it a hobby. I wouldn't.

"It's been off and on over the years." Like alcohol and happiness.

She nods. Is that good enough? Yes? No?

"Do you ever feel guilty about your sketching?"

Pardon?

She can see I'm confused again. She does the head tilt. Straightens. Puts her hands together. Protective triangle.

"You draw well," she says. "And that takes practice."

Right. But why does this make you nervous?

"Do you ever feel guilty about the time you spend drawing?"

Why would I? It's a hobby. It's supposed to be a waste of time.

"No." Do you feel guilty about playing the guitar?

"Okay. Then do you ever feel guilty that you haven't spent more time at it? You obviously have talent. Have you ever felt guilty that you haven't developed that talent more fully?"

You mean like Picasso and Rembrandt? Ha!

"I never wanted to be an artist – if that's what you are asking."

I pause to see if she will react. She doesn't.

"I'm happy with my life." Except when I'm not. "There's no glory in it but that's fine by me. I don't have any regrets."

Do you?

She goes stone face.

What? You expected me to whine about lost opportunities? Undeserved obscurity? Not a chance. I deserve every grain of obscurity I've amassed. So, forget it. I like what I do. Period.

"You draw a lot of women."

Yup. We've been here before.

"And ducks."

Right. I knew it.

"I wonder," she says, "about the ducks."

*

So here we are, doing circuits in the park. The sun is out but it's still chilly in the shade. Sally has a black jacket that goes with her skirt. And I have my fleece. We look like a duchess walking with her gardener in the public section of her estate. I am pointing out the flowers that are coming along very nicely thanks to my diligence and she is nodding condescendingly. Yes, yes. Keep it beautiful. We must keep the public happy. Attendance is up and we do need the money. Everything is so expensive these days. Do you think we should raise the entrance fee?

In reality, she has just told me about the death of her father in January. Heart attack. She's not sure what her mother will do. She is not an easy woman – her mother. Proud. Stern. She lives in Vancouver – in a condo – alone, now. She seems to be doing fine, so far, but it is difficult to tell. She is a woman who shows no emotion – proud, stern.

I don't know why she is opening up like this. Is it the fresh air? The park? The ducks? I told her about Julia's last visit and her strange mood, the death of the old woman up north, the new baby, our walk by the river and the ducks landing on the water? She perked up at the mention of the ducks. They were just ducks – rivers have ducks – but if she wants to focus on them, fine. The ducks arrived. And Sally started talking about her father.

Was that really it? Two ducks on the water? I don't know. Even when she opens up she is guarded. Is she on my side now? Or is this a ploy? Another tactic to draw me out? I haven't been as open as I could be. But that shouldn't matter. I've been honest about what counts. The issue is Julia, not me.

*

"I'm thinking about bringing my mother to Montreal."

We are sitting on a bench. By the water. There are five or six ducks. Sally has her arms and legs crossed. She appears to be watching something in the distance. An old woman walking with her little white dog. Or is it the young mother with the stroller? I am in my standard slouch, looking at the ducks and watching Sally from the corner of my eye. We look now like a duchess with her good-for-nothing cousin who has lost his title – disinherited by papa – and he wants to borrow some money. She doesn't want to give it to him. So, he is slouched and sulking. She is musing about the Queen.

"To live with you?" I ask. That doesn't sound like much fun.

"God, no." She uncrosses her legs, turns and looks at me. "Just to have her closer."

Sorry. I didn't mean to frighten you.

She stares at me for a moment then lets her gaze drift toward the ducks.

"Vancouver is so far away. I don't like the thought of her being there alone."

Why? You are here alone. And that doesn't seem to be a problem.

"It would be easier if she were closer. She could sell her condo and buy something here. Or rent. I'm not sure she would like the winter. She might not want to stay."

That would be the ideal situation, wouldn't it? For her to come and leave. You would have tried. What more could you do?

"How old is she?"

Sally turns at the sound of my voice. I glance at her and she lets her gaze drift away again.

"Sixty-eight."

Hmm.

"And her health?"

"Is good. It was my father who pushed himself. My mother has always been a swan."

So, sixty-eight, in good health and a swan.

"I assume you are asking for advice."

She turns to me yet again and smiles. Nice. Almost human.

Okay. I won't charge you for this.

"Ask her to visit and leave it at that."

*

We are walking again. It is past noon and I suggested we get some of those excellent croissants – my treat. Sally hesitated for a second – as if the location of the bistro were a secret – but now we are walking back to the office with croissants and cookies and coffee. At least, I am. The duchess is empty handed.

"What do you do to relax?" she asks. "Other than draw."

I don't draw, I sketch. And I don't sketch to relax. I sketch to find things out – but I'll let that pass.

"I walk. That's a big one." The biggest.

The world would be a better, calmer, happier place if more people walked.

"And I throw darts." Next in line. But I can't recommend it for everyone.

And I read. Don't watch TV. Listen to music, sometimes.

Sit empty-headed a lot.

"Throw darts?"

She seems puzzled. What's puzzling about darts?

"I've got a dartboard in my office."

She stops walking.

"Do you play darts with your clients?"

She is looking at me like I just admitted to serving scotch at the beginning of each session.

"Some have asked. But I don't like the idea of an angry client with a dart in hand. Plus, amateurs ruin good darts. I hate that."

We start walking again.

"Darts and drawing and walking," she says.

And reading.

"No yoga?"

I laugh.

"I touch my toes, sometimes. But not in a meditative way."

She doesn't smile.

"And no sports?"

Other than darts?

"No. I'm a soloist."

"I run alone," she says.

I know. Is solo running a sport?

She glances my way. "But, I admit, it's not always relaxing."

I look at her and smile.

"That's why I prefer to walk."

And here we are back at your building. End of walk. Not too long. And not too short. Just long enough. Good thing we didn't run.

*

I don't think Julia did it on purpose. I don't think she headed out with the idea that she would end up gone. I can't see that. She would have worried about Johnny and his wife and the baby. She wouldn't have done that to them. No. I can't see that. What I can see is her becoming careless. She was distracted when she visited me. The Index was down. So, I can see her paddling out too far. I can see her missing the change in the air – the extra chill, the edge of the storm. And when she did feel it the risk might have flickered in her mind. She might have felt the breeze, the damp, the chill – and she ignored it. She kept going. She knew it was a risk. And she didn't care.

I don't think she did it on purpose.

*

"Could you tell me about your dreams?"

We are sitting in the chairs not quite facing each other and – up until that question – things have been relaxed. The recorder is on. Lunch was good and I'm happy I suggested it. We even have two extra cookies for later in the afternoon. Sally hasn't mentioned her mother or father since the park. Not directly. We've been talking about living on the coast – Vancouver, Halifax – anywhere maritime. The changeable weather. The rain. The air. And then, out of nowhere, my dreams.

"Why?" I don't see what my dreams have to do with this.

Sally blinks.

"Don't you discuss dreaming with your clients?"

"Sometimes. But that's different."

"How? You are my client. And I am asking about your dreams."

Yes, I am. And, yes, you are. And, no, I don't talk about my dreams – to anyone.

"I don't see the relevance."

She cracks a smile.

"People seldom do."

Now she is sitting back. A pause. Hands up in the triangle.

"I can't force you to talk," she says. "But I think you should consider why you are refusing – if you are refusing. To put it bluntly, what are you afraid of?"

Nothing. Especially not you.

"I don't see what my dreams have to do with Julia's death."

Hands drop. Disbelief on her face.

"You know as well as I do that ..."

A pause. Stone face now.

"I have Julia's letters, your letter, your sketches and what you've told me in these sessions. Your dreams are one more source of information. Why would I ignore that source of information?"

I'm not asking you to ignore it. I am asking you why you think they are relevant. And you are telling me why. And I am sitting here thinking about what you are saying. Okay? I'm a reasonable guy. Don't rush me.

"Fair enough," I say. "But I'm still wondering about relevance."

She is trying to look patient.

"In this situation, Kit, I think you have to trust me to decide what is relevant."

*

"Have you read Basho?"

It is four o'clock and we have just come back from a break. I walked around the block a few times. Sally did I-know-not-what. The dream discussion didn't go all that well. I told her, well, nothing. I suspect she'll take a run at it again tomorrow, if there is a tomorrow. And that is a real question, not rhetorical. I think she's getting bored. Fed up might be a more accurate description. Fortunately, I don't consider that my problem.

Basho?

"I've got a book of his poems."

It was a gift. From Julia.

"The only poem I remember is the one about the frog and the pond."

Sally smiles.

"Everybody knows the frog poem. It's not his best. People try to read too much into it."

Okay. If you say so.

"But it was the start," she says, obviously warming to the topic. "He got steadily better – more confident. In his early poems he is trying to prove something. Later, he is simply writing."

She pauses and seems to relax.

"*The Narrow Road to the Deep North* is good."

She pauses to see if I recognize the title. I do, sort of. So I give her a sort-of look.

"There's a haiku in it that I especially like," she says. "He wrote it after passing through Shiogama on his way north. The Japanese is: natsugusa ya tsuwamono-domo ga yume no ato."

Another pause.

"You don't know any Japanese, do you?"

I shake my head. Not a chance.

"Some people try to keep the syllable count when they translate haiku but that doesn't make any sense to me. The languages are too different. I think it's more important to capture the images and the emotion."

Sure. Whatever.

"He wrote that poem at the ruins of a castle – a place where there was a famous battle. In *The Narrow Road* it comes just after he visited the Matsushima Islands – a place he called the most beautiful spot in Japan. The contrast was intentional I am sure."

I'll take your word for it. And so?

"I would translate it this way: Summer grass – that's what's left of warrior dreams."

She is watching me. Am I supposed to react to that?

"Japan is a warrior culture, you know."

Okay. Samurai and all that. Sure.

"So, he is saying something wide and deep with that haiku."

Social commentary. And personal fate. Right.

"That one is a favourite but his deathbed poem – his last – is the one I thought you would be interested in."

Another glance. I am listening. Keep talking.

"It goes: tabi ni yande yume wa kareno wo kake meguru."

She tilts her head.

I haven't learned Japanese in the last couple of minutes. You will have to translate, please.

"He was on the road again but he got ill in Osaka and had to stop. He was sick in bed and he knew he was dying. One of his students wrote the poem down for him. In English, it goes like this:

"Sick from travel – my dreams circle over desolate fields."

She looks at me and gives me a minute to think about it. I'm not sure what she is driving at. Dreams? Fatigue? Desolation? I can't think of anything to say.

After a long silence she reaches over to the desk and takes something out of the billows. She glances at it as if to double check.

"Tell me what you think about this," she says as she hands me the pages.

It is one of Julia's letters. A familiar one.

*

Hello you,

It is very early. The sun has begun to lighten the sky but it hasn't yet topped the horizon. In a few minutes I will go for my morning walk to watch the sun rise over the Pacific but I have to write this note first because I have a question for you, an important question that insists on becoming ink on paper before I bury it again. Questions can be like that, can't they? If only answers were so insistent.

The question I want to ask you is going to have to wait for a moment because I have to tell you about a dream first. It arrived this morning – the dream, not the question. The question has been hovering for months. This is not an evasion. Trust me.

In my dream I am walking in a marshy area at the edge of a large river – the Ottawa? – collecting reeds to make a basket. Why I want to make a basket, I don't know. But that is what I am doing. It is evening and the sun has disappeared below the line of trees on the far side of the river. The growing darkness makes it difficult for me to see, so I am moving very slowly through the water. It is getting deeper – up to my thighs. Suddenly there is a loud splashing and two ducks rise out of the reeds into the air. I am startled, step back and lose my balance. I turn and with my arm I hit something large that moves when I fall against it. It is a reed boat.

The boat is long and flat with an extended prow at one end. There is a slight depression in the middle with enough room for one person. I drop the reeds I have gathered onto the boat and then climb aboard. It seems made for lying down, so I do. It is very comfortable. Once I am settled the boat begins to move forward of its own, slipping out of the reeds into the river.

I lie quietly in the boat as it floats into the open water. I look briefly at the shoreline I have just left and I have the impression there is someone on the bank waving to me. I don't wave back. Instead, I watch for a moment then turn back to face the open water. The boat drifts toward the centre of the river then begins to move slowly upstream – against the current! As I move with the boat in the dark I hear the words "Finally, I am getting somewhere". And with those words, I wake up.

Odd, isn't it?

Finally, I am getting somewhere. As if all this time I have been in the same place. And even odder is the fact that as soon as I woke up from the dream I knew that it was you who was waving at me from the shore. Staying behind once again.

And now my question.

Will you come and visit me here? I know you would hate Tokyo but you would love the rest of Japan. You could visit the temples in Kyoto or go north to Hokkaido. Where I am now is so beautiful and magnificent at the same time. We could visit Matsushima – it isn't far – Basho called it the most beautiful place in Japan. If you came you would never want to leave. You should come.

Yes, you should come. My room is too small and it is against the rules to have guests, but I could find a cheap place for you to stay nearby. I would really like to have you here to see what I am seeing – the mountains and the hills and the ocean and the fishermen and the blossoms and birds and, above all else, the people. We could go for long walks by the ocean, take the ferry across to the Urato Islands or head back inland through the hills. We could drink tea for hours in a tea room or wander the streets being followed by the children who want to practice their English. We could talk all night. Or just sit and watch the stars.

You would see. Everything is different. You should come.

Please come.

Love -- Julia

September

1

The woman beside me thinks I'm strange. She's in her sixties – grey and loose and comfortable – and she's going to visit her mother in Oban. Her father died ten years ago although it-seems-like-longer but just-like-yesterday at the same time. It surely-is-strange the way it goes. Her mother still lives by herself and it's-a-worry. There's no one nearby to help – neighbours, of course, but no family. Her brother and her sister both moved away – London and Dundee. Why anyone would want to live in London is a mystery to her. She moved to Canada with her husband thirty-two years ago – he's dead, too – like her father – industrial accident – she didn't specify the industry or the accident – and now she lives in Cobourg which is a beautiful spot – a whiff of home. There's a Highland Games every summer – a wee thing but lots of fun. She tries to get back to Scotland every second year. With her mum getting on she doesn't want to miss a chance. But there is the cost.

And with that she settled down. I guess she was nervous. Maybe it was me – my vibes are kind of strained. Or maybe she doesn't like flying. Or maybe she was just being sociable. It doesn't matter. I didn't feel like talking so I took out my book and I've been reading ever since.

The aisle seat has a guy in his twenties – I'm stuck in the middle – last minute booking – serves me right. Old woman at the window. Young guy on the aisle. He is sullen. Curly hair. Wispy beard. He hasn't said a word since he arrived so I don't know whether he even speaks English. He's got headphones on and his eyes are closed so he may be asleep. The woman on my left is definitely snoozing. It didn't take her long once she figured out I didn't want to talk. Or listen. She leaned over when she saw I had a book and tried to see what it was. Is that a novel, she asked? No. I smiled and held up the cover. Military methods, I said. She read the title. Oh. She hesitated. I like Maeve Binchy, she said. And that was that.

I think it was the smile that did it. A little bit crooked and less than sincere. She probably thinks I'm CSIS or CIA. Or just some kind of military nut. Whatever she thinks, the book/smile combination has shut her down and that is fine by me. I've been reading and thinking and reading – flipping back and forth between the sections – the commentary and the text. It's interesting stuff – curious, as Alf would say – but I'm not convinced it means what they say it means. Set a stone tumbling downhill and that is that. Really? Are you sure?

I bought a copy a few months ago, as a follow-up on Montreal, but I left it in the den collecting dust until I felt the need. Emergency provisions, I guess you could say. And there it sat – silent on the desk – until I got this anxious feeling. I was getting ready to leave for the airport and for some reason the book came to mind – the circle and trident on the cover. I ignored it at first – travel light is the rule – and I was literally going out the door when my gut hit panic mode. So, I went back and picked it up. Once I had the book in my backpack I felt better.

The fact is – I am nervous. There's no point pretending. It's not the flight or the height or having all that water beneath us. Planes have been around for a while. And human error can kill you anywhere – the bathtub, for example. I'm not worried that way. It's not the flying. It's the arrival.

I have my plan – last minute, true, but all the same I *am* prepared. My rooms are booked and I've got the bus schedule, city maps and guidebooks. Money. I have enough cash to start with and they do have bank machines – I checked. It's none of that. The logistics I have figured out. And anything unexpected – well – I can ask. The inhabitants are human. Or so I'm told. But maybe – only maybe – I should have told Alf I am coming.

* I think I fell asleep. After the meal everyone closed up shop except for me and a couple of hard core insomniacs. I don't know what they were doing but I went back to reading. And circling. And sitting empty headed. I read a few pages and wondered, then looked at the city maps and then the guidebooks and then back at my book. Read, pause, muse and repeat. Eventually, I fell asleep. Or that's what I deduce from the fact that the book is at my feet.

There was an announcement just now. Maybe. It might have been a dream. Or me talking in my sleep. Hope not. The woman beside me is awake and looking out the window. Maybe it was her. It's dark so I don't know what she hopes to see out there. Stars, I guess. Or clouds. There's no moon as far as I can tell. Maybe there are islands down below with village lights. Or ships on the sea. Fishing boats. Submarines.

I wonder where we are.

My daughter who knows how to travel.

That's what woke me up. Those words. Which means it was me.

I hope I didn't say it aloud.

Probably not.

I hope.

It's what Margaret called Julia – her daughter who knew how to travel. She took her in – up north – after kids trashed Julia's place. She came over and found Julia sitting on the floor holding the pieces of a broken vase and crying. Margaret told Julia to come live with her – which she did. And things went better after that.

Her daughter who knows how to travel.

Hmm.

Double hmm.

I don't know how to travel. But I'm learning. I think.

Sally said I should make the trip. At the end of May she mailed me a book with haiku and drawings and told me I should try it in Edinburgh. It's a tradition, she said. Travel, poems and sketches. It would suit you.

It was her way of nudging me. A bit unsubtle for Sally but it had its effect and that's what counts. I sent her a thank-you note and told her I would think about it. And I did. And here I am – enroute to the land of haiku – or another sea-bound place even more suitable at the moment. I do have a sketchbook. And I do know that I will jot notes. But I don't think I'll count syllables.

*

My daughter who knows how to travel.

Sally didn't ask about Julia's time up north – not directly. It came out in bits and pieces as I sketched. I thought she would be interested in the child – the one who was killed in the accident – but she sat there stone faced through the whole story. At the end, she said a big nothing. Maybe she already knew the punchline.

She will come home – that's what Margaret said. The little girl fell off the back of a snowmobile and hit a rock beneath the snow and died. Everyone was wailing except Margaret. She took Julia on a long walk into the barrens – snow and rock and sky – and she explained that when a child died like that it would come back. It would be reborn. The child would come home.

I don't think Sally got it. Or maybe she did. In any case, she didn't show any interest. I told her Johnny named the baby Margaret – she was born about a year after Margaret died – but that didn't even raise an eyebrow with Sally. No blinks. No head tilts. Nothing.

It was a bit odd.

On the one hand, maybe she wanted me to talk things through on my own. She didn't want to interfere. I can understand that.

On the other hand, maybe she just didn't get it. That's a possibility. And it raises the question – was there anything to get?

*

It's still dark outside.

The woman beside me is resting or sleeping. The young guy, too. I should sleep but I can't. I don't feel like reading. I don't feel like doing anything. Eyes open. Mind blank.

I don't know why I am doing this.

Where exactly am I going?

Paris? Peru? Iraq? Iran?
And why?

2

The cabby was a bit surprised. I had him drop me off at the art gallery and he said, Are you sure? It doesn't open till ten. I said I knew – which I didn't – but that didn't matter. It was a quarter to seven and this was where I wanted to be. The hotel's just a few minutes away on Gray. The university is up the hill. I've got myself a bench by the River Kelvin and I could stay here all day if I didn't need to eat. It's about seven-thirty now and I figure I'll wait until eight before dumping my stuff. Then out to breakfast like a local.

So far I like the feel of the city – the airport, the cab ride, and less than an hour on a bench in Kelvingrove Park. It may be different elsewhere but where I am at the moment with the old stone buildings and the river running down and the rolling slopes edged by walking paths – the trees, the sun and the shadow – it's wabi sabi Glasgow – if that makes any sense. Which it doesn't. But that's okay.

Must be Sally's influence. She said she's never been to Scotland but maybe someday. She's got to do Kyoto first. I think her sessions with me have stirred things up. That may be part of the explanation. That and her father dying – and thinking about her mother – and getting older. It's never one thing. It's the accumulation. And the trigger. Maybe I'm the trigger. Who knows? She's not going anywhere yet. But I am.

*

A woman came down the hill a while ago singing. She was lean with long red hair that caught the light when she came out of the shadows. Middle earth. Middle aged. She was wearing a long skirt and cape and her hands were hidden, clasped behind her back. I don't think she saw me. Or if she did she didn't care. She kept up her song and walked toward the art gallery swaying slowly. I turned away for a minute to watch a flock of pigeons arrive and when I looked back she had disappeared.

Her I will sketch later – once I've stretched out the flight knots and finished my yawns. I might even write a syllable or two. Or seventeen. We'll see. For now I'm taking in the sun, listening to the birds, watching the leaves on the trees. There's a breeze rising, getting things moving. It's the first day of fall and the signals are coming in strong and clear. Just the way they are supposed to.

*

Alf says 'Glasgow' means 'the place you toss the bodies'. I know he's joking – Edinburgh-Glasgow-special-love – but the sentiment is supposed to fit the facts and it doesn't. Glasgow is supposed to be Broken Town – like Buffalo or Hamilton – but that's not the way it feels. There's too much history looming – old stone and wrought iron gates and something wandering across the grass – long coats and fancy hats – professors strolling – gesturing with their canes as they debate the works of Adam Smith. Something like that. Old ghosts that won't quite fade away.

I've done a sketch of the riverbank and the river and the bridge. I've got a few people walking but I haven't done any faces yet. The people are moving too quickly to catch more than the motion. I got one cyclist leaning into a curve. He was going way too fast – downhill – and the edges of his jacket were flapping out behind him. He had a cap and a beard and a backpack. A student, no doubt. Early morning class. The speed of thought. In pencil.

The woman from Oban said you'll find it different here. It was a parting spark of sociability as we got off the plane. She felt safe, I guess, back on home ground. If you want the real gift of Scotland, she said, go to the Hebrides. The Isle of Mull will do but the further out the better. You'll know what I mean once you get there.

I thanked her and said I would keep it in mind. That seemed to satisfy her, although it tightened my gut a bit. I have no plans beyond the next couple of days. Equinox in Glasgow. Bus to Edinburgh tomorrow. And the following day I knock on Alf's door. Amen. Beyond that is unknown territory. The Hebrides is a possibility but so are Paris and Peru. I might even panic and fly home. Who knows? It all depends on Alf. And the baby.

*

Angela helped me pick out a few outfits. I sent two sleepers in July – infant size – pink and yellow – together with a cloth rabbit about the size of my hand. I also bought some bigger outfits to bring with me – a little dress and a white sleeper and a matching sweater and hat. I figured I could always mail them if I decided I couldn't afford the trip. Plus, I didn't want to ask Angela for help a second time – not that she would have minded – she was laughing and oohing the whole time. She jabbered on about my visiting and ended the conversation by saying she'd bust my butt if I didn't deliver that stuff to the baby myself. I mean it, doc. You gotta go or I'll report you for sexual harassment. Angela, that's not a joke. You're right, she said. It isn't. She wasn't smiling.

She's been nasty since I got back from Montreal. I wouldn't talk to her about my time there and she didn't respond well. She asked. And asked again. I said it wasn't fun but I was glad I went. What? she said. Did you get dumped? Did you see them both? Yes, I saw them both. Doc! Are you stupid or what? I told you two was too many. You couldn't handle one. What makes thing you can make it with two? I gave her a hard look at that one but she didn't care. She was angry and she didn't give a shit. The rock lady's gone, she said. There's nothing you can do about that. But don't fuck-up again. Think about what you are doing, doc. You need to get your head straight before you mess with anyone else. Angela, it's not like that. Is that right? What's it like, doc? It's like work, Angela. That's what it's like. Isn't everything, doc? No, not everything is like work. You are kidding yourself, doc. Life is work. And then she spilled her soup.

*

I didn't ask Sally about the book. I figured there was no point until after I had read it and I didn't want to read it at the time. Now that I have read it I don't want to talk to her about it. So, that folds up very nicely.

Taking whole. I'm sure something will come to me sooner or later. I've done a few sketches of Sun Tzu – today's version – a phantom in the arms trade wearing a white suit and a Panama hat. Subtle, subtle.

He has a private jet but never uses it. Others do. Misdirection is the key. If they believe they know where you are that is their loss, your gain. Like a hawk's call where there is no hawk. Subtle, subtle.

I've got him in a hammock reading poetry. There's a small round table beside him with a tea bowl and pot of tea. Some kind of food on a plate. Looks like kibbles. I'm not very good at foreign foods.

He's in his eighties. No more fieldwork for him. Of course, the field is everywhere these days so the hammock's as good a place as any. And the poetry? I can't read the title. I don't think it's English.

A moustache, of course. And a little chin beard. Some stereotypes live forever. He used to wear a disguise – the adept does not reveal himself – but now that he's learned subtlety no one believes he's the guy anyway.

A haiku would make sense but I can't think of anything. Maybe a quote from *The Art of War*? A limerick? A couplet rhymed? I'm drawing a blank – so there's an empty space where the words ought to be.

*

It's nine-thirty and I'm still where I started. My butt is sore and I'm getting hungry but I can't seem to work up the energy to do anything more than watch the sunlight shift its angle. It's a long way across the Atlantic and I guess I haven't caught up with myself yet. Part of me is hanging over Iceland waiting for the Vikings to leave. They're heading west and I am heading east and I want to make sure they aren't fucking around. Never turn your back on a Viking.

I'm drifting. Don't know why. Two young mums with strollers just went past and their conversation floated my way. They were talking about their husbands and the air was sour. No one needs an extra child – especially one that drinks. You would think they might act their age – somewhere other than in bed – and even there – he's like a fourteen year old, you know – all he wants is ....

And with that they drifted out of range.

So, I don't know who to sympathize with. The kids in the strollers, I suppose. That's the life you are heading for, children. Pay attention and maybe you'll have more fun than ma and da. Or maybe not.

I think I should lie down for a while – stretch out in the sun and let my mind catch up with my body. It shouldn't take long. No more than a day or two. Then maybe I'll be able to act my age.

*

I don't think Angela is jealous. I think she's afraid I'll fuck-up and somehow that will reflect on her. It will be like she failed. She has this thing – not my mother, not my sister – definitely not my lover – more like my analyst. She's invested. But I don't need another analyst. I've already got Alf and Sally – and Julia (hanging on in the ether). Three's enough. No. Three's too many but I'm stuck with them. And I'm stuck with Angela, too.

Why does everyone think I need help?

I don't need help. I need breakfast.

3

Downtown. This isn't as romantic as Kelvingrove – fewer ghosts – but there's enough tired brick and sleeping stone to house a few. Narrow streets. Lots of convenient shadows. Enjoy it while you can, folks. Sooner or later a developer is going to show up and turn everything into condos. It's already happening. Condos and logos. A glass and metal future. I'm sure the ghosts will take the hint and wander elsewhere, bringing the wabi sabi with them. Out to the Hebrides, I suppose.

But lunch was good. The sun is out. And the walking is satisfactory. I splurged and went through St. Mungo's before lunch. It's a curious mix of artifacts and ecumenical fervour – not sure I understand the point – and I'm not sure Old Mungo would approve – being a proselytizer himself. It's educational, I suppose, but a little too earnest for my taste. Ah, well, that's the way the pendulum is swinging right now. Soon enough it will slip back into parochialism – as is only right. If you can't be yourself, who can you be?

David Livingstone, perhaps?

Look at that. This place is full of surprises. I didn't know Livingstone was a Scot. I assumed he was English – like Scott of the Antarctic. Well, they are both dead now but Livingstone has a statue – and a fine one it is. I'm sure it's what he was hoping for as he gazed calmly at the waters of Victoria Falls. A tall bronze memorial, he thought, in the heart of Glasgow. That would be nice. And he got his wish. Home again.

I wonder what he thinks of the traffic? It's a steady pressure around here – just like Montreal. White sound and grey and brass. Everyone thinks they are going to win – taking the curves – if they don't lose. Smooth and rushing, pushing it hard, leaning forward – like the water above Victoria Falls.

And so it goes.

*

Now there's a strange one.

I'm coming back into the square – out of the cemetery where I've spent the last half hour reading names – none I recognized other than John Knox but lots of fancy stones for the dead. Celtic crosses and the like. I hope they're satisfied.

She seems happy enough – sitting there in the sun, talking to herself. She's tiny and grey and she's got the mandatory bags filled with junk beside her on the bench but she doesn't have that air of ordinary befuddlement. It's more like she wandered out of the graveyard and is asking herself where everybody went. They aren't here. That's for sure. The square is almost empty except for the two of us, a few skateboarders across the way and some suits moving with intent toward the Cathedral – an appointment with God?

Hmm. Maybe not so strange after all. Those bags are in good shape –cloth – and they look to be filled with groceries, not trash. Plus, she is very well dressed – a dark grey skirt, white blouse and multi-coloured sweater that looks like it would cost more than my monthly rent. Her hair is wavy and grey and she has gathered it neatly at the back with a large silver barrette. She almost looks distinguished – except for the tilt in her aura. An old clan aristocrat? Hmm. She's noticed me looking at her. Do I turn away? Or go in for a closer look?

"Now look at those eyes!"

She's pointing at me. Okay. I'm committed. In for a closer look.

"Pardon?"

My eyes are brown. Hers are that dark blue I have begun to notice as a local feature. Intense in an off-balance way.

"Now, what are you about?" she says, except she says 'aboot' and phrases it a little differently – something like – and, now then, young man, what are you aboot on this glorious day with those old oak eyes of yours? It's a bit of a blur so I'll stick with the shorter version.

What am I about? Nothing. And I say as much.

"You needn't be shy," she says. "I'll not tell the dead."

It sounds like "I'll not tell the deed" but I'm sure that's not what she meant. Her voice quivers a bit. I suppose not telling the dead is a local expression – the same as not telling anyone – or that's how I am taking it. Anyway, I don't want to get into a long explanation of why I'm in Scotland – Julia, Alf, the baby and all that – so I say I'm here to play darts.

"Not in Glasgow," she says and gives me a crooked look.

True enough. "I'm heading to Edinburgh tomorrow."

She spits to the side and says, "That's a place to toss a body."

I'm serious. She is a well-dressed, slightly odd old woman sitting on a bench in Cathedral Square with two bags of groceries at her side. She could be my grandmother. But when I mention Edinburgh she turns to the side and spits. Real spit, not just dribble. Then she says the bit about the bodies. I know she couldn't possibly have said what I thought she said, so I look at her in my style of crooked and say, "Pardon?"

She looks down at where she spat, then up at me.

"I'm not a judge," she says. "Stop asking for pardon."

Then she winks.

"You have some looking to do before you get to play your darts, young man."

Okay. Whatever. Maybe toss a body has something to do with darts. Or maybe I misheard her completely. Toss a party? I don't know. In any case, it's true I have some looking to do before I get to play darts. I have to find Alf's place, among other things. So, I smile and say, "Maybe so."

She smiles back in a way that makes me feel a bit silly.

"It's all downhill from here," she says and motions with her hand toward the Clyde.

"By the river is good," she says. "By the sea is better."

She gives me a squinty look.

I raise my eyebrows to show I'm listening. Then I notice she has a ring on her right hand. It is silver with a large black stone. She sees me looking at her ring and holds up her hand. On either side of the black stone is a small green gem.

"You could try the Hebrides," she says, lowering her ring hand. "If you don't mind a journey."

For darts?

When I don't respond she puts her hands under the straps of her bags and stands up. The bags stay sitting on the bench on either side of her. She is a tiny woman and looks like she couldn't possibly carry two heavy bags filled with groceries.

"But if you're in a hurry," she says, "then climb Arthur's Seat."

I am about to say 'pardon' but think better of it. Maybe her next sentence will make more sense.

She steps away from the bench and the two bags slip off simultaneously. They swing beside her and I twitch sympathetically at the tug on her arms. It flashes through my mind that I should offer to help but a voice behind me says, "You must be kidding." Clear as day. I look around. No one is there.

"You're a quiet one," she says.

I look back at her. The bags have settled on either side, almost touching the ground. She is steady as a rock. She doesn't need my help.

"With those eyes of yours," she says, "you might have a chance."

A chance at what?

I smile and wink at her. It seems like the right thing to do.

She winks back.

"Don't mind me," she says. "Winter's coming on."

And away she goes.

*

It's dark now. I had supper at a place on Byre and I've been sitting here on my River Kelvin bench for an hour or so watching the light fade and the dark thicken. It was sunny most of the day but clouds started coming in just before supper and now it feels like rain – damp and heavy. The circles of light from the lamp posts add to the enclosed feeling instead of breaking it up. It is very quiet. I suppose everyone is already where they want to be for the evening – somewhere warm and dry. And I am where I started the day – chill and dark. Exactly where I want to be.

I wonder where the singing woman with the cape is now. I still haven't come up with a haiku for her. It may take a while. I had a good walk along the Clyde on the way back from downtown and I was mulling over the syllable thing all the way. It takes a lot to kill a river – and they've tried hard – but it's still flowing. Eighteen syllables. One too many. I could take out 'hard' but I don't want to. The book Sally gave me says it's not a rigid rule and I'm okay with that. But you can't count syllables until you have a few.

I'm sure something will come to me sooner or later. I checked out the bus station this afternoon – too far to carry luggage so I'll take a cab. I think I'll leave early. For some reason I feel like I need to get to Edinburgh sooner rather than later – not that it makes any sense – the buses run all day and a few hours shouldn't make any difference. I have lots of time – tomorrow's a free day – but I feel like I have to keep moving. It's not like anything turns on it but if I wait until the afternoon I think I'll miss out.

Miss out what? Well, that's the question.

4

The old woman said the child would come home. Sally didn't get it. Maybe she was playing dumb because it's not a particularly subtle idea. The child died. The child would come back – come home. I guess she couldn't make the connection. She didn't see what it had to do with Julia going north so I spelled it out.

"I know, I know," I said. "I'm not saying she believed it. What I'm saying is ... it's part of the context."

Head tilt.

Okay. Let me try this again.

"What I am saying is – it needs to be considered. It was on her mind when she went up north. Johnny and his wife named the baby Margaret and Julia was going for a visit. The old woman had come home. That's the idea. And that idea was on Julia's mind when she headed north. It seems to me to be a relevant fact."

The head tilt straightened. Stone face set in.

"It was on her mind," I said. "That's all I'm saying. Nothing more."

I paused. Still no reaction.

"But the fact that it was on her mind," I gave Sally a hard look. "I think that is important."

Blink. Blink.

"It's relevant," I said.

No response. Stone face. Unblinking.

"That's all I'm saying."

Right.

Sally needed time to think about it.

*

As bus stations go, Glasgow has a good one. No problem getting there and no problem leaving. And pleasant in between – for a bus station. Clean and quiet and fresh in the early morning. I settled up at the hotel last night and got to the bus station just after seven. There were a fair number of people who looked like regulars – back and forth between Glasgow and Edinburgh for work or whatever. It's less than an hour and not very expensive so I guess it's not surprising. All the same, I wonder how many people do that kind of thing. And why?

It's interesting to see the houses once you get out of the city. Near Glasgow they are newer, vertical blocks. Kind of ugly and probably cheap to build. As you get closer to Edinburgh there are more classic cottages – single storey or storey and a half. Squat. Low to the earth. I don't know what the change means but it must mean something given the rivalry between the two cities. There's a boundary out there somewhere – invisible but very real.

And then there are the fields and the hills. Hillocks, really – just bumps on the earth. Some look artificial – too symmetric to be geological – and each one has a sheep at the top surveying the early morning calm. Not exactly a tourist draw but definitely a local feature. The real scenery begins further out – the distant hills and far off villages with spires, country houses and grand estates. That's local life as it's supposed to be – unvisited.

I looked up Arthur's Seat last night and it turns out to be a hill in Edinburgh – odd name for a hill. From the photographs it looks like quite the climb – treeless and rising to a cliff-face built for jumping. Or tossing bodies. There must be a great view from the top – but what the old woman thinks I'll see from up there I do not know. She was an odd bit of scenery herself. In any case, the plan for today is to scout things out a bit. See where I am, where Alf is, where Arthur sits. I don't think I'll climb the hill until tomorrow. When I get to the top I'll see what I can see.

*

I wonder about that ring. She was proud to show it – pleased I had noticed. Silver, black and green. Are those Scottish colours? Some ancient clan from the Outer Hebrides? I don't know. It looked pretty old – the ring – and so did she – but they both carried their age well. I think you could say she was a little bit vain – the way she dressed and did her hair, her jewellery, the way she smiled.

It never fades. Not that that's a bad thing. It just sort of catches you off guard when vanity winks at you in its eighties. You would think at some point there would come a long sigh and goodbye-to-all-that. And there is sometimes. But lots of times, no. The centre holds. And holds. And holds. I guess it's all we've got, really. And, of course, with her, it's different. She's a couple of thousand years old and pleased with both her looks and her longevity – the Taoist Pict who lives in the Necropolis and comes out from time to time for a vanity stroll and a view of the newbies. Whatever.

I did a few sketches of her last night. I was wide awake thinking about what I've seen so far, so I figured I might as well do something useful – sketch. I've got her hand held aloft showing off the ring. And her finger pointing at my eyes as I came her way. A distant view of her sitting on the bench – before she saw me. And a front view of her standing with the bags on either side of her, still resting on the bench. Then three sketches of her walking away – ever further – through a crowd of younger beings.

Don't mind me. Winter's coming on.

*

Angela says I have a blind spot the size of a football. And maybe I do. I have a problem with the obvious. So what? The obvious takes care of itself. It's the subtle that needs discerning. Of course, there's the subtle and there's the subtle. Angela has a problem with either variety. She always thinks there's something more. She's used to nailing Big Things and so she's always looking around the corner to see the rest of the parade. But sometimes there's no one else – just that kid with the balloon, crying.

I have a present for Emily – a sunhat I found at a place in the market – and the outfits Angela and I picked out for the baby. And the stone, of course. The stones. I still haven't decided which one to give her. Not that it matters. I suppose I could give her both but then Emily would get upset – not a good way to start things off. One stone per person. That's the rule. Once I see her I'll know which one. It's not that important. It's just a stone.

5

She said, "Draw me a house by the sea."

I didn't get it.

"Sorry?"

"A house by the sea. Draw one."

"What kind?"

"Any kind. The way you picture it. However you picture a house by the sea – draw that kind."

Okay. Sure. A house by the sea.

So, I drew a squat wooden house – more wide than deep – a storey and a half with two dormers facing the water and a porch running the full width of the front – no railing – two steps down to grass and rock – the grass grown long – the rock smooth and bare, leading down to the water where a small beach spread as a white crescent with gentle waves rolling in and a pair of chairs sitting empty on the sand. Behind the house were a few trees and bushes and then a rising hill with outcrops of rock and more trees giving way to woods, thickening into forest as the side of the mountain rose above the house and the shore and the sea.

I handed the drawing to Sally.

She held it at arm's length and studied it for a minute. Head tilt. Straighten up. Other side. Straighten up. Smile.

"Very nice," she said.

"Thank you."

She put the drawing on the desk.

"Now tell me," she said.

A pause.

"Yes?"

"Why ..."

She glanced back at the drawing, at the lamp on her desk, the billows full of papers.

Why what?

She let her gaze drift to the window and then to the door. I shifted on my chair but I don't think she noticed. Her eyes were fixed on the doorframe. I cleared my throat. Slowly her attention came back to me.

"Why ..."

Spit it out. Stop playing around. Why what?

"Why wouldn't you want to live there?"

*

It's a foggy day on Arthur's Seat. Cool and damp. No rain. Just fog. Green and grey. And brown and grey. And grey. And grey. I passed a few runners on the way up – or they passed me to be exact. Struggling on the way up, bouncing half-out-of-control on the way down. It's a special kind of fun – killing your knees and ankles on a muddy, broken trail leading nowhere. There are crazies everywhere.

Now that I'm at the top I can understand the attraction – no matter where you look there's fog reaching into the distance – grey and grey and grey. And grey. You don't get that kind of view just anywhere. I suppose I should have come up yesterday while it was sunny but I was too tired. I explored a bit – figured out how to get to Alf's place. I didn't go far – a small circuit around the New Town and across to the Royal Mile. I have to admit the Castle's pretty impressive. Even from a distance you get the idea. Turrets. Walkable walls. Lots of stone and vertical drops. Exclusive neighbourhood. A nice place to visit but I wouldn't want to have to pay the heating bill.

I spent most of the afternoon in a coffee shop on Broughton, sketching and jotting, resting up. I started with the hills and the sheep. And then the houses. And then the fat guy on the bus who kept nodding off, head back, mouth open like he was waiting for someone to pour in a pint. I did a few of the Castle – impressionistic – the in-your-face feel of all that rock. Then I focused on the view from where I was sitting – the street, the pedestrians, the cars. Eventually I worked my way inside to the barista – a woman in her twenties with multiple piercings and hair that was getting away from her. She had tied it up with two scarves – one green, one yellow – but strands were falling out on all sides. I did it like Medusa.

The dark blue eyes keep showing up. Definitely a feature. I'm an obvious outsider with my dark brown. Julia's were green. It's just colours but it makes a difference if you're not used to seeing the odd-colour-out. The assumptions you make – green means alert, vivacious; light blue means electric, unstable; brown means mellow, maybe even deep; and I don't know what dark blue means, yet – crazy old lady, I guess. The barista had light blue eyes. She was lively. And a bit silly. The difference between a twenty-three second and a twenty-four second espresso. She was trying it out on a friend – scruffy beard, fewer piercings than her but more tattoos. He went all meditative and claimed he could tell the difference – bitterness and edge and lingering. I'm sure he nailed it. No doubt. I didn't get a good look at his eyes but I'm pretty sure they were dark blue.

*

Angela tried to get me to bring a camera. I want pictures, she said. Baby pictures. Lots of them. Sorry, I said. I don't do photos. It's against my religion. Doc, she said, you're going to see a baby. They'll be insulted if you don't take pictures. I pointed out that Alf has both a camera and the baby and despite that fact he hasn't sent me any photos so I wasn't worried about insulting anyone. I will bring home sketches, I said. I promise. Not good enough. You are such a jerk, doc. Right you are, Angela. But that's not likely to change soon. It's nothing to be proud of, doc. I'm not proud of it, Angela. I'm accepting.

*

I'm sure if I sit here long enough the fog will clear. Other than the runners and a pair of hiking Swedes I haven't seen anybody. A few crows. I brought a muffin, an apple and a bottle of water so I'm prepared for a long stay – at least until lunch. That gives me a few hours to see whatever I'm supposed to see. I hope it shows up soon. I've cooled down from the climb and this isn't exactly lounging weather. Chilly. And damp. I don't want to get a cold.

Sally was glad I was making the trip. Or that's what she told me and I think she meant it. But keep an open mind, she said using her best supportive-and-not-too-directive voice. Then she apologized. It was on the phone and I left a silence before I told her I wasn't insulted. My mind was open. Is open. It can't be any other way. I don't know what I'm looking for. And I have no expectations. So, it's pretty hard to have a closed mind.

That's not true. My mind is open but I do have hopes – about Alf and Gem – and about the girls. Emily Elaine.

Kathleen Julia. Musical names. That must be Gem. Alf would have called them Prima and Secunda to keep things neutral. Names are a burden, he says. They set a frame you have to carry with you all your life. I guess he doesn't like Alfred – too kingly. He's a psychoanalytic-Buddhist-anarchist at heart. He would have preferred to be called Nub or Nought. I have no idea what his middle name is. Probably Ernest.

I wonder if Sally has a middle name.

Meiko? Hiromi? Alice?

Something wind-like.

*

It's true I don't know what I'm looking for but I do want to find something. The old woman said life is sweet. Never forget life is sweet. Then she took Julia to live with her. And things got better. I know that's why she went up north – because of the old woman and Johnny and the baby. She would visit with her old friends. See the north and the ocean. See Margaret's grave. The baby. But, beyond that, what did she expect?

She wasn't clear. We were standing by the river, looking across at the Gatineau Hills. She told me she was going north. She told me about Johnny and his wife and the baby and Margaret. She said she was going to see the baby. She would fly up north to see the baby. That part was clear enough. But then she said, I'll be coming home. And she turned and she looked at me. I smiled and said, good. I'll be here. She smiled back, touched my hand and then faced the water again, looking across the river at the hills. The sun was bright, the water blue and there were white clouds in the sky. The leaves were turning red in the distance. It was a beautiful day. Julia would go north. And then she would come home.

*

Two crows just flew past – came in close then arced away without making a sound. I think they were taking a look at me, checking for scraps, doing the rounds. This place is pretty good as far as litter is concerned – meticulous Scots – so the crows have to work for their pickings. I suspect they don't mind. It keeps them out of trouble.

Sally said, turn it over. Walk away. Come back. And turn it over again.

Don't expect an answer. Take your time. Walk away. Do something else.

Then come back and turn it over again.

That part I understand. That's what this trip is about. Create some distance. Let things sit while I do other stuff – visit Alf and Gem, Emily and the baby. See Glasgow, Edinburgh, the Highlands. Who knows – maybe even the Hebrides. Explore. Travel. Visit. Run away. Hide. See what you can see. Then go back and turn it over again.

*

There is nothing like sitting in a fog to make you realize how hard stone is. My butt is killing me. The muffin's gone. I'm saving the apple. I could use a coffee but the nearest café is a bit of a hike and I'm not coming back up that trail – not today – so I'm not going down yet. I'll give it another half hour or so. Forty-five minutes at the most.

Three more runners have come up – a pair and a singleton – but no one else stupid enough to make that climb on a morning like this. The crows flew past again – further off. The same ones or different? Who knows? The fog is thick and I can't see where they go or where they come from. There must be dozens of them living around here. It's ideal crow territory – empty, desolate, filled with dead things. The kind of place crows dream of.

They probably take turns patrolling – checking for intruders – foreign crows and hawks and humans. I wonder if they form gangs. They are obviously social birds. And territorial. Gangs would make sense – colours and all that. Black. And Double-Black. Coded caws. Wing signals. But the fog could be a problem – keeping track of boundaries on days like this. One hill too far and suddenly the Triple-Blacks appear. A murder of crows. That's the phrase, isn't it? It starts with feather clubs, moves on to gangs and before you know it you've got a murder. Tumbling and cawing. Talons and beaks. Black feathers falling in a flurry. Territory is at stake. This is not a game. Someone is going to die.

*

The old woman said I might have a chance. And she suggested I try here. But she didn't put the two things together. There was no necessary connection so I could be operating under a misapprehension. The hike-up-here and the chance-at-seeing-whatever could be completely separate things. Independent events, as they say. It's a possibility. She wasn't exactly clear.

In any case, I have no idea what I'm looking for. People? Crows? Ghosts? I keep looking at the fog and the sky and the hillside. Maybe I should do a circuit of the summit. There could be something lying around – a message on a rock, a note in a bottle. It could be anything. Maybe I'll find buried treasure.

The wind is coming up. The fog is moving and that's hopeful. It isn't lifting – just shifting from right to left – but that's more activity than I've seen in a while. I don't want to get too excited but there's the possibility of a bright spot where the sun exists. Not yet, but sometime later today.

I've done a couple of sketches of the crows, a few rocks tumbling downhill, the old woman with the ring. I've got her standing at the summit looking out at the fog while someone climbs the hill toward her. A woman. They don't see each other but I do and so I'm the only one who can see the scene unfolding. It's a time-space thing. I'm outside and they are inside and the big question is – when they come together will the universe explode?

*

My wanderings around the top yielded a cigarette lighter, two beer cans and a pair of panties. I left the panties where they were. The owner may come back to get them. Right? Doesn't matter. I know they mean something but I'd rather not think about it.

Now I'm back where I began with a mobile fog flowing around me and the growing suspicion that I might have to come here again if I want to see whatever it is I'm supposed to see. Perseverance furthers. That's one thing Julia never said of me – that I didn't persevere. The problem was the opposite. I persevered too much. In one place. Doing the same thing. Over and over. For years.

Don't sink the Index. That's what she said. Stop dragging it down. Move. Circulate. Breathe. Pay attention.

Sure, my love, whatever you say.

*

The fog is thinning. Arthur is sitting. And the crows are
due for a return. I'm not waiting any longer. It is time to
move on. Don't worry, I'll come back before I leave. In the
meantime I've got some walking to do. And some sketching. And some visiting. Don't worry. I'm paying attention.
Here. There. Everywhere.

Paris. Peru. Iraq. Iran.

Don't you worry about a thing.

6

Today is over. And tomorrow is waiting in the wings.

Rain. And sun. And puddles. And people walking.

Stevie Wonder is in there somewhere. I've been humming him since I left the summit. Like a rock tumbling from a mountain a thousand miles high. That's how it works according to Sun Tzu – and he has a point. I started singing on my way down from Arthur's Seat and the ear-worm has been there ever since. It won't let go. But I don't mind. It's like the years have disappeared and she's on another trip to Japan or Korea or wherever – gone in search of awareness – coming back in a few months. I know it isn't true. But it feels okay.

I know it isn't true.

She's gone. She is not coming back. But all the same it feels okay.

Not sick. Healthy. Good.

*

This room is good. The ceiling's high. The walls thick. The windows tall. The heater is on a timer. It will go off soon. Ten o'clock. By then I'm supposed to be asleep. I've already been asleep. And awake. And asleep.

This chair is good – broad, leather, comfortable – not too saggy. Not a body trap. The extra beer at supper has done that job. A fine Scottish ale that deserved the encore – I'm not complaining – it was good – but my body is sunk in leather and my eyelids are trying to reach my chin. Down they go. Until I pry them open with my fingers one more time.

I'm too tired to read. I turned on the television for a few minutes when I came in – just to see if it was any better in Scotland. No such luck. It's the medium, not the message. Fade to black. I made some notes for the day and now I'm flipping through the sketchbook, trying to keep from zoning out completely. If I go to sleep now I'll wake up at three – and that would not be happy – so I'm trying to stay awake until at least eleven. Maybe. We'll see. I just want a decent sleep so I'm rested when I go to Alf's. Tomorrow is the day. Meet and greet. And anniversary.

It's hard to believe. One year down. It seems like longer.

And just-like-yesterday at the same time.

It surely is strange.

7

Everything interesting happens at dawn.

It's not quite light and the air is chilly and there's a mist over the water. Someone somewhere is singing opera. Or that's what it sounds like from where I am. She's on the far side of the park. She might even be in the gardens – jumped the fence or something. I don't know. This is a big place – two big places – the park and the gardens – and I'm in the corner by the pond. Her voice is soaring and coming in strong from the northeast. Not loud enough to waken people but a real serenade for a pre-dawn wanderer like me.

I've been here for over an hour watching the ducks and the gulls as they nod and stir and nod again. A few dog walkers and runners have come past but no fellow insomniacs. And no little-old-women asking about my eyes. No ghosts or visions either. Just ducks and gulls and dogs and the early rising inhabitants of this part of Edinburgh. And one singer of opera.

The singing started about fifteen minutes ago and began with what sounded like warm-ups. Now it is definitely a song but I don't recognize the tune. It might not be opera. In fact, it probably isn't because it seems vaguely familiar and opera is an ocean of ignorance for me. As far as I'm concerned opera is an early form of television – without the mute button – so ignorance is bliss and I'd like to keep it that way.

She has a good voice – at least at this distance – which means it is powerful and more or less on key. Is she old? Young? In between? Tall? Thin? Fat? Swift or slow? No idea. Not that it matters. But I am curious.

*

Okay. She's under a tree a little way in from the big gate, about as close to the centre of the park-garden as you can get without standing in the road that runs up the middle. I can't see her very clearly and I don't want to come too close in case she's the nervous type. She may have seen me already. It's light now and there's not much happening around here so I'm trying to look nonchalant. Just some-body out for an early morning walk. Not the sound police. I don't want to shut you down. This is your park not mine.

*

Maybe it's therapy. Voice yoga. I don't know. But whatever she calls it it works for me. She's mixing songs with exer-cises – melodies and leaping notes – tracking the missing instrumentals – lines and stutters and trills. A real hodge-podge of sound. Soprano, I guess, but not the high C kind. A little more fulsome, mellow. Mezzo-soprano? I don't know. It doesn't matter.

The last tune was a folk song I didn't recognize, then some free form lines and now she's onto – guess who – Stevie Wonder. No kidding. You are the sunshine of my life. That's why I'll always be around. She's got that one nailed. I think I'm tearing up. I haven't heard that song in ages and now I'm time travelling in Inverleith Park. Ted and the guys at the apartment. The stereo booming. Party time. Julia and her friends coming up the stairs. That's what was playing – Sunshine. Me hanging over the railing upside down and Julia looking up at my idiot grin while Stevie Wonder tells her she's the apple of my eye. Not that either of us knew it then. We hadn't even met. And with that kind of start ... say hello to the grinning fool ... it didn't seem too likely. It took the evening and then some to figure things out.

Wow. Everything's tumbling out now. Ted and darts and Wendy and Julia. South Korea and then Japan. And more Stevie Wonder. And more travel. Paris. Peru. You say your style of life's a drag. And that you must go other places. On and on. While I stayed behind. Never knowing. Waiting in the wings.

This is too much.

8

Just past noon and I am back at the graves. David Hume this time. It's a very fine structure for a philosopher. Nowadays he'd get a brass plaque at the university – if that – but in those days – it was another time and place – well, another time – back then philosophers got respect. I guess that says something. Although I'm not sure what.

So, Mr. Hume, what should I believe about all this? Philosophically speaking. Whatever I want, I suppose. It's either real or it isn't. And I can be as skeptical as I want. Positively Humean if I wish. It's up to me. It's all in the mind, after all. But no matter what I may choose to believe – or default into – it's all I've got right now.

Not quite. The other thing I've got is an afternoon to fill before I knock on Alf's door. Today is the day. I have to do it today. I can't put it off. And I'm not trying to – but time seems to be dragging. No, not dragging. Stretching. I have been sitting here for twenty minutes but it seems like hours. And it feels like nothing. Stopped. That's what it feels like. I'm here in a single quantum of time that won't tick forward. Waiting. Letting the moment fill up with nothing. And it is almost as if she is here with me. Not quite here – in the neighbourhood. Present – meaning – being here. And present – meaning – now. Being here now. Present. In the time-space bubble that makes this place what it is for the moment. Enduring. For the moment.

This is what I get for hanging out in graveyards.

9

So, here I am – and have been for the past fifteen minutes. Another minute and I'll ring the buzzer. Two at most. I'm not nervous. But it isn't the right time yet. Not quite. I need to do this properly and that means not too early. I don't want to interrupt their supper. That would be awkward. Of course, I have no idea what hours Alf works. It's ten past six so I assume he's home by now. Probably. If he's teaching his course he could be at the university. I don't know when he teaches – the time or the day. An evening class would make sense given that he works at the clinic all day.

Right. What are the chances?

I should have called. If he's not here it would not be good. Gem alone with the girls and me showing up unannounced. A stranger at the door. At least I have my accent. That would help. But I don't want to embarrass her. How believable is it that I would come all this way without even an email? Me, Kit, the guy who doesn't travel.

This is beginning to look like a stupid plan.

*

It's six-twenty. If I wait much longer the baby will be in bed. She may be there already for all I know. What time do babies go to bed? All the time – right? Except in the middle of the night. Or so I hear.

*

A blind spot the size of a football. Must be the hole in my head.

*

If I don't do it soon I'll have to wait until tomorrow and that will throw everything off. Today is today and that means today is the day I have to arrive. So, stop pissing around and walk up to the door and push the buzzer. Number 3. Go. Now. It's not that difficult. It's not that far.

*

The door's opening. And someone's coming out. Backing out. A woman in a long skirt and sweater. With a stroller. She's on the step, the sidewalk, looking back at the door – which is still wide open – magically. She's got the stroller turned, facing my way. And now there's a little girl in the doorway. She was holding the door open and now she's hopping out – both arms in the air as the door closes behind her. She's got long brown hair and it flies up as she jumps. She comes up beside the woman – her mother – and then skips to the front of the stroller. She looks to be singing.

That is Gem. It has to be. She looks older, thinner than in her wedding picture but there can be no doubt about it – that is definitely Gem. I would recognize her anywhere. And if that is Gem then that must be Emily up front. Long hair and oval face like her mother. Long skirt and sweater. What a pretty little girl. She is definitely her mother's daughter.

And in the stroller must be the baby. The seat is turned around and tilted back making it like a carriage, so I can't see her. But they are coming my way – all three of them – so I will see her soon enough. Seconds, not minutes. They are only a few doors down. Emily, the stroller and Gem.

I have the stones in my pockets – the bluish round one in my left and Julia's paperweight in my right. They are both small, smooth and beautiful in their own way. I will know which one to choose when I see her face.

*

Sally didn't say anything when I told her. She just blinked.

When I repeated myself she stopped blinking.

"What do you hope to find?" she asked

"I don't hope to find anything."

Head tilt.

"I have no expectations," I said.

Silence.

"But I will know what I see when I see it."

*

This is it. Gem looks distracted, weary. Emily is singing.

When the world goes
In a world glow

La dee
La-dee-la-dee-la-dee

La dee
La-dee-la-dee-la-dee

"Hello. Gillian?"

She's looking at me puzzled, on guard, protective.

"Gem?"

More puzzlement. But it is definitely her.

"I'm Kit. From Canada."

Thinking. Questioning.

"This must be Emily."

She smiles at me when I say her name. I smile back.

"And this is your new sister, Emily. Isn't it?"

We all look at the baby. I look at the baby.

"Isn't she beautiful?" I say to Emily. "Her name is Kathleen, isn't it?"

I look back at Gem who is beginning to look like she understands.

"I'm sorry to surprise you like this. I've come for a visit. I'm staying at a B&B on Dublin."

I look at the baby. Her eyes are wide open. Alert. Staring up at me.

And I think I'm going to die.

Today

I gave Sally a pen and ink sketch of Edinburgh – the view from Arthur's Seat with the Castle and St. Gile's Cathedral in the distance. It's a composite I put together from a bunch of rough sketches made over a few days. I did the climb five times in total. When the weather's good the view from up there is spectacular – but it's seldom good. So, it took a while.

I framed the sketch and gave it to Sally at the beginning of November. I figured she could hang it somewhere inconspicuous – in the hallway or inside a closet. I didn't say that, of course, but I know it may not be her thing so I don't expect to see it hanging in her office beside the Borduas. She could re-gift it for all I care. Maybe she'll give it to her mother as a peace offering. Who knows? It's the thought that counts.

I also gave her a couple of rough sketches with haiku. I had them in a big envelope and when she took them out there was a smile I hadn't seen before. I guess she was happy to see I had listened. Or maybe they're just better than the Edinburgh drawing. It's kind of stiff. I like the flow of the pencil sketches better and I guess Sally does too. She especially likes the old woman walking into the graveyard with her shopping bags. I did it on one of my trips up to Arthur's Seat. The old woman kept coming to mind so I did the sketch to get the image out of my head. It didn't work – although the sketch did – but I'm not sure about the text: The Old Pict returns from whence she came / Winter's coming on. The syllables aren't quite there – or the grammar – but Sally liked it. I suspect I'll do a few more before I drain that image of its halo.

I scanned all the sketches and kept copies for myself. I've never done that before. It felt kind of weird – treating scribbles a little too seriously – but it seemed like the right thing to do. I'll have to look into getting them printed on something better than photocopy paper. Maybe I'll make up a little album. Go into business with Angela. We'll see.

*

Alf emailed me photos when I got back. Alf and Gem and Emily and Kathleen. Me and Alf. Me and Gem. A picture of me on Princes Street with the Castle looming high in the background. A picture of me holding the baby.

I printed a set and gave them to Angela as a surprise. She almost gave me a kiss. She would have but I jumped back in time and she was too busy looking at the pictures to give it a second try. I don't think she was offended.

"Doc," she said. "This is great!"

She had the picture of me with the baby and was holding it up in the air like a trophy. I have to admit it was a good photo – except for my stupid grin. Plus, it made my ears look bigger than ever. She didn't seem to notice. I guess she was focussing on the baby. It's a great photo of Kathleen – her eyes are wide and she is looking up at my face – not quite nervous – just wondering.

Angela held it out for me to see again.

"Doc," she said. "You've grown up."

*

Today I'm sitting by the river at Kitchissippi Point looking out at the Deschênes Rapids and the Gatineau Hills. The trees are bare and the water is a dark cold blue rippled by a light breeze from the west. The sun is as high as it gets in late November. It's the middle of the day in the middle of the week and there's nobody here but me. And a few ducks.

The main migration ended a couple of weeks ago but there are a few stragglers paddling in the shallows in front of me. A group of geese is drifting further out. They'll all leave soon enough – before the snow comes for real and the ice starts to form – but I'll still be here.

Or maybe not. Sally raised the idea of a trip. Sort of. It was a general statement – I have been thinking about going somewhere. And that was it. No explanation. No invitation. But I think it was there – the question – down below the   I'm-just-thinking-aloud-it-doesn't-mean-anything. Sandwiched between that and the double blinks. It was lurking there – murmuring – would you like to come?

I'll have to think about it. I don't much like travel. And I don't think she does either. It would make for an odd trip – two stick-in-the muds on the road together. Plus, I've already exceeded my travel quota for the decade. I don't want to give myself a stroke.

So, I'm not pushing it. I'll see if she mentions it again.

*

The geese are coming in and the ducks are moving upstream. Noise-making time. Quacking and honking. I should have worn a scarf. The wind has come up and the sun isn't doing much for me. I may have to walk soon but I'd rather not. I don't want to go back to the office. And I don't feel like wandering. I need a little longer here. A few more minutes at least. I'm not expecting anything. I just want to sit.

Sally showed me another poem by Basho that she likes. She seems to be getting into the haiku translation thing – an unexpected bonus from our sessions, I guess. She says the first translation she read of that particular poem was terrible – flat, off base, small minded – so it slipped right past her. That was years ago. When she read it again in the summer she thought Basho couldn't have written something that bad so she found another translation and then she looked up the Japanese and – surprise, surprise – she saw the possibilities. She took out the dictionary, put on her stone face and gave it a shot.

I made that part up – the stone face bit. I suppose she could have done blinks and head tilts but they are more theatrics than anything else. She is one severe woman when it comes to things serious – and there is nothing more serious than translating haiku – so I picture her sitting erect at her desk, hand raised with a brush hovering over rice paper, ink stone at the side – and a face like pale marble. Something like that.

Anyway, she showed me the shitty version, the Japanese phonetics and then a word-for-word translation. Once I'd had a chance to marvel at the awfulness of that first version she showed me her take on Master Basho. The Japanese goes: yo o tabi ni / shiro kaku oda no / yukimodori. And her translation of her new favourite haiku goes like this:

Travelling through the world
Ploughing a field back and forth
We come and we go.

Yes, indeed.

I told her I would do a sketch to go with the poem. I am still working up to it. I have some paper. And new pencils. But sometimes you have to wait for everything to come together.

Acknowledgements

The author is grateful for permission to use the cover photo: "Water and Ice" © David G. Taylor (davidtaylorphotostudio.com)

The author thanks Brenda Taylor and Jessica Taylor for comments on draft versions of this novel. The author also thanks the staff of FriesenPress for editorial suggestions, cover and book design, and general assistance in the production of this book.

Finally, the author thanks Dark Horse, Manic Coffee and RCM's b espresso bar for providing excellent coffee and a comfortable public space for private writing.

The Author

Christopher A. Taylor is a Canadian writer currently living in Ontario. He has taught mathematics, practised law and worked in the software industry. His first collection of short fiction, *Travel Light & Other Stories*, was published in 2013. He has also published two collections of poetry: *Shedding Knowledge* (2007) and *This May Sound Strange* (2012).

CPSIA information can be obtained at www.ICGtesting.com
Printed in the USA
LVOW06s0535040215

425634LV00002B/32/P